The First Advance Comment on Tom Sharpe:

"Tom Sharpe's comedy is exuberantly—I don't suppose 'gloriously' can be the right word—base-hearted. His characters, quite by their own lights, get into relentlessly magnetic, intricately horrible fixes that no one but his characters could deserve or come out of. America has deserved Sharpe for some time, and now at last we have him. At his best…he is far more satisfying than Kingsley Amis or any other nasty Brit novelist since Evelyn Waugh."—Roy Blount, Jr.

Also available or forthcoming from Vintage Books: *Vintage Stuff, Wilt, Blott on the Landscape, The Great Pursuit* and *The Wilt Alternative.*

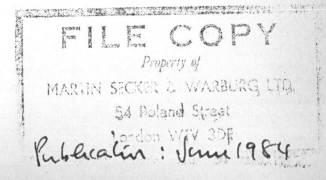

The Throwback

Tom Sharpe

Vintage Books
A Division of Random House
New York

First Vintage Books Edition, April 1984
Copyright © 1978 by Tom Sharpe

Library of Congress Cataloging in Publication Data
Sharpe, Tom.
The throwback.
I. Title.
[PR6069.H345T5 1984]   823′.914   83-40338
ISBN 0-394-72439-9 (pbk.)

Manufactured in the United States of America

Chapter one

It could be said of Lockhart Flawse when he carried his bride, Jessica, *née* Sandicott, across the threshold of 12 Sandicott Crescent, East Pursley, Surrey, that he was entering into married life with as little preparedness for its hazards and happiness as he had entered the world at five past seven on Monday, 6 September 1956, promptly killing his mother in the process. Since Miss Flawse had steadfastly refused to name his father even on the stinging nettles that composed her deathbed and had spent the hour of his delivery and her departure alternately wailing and shouting 'Great Scot!', it had devolved upon his grandfather to name the infant Lockhart after the great Scott's biographer and, at some risk to his own reputation, to allow Lockhart to assume the surname Flawse for the time being.

From that moment Lockhart had been allowed to assume nothing, not even a birth certificate. Old Mr Flawse had seen to that. If his daughter had been so obviously devoid of social discretion as to give birth to a bastard under a dry-stone wall while out cub-hunting, which dry-stone wall her horse had, more sensibly than she, refused, Mr Flawse was determined to ensure that his grandson grew up with none of his mother's faults. He had succeeded. At eighteen Lockhart knew as little about sex as his mother had known or cared about contraception. His life had been spent under the care of several housekeepers and later half a dozen tutors, the former chosen for their willingness to endure the bed and board of old Mr Flawse, and the latter for their other-worldliness.

Since Flawse Hall was situated on Flawse Fell close under Flawse Rigg some seventeen miles from the nearest town and on the bleakest expanse of moorland north of the Roman Wall, only the most desperate of housekeepers and other-worldly of tutors accepted the situation for long. There were other rigours than the natural. Mr Flawse was an extremely irritable man and the succession of tutors who had provided Lockhart with the most particular of general educations had done so under the strict proviso that Ovid was not to be included among the classics and that literature was to be dispensed with entirely.

Lockhart was to be taught the ancient virtues and mathematics. Mr Flawse was particularly hot on mathematics and believed in numbers as ferociously as his forefathers had believed in predestination and cattle-rustling. They formed in his opinion a firm foundation for a commercial career and were as entirely without obvious sexual connotations as were the features of his housekeepers. Since tutors, and other-worldly tutors at that, seldom combined a knowledge of both maths and the classics, Lockhart's education proceeded by fits and starts but was sufficiently thorough to defeat every attempt by the Local Authorities to provide him with a more orthodox schooling at public expense. The School Inspectors who ventured to Flawse Hall to obtain evidence that Lockhart's education was deficient came away confounded by his narrow erudition. They were unused to small boys who could recite their nineteen-times table in Latin and read the Old Testament in Urdu. They were also unused to conducting examinations in the presence of an old man who appeared to be toying with the trigger of an ostentatiously loaded shotgun aimed absent-mindedly in their direction. In the circumstances they felt that Lockhart Flawse, while hardly in safe hands, was educationally in excellent ones and that there was nothing to be gained, except in all probability a volley of buckshot, by attempting to take him into public care, a point of view that was shared by his tutors, who came less frequently with every passing year.

Mr Flawse made good their absence by teaching Lockhart himself. Born in 1887 at the height of the Empire, he still held those tenets to be true which had been commonplace in his youth. The British were the finest specimens of animal life that God and Nature had created. The Empire was still the greatest that had ever existed. Wogs began at Calais, and sex was necessary for procreation but was otherwise unmentionable and generally disgusting. The fact that the Empire had long since ceased to exist and that wogs, far from beginning at Calais, had reversed the process and in large measure ended at Dover, Mr Flawse ignored. He took no newspaper and, lacking any electricity at Flawse Hall, used this as an excuse for refusing to have even a transistor radio, let alone a television set, in the house. Sex, on the other hand, he couldn't ignore. Even at ninety he was consumed by guilt at his own excesses and the fact that these, like the Empire, had largely passed from reality to fantasy only made matters worse. In his mind Mr Flawse remained a profligate and maintained a regimen of cold baths and long walks to exercise his body and exorcize his soul. He also hunted and fished and shot and encouraged his bastard grandson in these healthy outdoor pursuits to the point where Lockhart could bring down a running hare at five hundred yards with a First World War 303 Lee-Enfield and a grouse at a hundred with a 22. By the time he was seventeen Lockhart had so decimated the wild life on Flawse Fell and the fish in the North Teen that even the foxes, carefully preserved from relatively painless death by gunshot to be hunted and torn to pieces by the hounds, found it difficult to make ends meet, and brought meets to an end by moving off to less exacting moors. It was largely in consequence of this migration, which coincided with the departure of his latest and most desirable housekeeper, that old Mr Flawse, resorting too heavily to the port bottle and the literary companionship of Carlyle, was urged by his personal physician, Dr Magrew, to take a holiday. The doctor was supported by Mr Bullstrode, the solicitor, at one of the monthly dinners at Flawse Hall which the old man had given for thirty years and which allowed him a forum for those vociferous disputations on things eternal, metaphysical, biological and generally slanderous. These dinners were his substitute for church attendance, and his arguments afterwards were his nearest approach to any recognizable religion.

'Damned if I will,' he said when Dr Magrew first mooted the idea of a holiday. 'And the fool who first said a change is as good as a rest didn't live in this benighted century.'

Dr Magrew helped himself to more port. 'You can't live in an unheated house without a housekeeper and expect to last another winter.'

'I've got Dodd and the bastard to look after me. And the house isn't unheated. There's coal in the drift mine up Slimeburn and Dodd brings it down. The bastard does the cooking.'

'And that's another thing,' said Dr Magrew, who rather suspected that Lockhart had cooked their dinner, 'your digestion won't stand the strain and you can't expect to keep the boy cooped up here for ever. It's time he saw something of the world.'

'Not till I find out who his father is,' said Mr Flawse malevolently. 'And when I do I'll horsewhip the swine to within an inch of his life.'

'You'll not be fit to horsewhip anyone unless you take our advice,' said Dr Magrew. 'Isn't that your opinion, Bullstrode?'

'Speaking as your friend and legal adviser,' said Mr Bullstrode glowing in the candlelight, 'I would say that I would regret the premature ending of these pleasant occasions by virtue of an obstinate disregard for the weather and our advice. You're not a young man and the question of your will ...'

'Damn my will, sir,' said old Mr Flawse, 'I'll make a will when I know whom I'm settling my money on and not before. And what is this advice you offer so readily?'

'Take a cruise,' said Mr Bullstrode, 'somewhere hot and sunny. I'm told the food is excellent.'

Mr Flawse stared into the depths of the decanter and considered the proposition. There was something in what his friends advised and besides there had recently been complaints from several tenant farmers that Lockhart, lacking any more fleet-footed quarry, had taken to pot-shooting sheep at fifteen hundred yards, complaints that had been confirmed by Lockhart's cuisine. They had had underdone mutton too frequently of late for Mr Flawse's digestion and conscience, and besides Lockhart was eighteen and it was high time he got shot of the lad before someone got shot by him. As if to reinforce this opinion there came the sound from the kitchen of Mr Dodd's Northumbrian pipes playing a melancholy air while Lockhart sat opposite him listening, just as he listened to Mr Dodd's stories of the grand old days and the best way to poach pheasant or tickle trout.

'I'll think about it,' Mr Flawse said finally.

That night a heavy fall of snow decided him, and Dr Magrew and Mr Bullstrode came down to breakfast to find him in a more amenable mood.

'I'll leave the arrangements to you, Bullstrode,' he said as he finished his coffee and lit a blackened pipe. 'And the bastard will go with me.'

'He'll need a birth certificate to get a passport,' said the solicitor, 'and ...'

'Born in a ditch and die in a dyke. I'll only register him when I know who his father is,' said Mr Flawse glowering.

'Quite,' said Mr Bullstrode who didn't want to go into the question of horsewhipping so early in the morning. 'I suppose we could still have him put on your passport.'

'Not as his father,' snarled Mr Flawse, the depths of whose feelings for his grandson were partly to be explained by the terrible suspicion that he himself might not altogether be devoid of responsibility for Lockhart's conception. The memory of one drunken encounter with a housekeeper who had seemed on recollection to have been younger and more resistant than her daytime appearance had led him to expect still haunted his conscience. 'Not as his father.'

'As his grandfather,' said Mr Bullstrode. 'I'll need a photograph.'

Mr Flawse went through to his study, rummaged in a bureau drawer and returned with one of Lockhart aged ten. Mr Bullstrode studied it dubiously.

'He's changed a lot since then,' he said.

'Not to my knowledge,' said Mr Flawse, 'and I should know. He was ever a gormless lout.'

'Aye, and for all practical purposes a non-existent one,' said Dr Magrew. 'You know he's not registered on the National Health system, and if he's ever taken ill I can foresee considerable difficulties in the matter of obtaining treatment.'

'He's never known a day's illness in his life,' Mr Flawse retorted. 'A healthier brute it would be difficult to find.'

'He could have an accident,' Mr Bullstrode pointed out.

But the old man shook his head. ' 'Tis too much to be hoped for. Dodd's seen to it he knows how to handle himself in an emergency. You'll have heard the saying that a poacher makes the best gamekeeper?' Mr Bullstrode and Dr Magrew had. 'Well, Dodd's the reverse. He's a gamekeeper who would make the best poacher,' continued Mr Flawse, 'which is what he has made of the bastard. There's not a bird nor beast safe within twenty miles when he's abroad.'

'Talking of abroad,' said Mr Bullstrode, not wishing as a solicitor to be privy to Lockhart's illegal activities, 'where would you like to go?'

'Somewhere South of Suez,' said Mr Flawse whose memory

for Kipling was not what it had been. 'I'll leave the rest to you.'

Three weeks later Lockhart and his grandfather left Flawse Hall in the ancient brougham Mr Flawse used for his more formal means of transport. As with everything else modern he eschewed the motor car. Mr Dodd sat up front at the reins, and behind was tied the cabin trunk Mr Flawse had last used in 1910 on a voyage to Calcutta. As the horses clattered down the metalled track from the Hall, Lockhart was in a state of high expectation. It was his first journey into the world of his grandfather's memories and his own imagination. From Hexham they took the train to Newcastle and from Newcastle to London and Southampton, Mr Flawse all the way complaining that the London North-Eastern Railway wasn't what it had been forty years before and Lockhart astonished to discover that not all women had partial beards and varicose veins. By the time they reached the ship old Mr Flawse was exhausted to the point of twice supposing, thanks to the complexion of two ticket collectors, that he was already back in Calcutta. It was with the greatest difficulty and the least examination of his passport that he was helped up the gangway and down to his cabin.

'I shall dine here in the stateroom,' he told the steward. 'The boy will sup aloft.'

The steward looked at the 'boy' and decided not to argue that the cabin was not strictly a stateroom, nor that dinners in cabins were things of the past.

'We've got one of the old sort in Number 19,' he told the stewardess afterwards, 'and when I say old I mean old. Wouldn't surprise me if he sailed on the *Titanic*.'

'I thought they all drowned,' said the stewardess, but the steward knew better. 'Not all. That old sod's a survivor if ever I saw one and his ruddy grandson's like something out of the Ark and I don't mean something cuddly.'

That evening as the *Ludlow Castle* sailed down the Solent, old Mr Flawse dined in his stateroom, and it was Lockhart, dressed conspicuously in tails and white tie which had once belonged to a larger uncle, who made his way up to the First Class Dining Saloon and was conducted to a table at which sat Mrs Sandicott and her daughter Jessica. For a moment, stunned by Jessica's beauty, he hesitated, then bowed and sat down.

Lockhart Flawse had not fallen in love at first sight. He had plunged.

Chapter two

And Jessica followed suit. One look at this tall, broad-shouldered young man who bowed and Jessica knew she was in love. But if with the young couple it was love at first sight, with Mrs Sandicott it was calculation at second. Lockhart's appearance in white tie and tails and his general air of incoherent embarrassment had a profound effect upon her, and when during the meal he managed to stammer that his grandfather was dining in their stateroom Mrs Sandicott's suburban soul thrilled to the sound.

'Your stateroom?' she asked. 'You did say your stateroom?'

'Yes,' mumbled Lockhart, 'you see he's ninety and the journey from the Hall fatigued him.'

'The Hall,' murmured Mrs Sandicott and looked significantly at her daughter.

'Flawse Hall,' said Lockhart. 'It's the family seat.'

Once again Mrs Sandicott's depths were stirred. The circles in which she moved did not have family seats and here, in the shape of this angular and large youth whose accent, acquired from old Mr Flawse, went back to the late nineteenth century, she perceived those social attributes to which she had long aspired.

'And your grandfather is really ninety?' Lockhart nodded. 'It's amazing that such an elderly man should be taking a cruise at his time of life,' continued Mrs Sandicott. 'Doesn't his poor wife miss him?'

'I really don't know. My grandmother died in nineteen thirty-five,' said Lockhart, and Mrs Sandicott's hopes rose even higher. By the end of the meal she had winkled the story of

Lockhart's life from him, and with each new piece of information Mrs Sandicott's conviction grew that at long, long last she was on the brink of an opportunity too good to be missed. She was particularly impressed by Lockhart's admission that he had been educated by private tutors. Mrs Sandicott's world most certainly did not include people who had their sons educated by tutors. At best they sent them to Public Schools. And so, as coffee was served, Mrs Sandicott was positively purring. She knew now that she had not been wrong to come on the cruise and when finally Lockhart rose and lifted her chair back for her and then for Jessica, she went down to her cabin with her daughter in a state of social ecstasy.

'What a very nice young man,' she said. 'Such charming manners and so well brought up.'

Jessica said nothing. She did not want to spoil the savour of her feelings by revealing them. She had been overwhelmed by Lockhart but in a different way to her mother. If Lockhart represented a social world to which Mrs Sandicott aspired, to Jessica he was the very soul of romance. And romance was all in all to her. She had listened to his description of Flawse Hall on Flawse Fell close under Flawse Rigg, and had garnished each word with a new significance that came from the romantic novels with which she had filled the emptiness of her adolescence. It was an emptiness that amounted to vacuity.

At eighteen Jessica Sandicott was endowed with physical charms beyond her control and an innocence of mind that was both the fault and despair of her mother. To be more precise, her innocence resulted from the late Mr Sandicott's will in which he had left all twelve houses in Sandicott Crescent 'to my darling daughter, Jessica, on her reaching the age of maturity'. To his wife he bequeathed Sandicott & Partner, Chartered Accountants and Tax Consultants, of Wheedle Street in the City of London. But the late Mr Sandicott's will had bequeathed more than these tangible assets. It had left Mrs Sandicott with a sense of grievance and the conviction that her husband's premature death at the age of forty-five was proof positive that she had married no gentleman, the proof of his ungentlemanliness lying in his failure to depart this world at least ten years earlier when she was still at a reasonably remarriageable age, or, failing that, to have left her his entire fortune. From this misfortune Mrs Sandicott had formed two resolutions. The first was that her next husband would be a very rich man with a life expectancy of as few years as possible and preferably with a terminal illness; the second to see that Jessica reached the age of maturity as slowly as a religious education could delay. So far she had failed in her first objective and only partly succeeded in her second.

Jessica had been to several convents, and the plural was indicative of her mother's partial failure. At the first she had developed a religious fervour of such pronounced proportions that she had decided to become a nun and subtract her own worldly possessions by adding them to those of the Order. Mrs Sandicott had removed her precipitately to a less persuasive convent and for a time things looked distinctly brighter. Unfortunately, so did several nuns. Jessica's angelic face and innocence of soul had so combined that four nuns fell madly in love with her and the Mother Superior, to save their souls, had requested that Jessica's disturbing influence be removed. Mrs Sandicott's self-evident argument that she wasn't to blame for her daughter's attractions and that if anyone ought to be expelled it was the lesbian nuns cut no ice with the Mother Superior.

'I do not blame the child. She was made to be loved,' she said with suspicious emotion and in direct contradiction to Mrs Sandicott's views on the subject. 'She will make some good man a wonderful wife.'

'Knowing men rather more intimately than I hope you do,' riposted Mrs Sandicott, 'she will marry the first scoundrel who asks her.'

It was a fatefully accurate prediction. To protect her daughter from temptation and to maintain her own financial income from the rents of the houses in Sandicott Crescent, Mrs Sandicott had confined Jessica to her home and a correspondence course in typing. By the time Jessica reached eighteen it was still impossible to say of her that she had reached the age of maturity. If anything she had regressed and while Mrs Sandicott supervised the running of Sandicott & Partner, the partner being a Mr Treyer, Jessica sank back into a literary slough of romantic novels populated entirely by splendid young men. In short she lived in a world of her imagination, the fecundity of which was proven one morning when she announced that she was in love with the milkman and intended to marry him. Mrs Sandicott studied the milkman next day and decided that the time had come for desperate measures. By no stretch of her own imagination could she visualize the milkman as an eligible young man. Her arguments to this effect, backed by the fact that the milkman was forty-nine, married and the father of six children, and hadn't been consulted by his bride-to-be in any case, failed to influence Jessica.

'I shall sacrifice myself to his happiness,' she said. Mrs Sandicott determined otherwise and promptly booked two tickets on the *Ludlow Castle* in the conviction that whatever else the ship might have to offer in the way of possible husbands for her daughter, they couldn't be less eligible than the milkman. Besides, she had herself to think of, and cruise liners were notoriously happy hunting-grounds for middle-aged widows with an eye to the main chance. That Mrs Sandicott's own eye was fastened on an ancient and potentially terminal old man with money only made the prospect of the voyage the more desirable. And Lockhart's appearance had heralded the mainest chance of all, an eligible and evidently half-witted young man for her idiot daughter and in his stateroom a gentleman of ninety with an enormous estate in Northumberland. That night Mrs Sandicott went to sleep a cheerful woman. In the bunk above Jessica sighed and murmured the magical words, 'Lockhart Flawse of Flawse Hall on Flawse Fell close under Flawse Rigg.' They formed a litany of Flawse to the religion of romance.

On the boat-deck Lockhart leant on the rail and stared out over the sea, his heart filled with feelings as turbulent as the white wake of the ship. He had met the most wonderful girl in the world and for the very first time he realized that women were not simply unprepossessing creatures who cooked meals, swept floors and, having made beds, made strange noises in them late at night. There was more to them than that but what that something more was Lockhart could only guess.

His knowledge of sex was limited to the discovery, made while gutting rabbits, that bucks had balls and does didn't. There

14

appeared to be some connection between these anatomical differences that accounted for ladies having babies and men not. On the one occasion he had attempted to explore the difference further by asking the tutor in Urdu how Mizriat begat Ludin in Genesis 10:13 he had received a clout across the ear that had temporarily deafened him and had given him the permanent impression that such questions were better left unasked. On the other hand he was aware that there was such a thing as marriage and that out of marriage came families. One of his distant Flawse cousins had married a farmer from Elsdon and had subsequently raised four children. The housekeeper had told him as much and no more, except that it had been a shotgun marriage which had merely deepened the mystery, shotguns in Lockhart's experience being reserved for putting things to death rather than bringing them to life.

To make matters even more incomprehensible, the only occasions on which his grandfather had permitted him to visit his relatives, had been to their burials. Mr Flawse enjoyed funerals immensely. They reinforced his belief that he was hardier than any other Flawse and that death was the only certainty. 'In any uncertain world we can take consolation in the verity, the eternal verity, that death comes to us all in the end,' he would tell a bereaved widow to terrible effect. And afterwards, in the jaunting-cart he used for such outings, he would expatiate glowingly to Lockhart on the merits of death as preserver of moral values. 'Without it we would have nothing to stop us from behaving like cannibals. But put the fear of death up a man and it has a wondrously purgative effect.'

And so Lockhart had continued in ignorance of the facts of life while acquiring extensive knowledge of those of death. It was left to his bodily functions and his feelings to guide him in quite contrary directions in the matter of sex. Lacking a mother and loathing most of his grandfather's housekeepers, his feelings for women were decidedly negative. On the more positive side he got a great deal of pleasure from nocturnal emissions. But their significance escaped him. He didn't have wet dreams in the presence of women and he didn't have women at all.

And so leaning on the guard rail staring down at the white foam in the moonlight Lockhart expressed his new feelings in images he knew best. He longed to spend the rest of his life shooting things and laying them at Jessica Sandicott's feet. With this exalted notion of love Lockhart went down to the cabin where old Mr Flawse, clad in a red flannel nightgown, was snoring noisily, and climbed into bed.

If Mrs Sandicott's expectations had been aroused by Lockhart's appearance at dinner they were confirmed by old Mr Flawse at breakfast. Dressed in a suit that had been out of fashion as far back as 1925, he cut a swathe through subservient waiters with an arrogance far older than his suit and, taking his place with a 'Good morning to you, ma'am', surveyed the menu with disgust.

'I want porridge,' he told the headwaiter who hovered nervously, 'and none of your half-boiled mush. Oats, man, oats '

'Yes, sir, and what to follow?'

'A double ration of eggs and bacon. And find some kidneys,' said Mr Flawse to the prognostic delight of Mrs Sandicott, who knew all there was to know about cholesterol. 'And by double I mean double. Four eggs and a dozen rashers. Then toast and marmalade and two large pots of tea. And the same goes for the boy.'

The waiter hurried away with this lethal order and Mr Flawse looked over his glasses at Mrs Sandicott and Jessica.

'Your daughter, ma'am?' he inquired.

'My only daughter,' murmured Mrs Sandicott.

'My compliments to you,' said Mr Flawse without making it clear whether he was praising Mrs Sandicott for her daughter's beauty or her singularity. Mrs Sandicott blushed her acknowledgement. Mr Flawse's old-world manners were almost as enchanting to her as his age. For the rest of the meal there was silence broken only by the old man's denunciation of the tea as weaker than well-water and his insistence on a proper pot of breakfast tea you could stand your spoon up in. But if Mr Flawse appeared to be concentrating on his bacon and eggs and tea that contained enough tannin to scour its way through a blocked sewer-pipe, his actual thoughts were elsewhere and moved along lines very similar to those of Mrs Sandicott though with a rather different emphasis. In the course of his long life he had learnt to smell a snob a mile off and Mrs Sandicott's deference suited him well. She would, he considered, make an excellent housekeeper. Better still, there was her daughter. She was clearly a gormless girl, and just as clearly an ideal match for his gormless grandson. Mr Flawse observed Lockhart out of the corner of a watery eye and recognized the symptoms of love.

'Sheeps' eyes,' he muttered aloud to himself to the confusion of the hovering waiter, who apologized for their not being on the menu.

'And who said they were?' snapped Mr Flawse and dismissed the man with a wave of a mottled hand.

Mrs Sandicott absorbed all these details of behaviour and calculated Mr Flawse to be exactly the man she had been waiting for, a nonagenarian with an enormous estate, and therefore an enormous bank account, and an appetite for just those items on the menu best suited to kill him off almost immediately. It was therefore with no affectation of gratitude that she accepted his offer of a stroll round the deck after breakfast. Mr Flawse dismissed Lockhart and Jessica to go and play deck quoits, and presently he and Mrs Sandicott were lapping the promenade deck at a pace that took her breath away. By the time they had covered the old man's statutory two miles, Mrs Sandicott's breath had been taken away for other reasons. Mr Flawse was not a man to mince his words.

'Let me make myself plain,' he said unnecessarily as they took their seats in deckchairs; 'I am not overgiven to delaying my thoughts. You have a daughter of marriageable age and I have a grandson who ought to be married. Am I right?'

Mrs Sandicott adjusted the blanket round her knees and said with some show of delicacy that she supposed so.

'I am so, ma'am,' said Mr Flawse, 'I know it and you know it. In truth we both know it. Now, I am an old man and at my age I cannot expect a sufficient future to see my grandson settled according to his station. In short, ma'am, as the great Milton expressed it "in me there's no delay". You take my meaning?'

Mrs Sandicott took it and denied it simultaneously. 'You're quite remarkably fit for your time of life, Mr Flawse,' she said encouragingly.

'That's as may be, but the Great Certainty looms,' said Mr Flawse, 'and 'tis equally certain that my grandson is a nincompoop who will in a short time, being my only heir, be a rich nincompoop.'

He allowed Mrs Sandicott to savour the prospect for a moment or two. 'And being a nincompoop he needs a wife who has her head screwed on the right way.'

He paused again and it was on the tip of Mrs Sandicott's tongue to remark that Jessica's head, if screwed on at all, had been screwed on against the thread, but she restrained her words.

'I suppose you could say that,' she said.

'I can and I do,' continued Mr Flawse. 'It has ever been a Flawse trait, ma'am, in choosing our womenfolk, to take cognizance of their mothers, and I have no hesitation in saying that you have a shrewd head for business, Mrs Sandicott, ma'am.'

'It's very kind of you to say so, Mr Flawse,' Mrs Sandicott simpered, 'and since my poor husband died I have had to be the breadwinner. Sandicott & Partner are chartered accountants and I have run the business.'

'Exactly,' said Mr Flawse. 'I have a nose for these things and it would be a comfort to know that my grandson was in good hands.' He stopped. Mrs Sandicott waited expectantly.

'And what hands did you have in mind, Mr Flawse?' she asked finally, but Mr Flawse had decided the time had come to feign sleep. With his nose above the blanket and his eyes closed he snored softly. He had baited the trap. There was no point in watching over it and presently Mrs Sandicott stole quietly away with mixed feelings. On the one hand she had not come on the cruise to find a husband for her daughter; she had come to avoid one. On the other, if Mr Flawse's words meant anything he was looking for a wife for his grandson. For one wild moment Mrs Sandicott considered Lockhart for herself and instantly rejected him. It was Jessica or no one, and the loss of Jessica would mean the loss of the rent of the twelve houses in Sandicott Crescent. If only the old fool had proposed to her she would have seen things in a different light.

'Two birds with one stone,' she murmured to herself at the thought of a double killing. It was worth calculating about. And so, as the two young lovers gambolled on the sun-deck, Mrs Sandicott ensconced herself in a corner of the First Class Lounge and calculated. Through the window she could keep an eye on the blanketed figure of Mr Flawse recumbent in the deckchair. Every now and again his knees twitched. Mr Flawse

18

had given way to those sexual excesses of the imagination which were the bane of his non-conformist conscience, and for the first time Mrs Sandicott figured in them largely.

Chapter three

Imagination played a large part in the love that blossomed between Lockhart and Jessica. Having plunged they sported like water babies in the swimming pool or frolicked at deck tennis and as each day passed, and the ship steamed slowly south into equatorial waters, their passion grew inarticulately. Not entirely inarticulately but when they spoke during the day their words were matter-of-fact. It was only at night, when the older generation danced the quickstep to the ship's band and they were left alone to stare down at the white water swirling from the ship's side and invest one another with those qualities their different upbringings had extolled, that they spoke their feelings. Even then it was by way of other people and other places that they told one another what they felt. Lockhart talked of Mr Dodd and how at night he and the gamekeeper would sit at the settle in the stone-flagged kitchen with the black iron range glowing between them while the wind howled in the chimney outside and Mr Dodd's pipes wailed inside. And of how he and Mr Dodd would herd the sheep or stalk game in the wooded valley known as Slimeburn where Mr Dodd dug coal from a drift mine that had first been worked in 1805. Finally there were the fishing expeditions on the great reservoir fringed with pine that stood a mile from Flawse Hall. Jessica saw it all so clearly through a mist of Mazo de la Roche and Brontë and every romantic novel she had ever read. Lockhart was the young gallant come to sweep her off her feet and carry her from the boredom of her life in East Pursley and away from her mother's cynicism to the ever-ever land of Flawse Hall on Flawse Fell close under Flawse Rigg where the wind blew fierce and the snow lay thick outside but all within was warm with old wood and dogs and the swirl of Mr Dodd's Northumbrian pipes and old Mr Flawse sitting at the oval mahogany dining-table disputing by candlelight questions of great moment with his two friends, Dr Magrew and Mr Bullstrode. In the tapestry woven from Lockhart's words she created a picture of a past which she dearly longed to make her future.

Lockhart's mind worked more practically. To him Jessica was an angel of radiant beauty for whom he would lay down, if not his own life, at least that of anything which moved within range of his most powerful rifle.

But while the young people were only implicitly in love, the old were more outspoken. Mr Flawse, having baited the trap for another housekeeper, waited for Mrs Sandicott's response. It came later than he had expected. Mrs Sandicott was not a woman to be hustled and she had calculated with care. Of one thing she was certain. If Mr Flawse wanted Jessica for his daughter-in-law he must take her mother for his wife. She broached the subject with due care and by way of the mention of property.

'If Jessica were to marry,' she said one evening after dinner, 'I would be without a home.'

Mr Flawse signalled his delight at the news by ordering another brandy. 'How so, ma'am?' he inquired.

'Because my poor dear late husband left all twelve houses in Sandicott Crescent, including our own, to our daughter and I would never live with the young married couple.'

Mr Flawse sympathized. He had lived long enough with Lockhart to know the hazards of sharing a house with the brute. 'There is always Flawse Hall, ma'am. You would be very welcome there.'

'As what? A temporary guest or were you thinking of a more permanent arrangement?'

Mr Flawse hesitated. There was an inflexion in Mrs Sandicott's voice which suggested that the permanent arrangement he had in mind might not be at all to her liking. 'There need be nothing temporary about your being a guest, ma'am. You could stay as long as you liked.'

Mrs Sandicott's eyes glinted with suburban steel. 'And what precisely would the neighbours make of that, Mr Flawse?'

Mr Flawse hesitated again. The fact that his nearest neighbours were six miles off at Black Pockrington, and that he didn't give a tuppenny damn what they thought, presented a prospect that had lost him too many housekeepers already and was unlikely to appeal to Mrs Sandicott.

'I think they would understand,' he prevaricated. But Mrs Sandicott was not to be fobbed off with understandings. 'I have my reputation to think of,' she said. 'I would never consent to staying alone in a house with a man without there being some legal status to my being there.'

'Legal status, ma'am?' said Mr Flawse and took a swig of brandy to steady his nerves. The bloody woman was proposing to him.

'I think you know what I mean,' said Mrs Sandicott.

Mr Flawse said nothing. The ultimatum was too clear.

'And so if the young couple are to be married,' she continued remorselessly, 'and I repeat "if", then I think we should consider our own futures.'

Mr Flawse did and found it an uncertain one. Mrs Sandicott was not a wholly unattractive woman. Already in his dozing fantasies he had stripped her naked and found her plump body very much to his taste. On the other hand wives had disadvantages. They tended to be domineering and while a domineering housekeeper could be sacked a wife couldn't, and Mrs Sandicott for all her deference seemed to be a strong-minded woman. To spend the rest of his life with a strong-minded woman was more than he had bargained for, but if it meant getting the bastard Lockhart off his hands it might be worth the risk. Beisdes there was always the isolation of Flawse Hall to tame the strongest-minded woman and he would have an ally in Mr Dodd. Yes, definitely an ally in Mr Dodd and Mr Dodd was not without resource. And finally if he couldn't sack a wife nor could the wife leave like a housekeeper. Mr Flawse smiled into his brandy and nodded.

'Mrs Sandicott,' he said with unaccustomed familiarity, 'am I right in supposing that it would not come averse to you to change you name to Mrs Flawse?'

Mrs Sandicott beamed her assent. 'It would make me very happy, Mr Flawse,' she said, and took his mottled hand.

'Then allow me to make you happy, ma'am,' said the old man, with the private thought that once he'd got her up to

21

Flawse Hall she'd get her fill of happiness one way or another. As if to celebrate this forthcoming union of the two families the ship's band struck up a foxtrot. When it had finished Mr Flawse returned to more practical matters.

'I must warn you that Lockhart will need employment,' he said. 'I had always intended to keep him to manage the estate he will one day inherit but if your daughter has twelve houses . . .'

Mrs Sandicott came to his rescue. 'The houses are all let and at rents fixed by the Rent Tribunal on long leases,' she said, 'but dear Lockhart could always join my late husband's firm. I understand he is clever with figures.'

'He has had an excellent grounding in arithmetic. I have no hesitation in saying so.'

'Then he should do very well at Sandicott & Partner, Chartered Accountants and Tax Consultants,' said Mrs Sandicott.

Mr Flawse congratulated himself on his foresight. 'Then that is settled,' he said. 'There remains simply the question of the wedding.'

'Weddings,' said Mrs Sandicott, emphasizing the plural. 'I had always hoped that Jessica would have a church wedding.'

Mr Flawse shook his head. 'At my age, ma'am, there would be something incongruous about a church wedding to be so closely followed by a funeral. I would prefer a more cheerful venue. Mind you, I disapprove of registry offices.'

'Oh so do I,' Mrs Sandicott agreed, 'they are so unromantic.'

But there was nothing unromantic about the old man's reluctance to see Lockhart married in a registry office. It had dawned on him that without a birth certificate it might be impossible to marry the swine off at all. And besides there was still the fact of his illegitimacy to be concealed.

'I see no reason why the Captain shouldn't marry us,' he said finally. Mrs Sandicott thrilled at the notion. It combined speed and no time for second thoughts with an eccentricity that was almost aristocratic. She could boast about it to her friends.

'Then I'll see the Captain about it in the morning,' said Mr Flawse, and it was left to Mrs Sandicott to break the news to the young couple.

She found them on the boat-deck whispering together. For a moment she stood and listened. They so seldom spoke in her presence that she was curious to know what they did say to one another in her absence. What she heard was both reassuring and disturbing.

'Oh, Lockhart.'

'Oh, Jessica.'

'You're so wonderful.'

'So are you.'

'You really do mean that?'

'Of course I do.'

'Oh, Lockhart.'

'Oh, Jessica.'

Under the gleaming moon and the glittering eye of Mrs Sandicott they clasped one another in their arms and Lockhart tried to think what to do next. Jessica supplied the answer.

'Kiss me, darling.'

'Where?' said Lockhart.

'Here?' said Jessica and offered him her lips.

'There?' said Lockhart. 'Are you sure?'

In the shadow of the lifeboat Mrs Sandicott stiffened. What she had just heard but couldn't see was without doubt nauseating. Either her future son-in-law was mentally deficient or her daughter was sexually more sophisticated, and in Mrs Sandicott's opinion positively perverse, than she had ever dreamt. Mrs Sandicott cursed those damned nuns. Lockhart's next remark confirmed her fears.

'Isn't it a bit sticky?'

'Oh, darling, you're so romantic,' said Jessica, 'you really are.'

Mrs Sandicott wasn't. She emerged from the shadows and bore down on them. 'That's quite enough of that,' she said as they staggered apart. 'When you're married you can do whatever you like but no daughter of mine is going to indulge in obscene acts on the boat-deck of a liner. Besides, someone might see you.'

Jessica and Lockhart stared at her in amazement. It was Jessica who spoke first.

'When we're married? You really did say that, mummy?'

'I said exactly that,' said Mrs Sandicott. 'Lockhart's grandfather and I have decided that you should . . .'

She was interrupted by Lockhart who, with a gesture of

chivalry that so endeared him to Jessica, knelt at his future mother-in-law's feet and reached out towards her. Mrs Sandicott recoiled abruptly. Lockhart's posture combined with Jessica's recent suggestion was more than she could stomach.

'Don't you dare touch me,' she squawked and backed away. Lockhart hastened to his feet.

'I only meant . . .' he began but Mrs Sandicott didn't want to know.

'Never mind that now. It's time you both went to bed,' she said firmly. 'We can discuss arrangements for the wedding in the morning.'

'Oh, mummy . . .'

'And don't call me "mummy",' said Mrs Sandicott. 'After what I've just heard I'm not at all sure I *am* your mother.'

She and Jessica left Lockhart standing bemused on the boat-deck. He was going to get married to the most beautiful girl in the world. For a moment he looked round for a gun to fire to announce his happiness but there was nothing. In the end he unhooked a lifebelt from the rail and hurled it high over the side into the water and gave a shout of joyful triumph. Then he too went down to his cabin oblivious of the fact that he had just alerted the bridge to the presence of 'Man Overboard' and that in the wake of the liner the lifebelt bobbed frantically and its warning beacon glowed.

As the engines went full astern and a boat was lowered, Lockhart sat on the edge of his bunk listening to his grandfather's instructions. He was to marry Jessica Sandicott, he was to live in Sandicott Crescent, East Pursley, and start work at Sandicott & Partner.

'That's marvellous,' he said when Mr Flawse finished, 'I couldn't have wished for anything better.'

'I could,' said Mr Flawse, struggling into his nightgown. 'I've got to marry the bitch to get rid of you.'

'The bitch?' said Lockhart. 'But I thought . . .'

'The mother, you dunderhead,' said Mr Flawse and knelt on the floor. 'Oh Lord, Thou knowest that I have been afflicted for ninety years by the carnal necessities of women,' he cried. 'Make these my final years beneficent with the peace that passes all understanding and by Thy great mercy lead me in the paths of righteousness to the father of this my bastard grandson, that I may yet flog the swine within an inch of his life. Amen.'

On this cheerful note he got into bed and left Lockhart to undress in the darkness, wondering what the carnal necessities of women were.

Next morning the Captain of the *Ludlow Castle*, who had spent half the night searching for the Man Overboard and the other half ordering the crew to check the occupants of all cabins to ascertain if anyone had indeed fallen over the side, was confronted by the apparition of Mr Flawse dressed in a morning suit and grey topper.

'Married? You want me to marry you?' said the Captain, when Mr Flawse had made known his request.

'I want you to conduct the ceremony,' said Mr Flawse. 'I have neither the desire to marry you nor you to marry me. Truth be told, I don't want to marry the damned woman either, but needs must when the devil drives.'

The Captain eyed him uncertainly. Mr Flawse's language, like his costume, not to mention his advanced age, argued a senility that called for the services of the ship's doctor rather than his own.

'Are you sure you know your own mind on this matter?' he asked when Mr Flawse had further explained that not only was the marriage to be between himself and Mrs Sandicott but between his grandson and Mrs Sandicott's daughter. Mr Flawse bristled. 'I know my own mind, sir, rather better than it would appear you know your own duty. As Master of this vessel you are empowered by law to conduct marriages and funerals. Is that not so?'

The Captain conceded that it was, with the private reservation that in Mr Flawse's case his wedding and burial at sea were likely to follow rather too closely for comfort.

'But wouldn't it be better if you were to wait until we reach Capetown?' he asked. 'Shipboard romances tend to be very transitory affairs in my experience.'

'In your experience,' said Mr Flawse, 'I dare say they do. In mine they don't. By the time you reach four-score years and ten any romance is in the nature of things bound to be a transitory affair.'

'I see that,' said the Captain. 'And how does Mrs Sandicott feel about the matter?'

'She wants me to make an honest woman of her. An impossible task in my opinion but so be it,' said Mr Flawse. 'That's what she wants and that's what she will get.'

Further argument merely resulted in Mr Flawse losing his temper and the Captain submitting. 'If the old fool wants the wedding,' he told the Purser later, 'I'm damned if I can stop him. For all I know he'll institute an action under Maritime Law if I refuse.'

And so it was as the ship sailed towards the Cape of Good Hope that Lockhart Flawse and Jessica Sandicott became Mr and Mrs Flawse while Mrs Sandicott achieved her long ambition of marrying a very rich old man with but a short time to live. Mr Flawse for his part consoled himself with the thought that whatever disadvantages the ex-Mrs Sandicott might display as a wife, he had rid himself once and for all of a bastard grandson while acquiring a housekeeper who need never be paid and would never be able to give notice. As if to emphasize this latter point he refused to leave the ship while she lay in Capetown, and it was left to Jessica and Lockhart to spend their honeymoon chastely climbing Table Mountain and admiring one another from the top. When the ship set out on the return voyage only their names and their cabins had changed. Mrs Sandicott found herself closeted with old Mr Flawse and prey to those sexual excesses which had previously been reserved for his former housekeepers and of late for his imagination. And in her old cabin Jessica and Lockhart lay in one another's arms as ignorant of any further purpose in their marriage as their singular upbringings had left them. For another eleven days the ship sailed north and by the time the two married couples disembarked at Southampton, it could be said that, apart from old Mr Flawse, whose excesses had taken some toll of his strength and who had to be carried down the gangway in a wheelchair, they were all entering upon a new life.

Chapter four

If the world of Flawse Hall on Flawse Fell close under Flawse Rigg, Northumberland, had played a large part in persuading Jessica that Lockhart was the hero she wanted to marry, the world of Sandicott Crescent, East Pursley, Surrey, had played no part in Lockhart's choice at all. Used as he was to the open moors of the Border country where the curlews, until he shot them, cried, Sandicott Crescent, a cul-de-sac of twelve substantial houses set in substantial gardens and occupied by substantial tenants with substantial incomes, was a world apart from anything he knew. Built in the thirties as an investment by the foresighted if late Mr Sandicott, the twelve houses were bordered to the south by the Pursley Golf Course and to the north by the bird sanctuary, a stretch of gorse and birch whose proper purpose was less to preserve bird life than to maintain the property values of Mr Sandicott's investment. In short it was an enclave of large houses with mature gardens. Each house was as different in style and similar in comfort as the ingenuity of architects could make it. Pseudo-Tudor prevailed, with an admixture of Stockbroker Spanish Colonial, distinguished by green glazed tiles, and one British Bauhaus with a flat roof, small square windows and the occasional porthole to add a nautical air. And everywhere trees and bushes, lawns and rockeries, rose bushes and ramblers were carefully clipped and trimmed to indicate the cultivation of their owners and the selectness of the district. All in all, Sandicott Crescent was the height of suburbia, the apex of that architectural triangle which marked the highest point of the topographical chart of middle-class ambition. The result was that the rates were enormous and the rents fixed. Mr Sandicott for all his prudence had not foreseen the Rent Act and Capital Gains Tax. Under the former there was no way of evicting tenants or increasing the rent they paid to a financially profitable sum; under the latter the sale of a house earned more for the Exchequer than it did for the owner; together the Rent Act and the tax nullified all Mr Sandicott's provisions for his daughter's future. Finally, and most aggravatingly of all, from Mrs Sandicott's point of view, the inhabitants of the Crescent took plenty of exercise, ate sensible diets and generally refused to oblige her by dying.

It was in large part the knowledge that she was saddled with twelve unsaleable houses whose combined rents barely covered the cost of their maintenance that had persuaded Mrs Sandicott that Jessica had reached the age of maturity she had so assiduously delayed. If Mr Flawse had rid himself of the liability of Lockhart, Mrs Sandicott had done much the same with Jessica and without further inquiry into the extent of Mr Flawse's fortune. It had seemed enough that he owned five thousand acres, a Hall and had but a short life expectancy.

By the time they had disembarked she had begun to have doubts. Mr Flawse had insisted on immediately catching a train to London and thence to Newcastle and had absolutely refused to allow Mrs Flawse to collect her belongings first or to drive him north in her large Rover.

'Ma'am,' he said, 'I place no faith in the infernal combustion engine. I was born before it and I do not intend to die behind it.' Mrs Flawse's arguments had been countered by his ordering the porter to put their baggage on the train. Mr Flawse followed the baggage and Mrs Flawse followed him. Lockhart and Jessica were left to move straight into Number 12 Sandicott Crescent with the promise to have her belongings packed and sent by removal van to Flawse Hall as quickly as possible.

And so the young couple started their married but unorthodox life in a house with five bedrooms, a double garage and a workshop in which the late Mr Sandicott, who had been handy with tools, had made things. Each morning Lockhart left the house, walked to the station and caught the train to London. There in the offices of Sandicott & Partner he began his apprenticeship under Mr Treyer. From the start there were difficulties. They lay less with Lockhart's ability to cope with figures – his limited education had left him mathematically exceedingly proficient – than in the directness of his approach to the problems of tax avoidance, or as Mr Treyer preferred to call it, Income Protection.

'Income and Asset Protection,' he told Lockhart, 'has a more positive ring to it than tax avoidance. And we must be positive.'

Lockhart took his advice and combined it with the positive simplicity his grandfather had adopted towards matters of income tax. Since the old man had transacted all possible business in cash and had made a habit of hurling every letter from the Income Tax authorities into the fire without reading it while at the same time ordering Mr Bullstrode to inform the bureaucratic swine that he was losing money not making it, Lockhart's adoption of his methods at Sandicott & Partner, while initially successful, was ultimately catastrophic. Mr Treyer had been delighted at first to find his IN tray so empty, and it was only his early arrival one morning to discover Lockhart using the toilet as an incinerator for all envelopes marked, 'On Her Majesty's Service' that alerted him to the cause of the sudden cessation of final demands. Worse still, Mr Treyer had long used what he called his Non-Existent Letter device as a means of confusing Income Tax officials to the point where they had nervous breakdowns or demanded to be transferred to other correspondence. Mr Treyer was proud of his Non-Existent Letter technique. It consisted of supposed replies which began 'Your letter of the 5th refers . . .' when in fact no letter of the 5th had been received. The consequent exchange of increasingly acrimonious denials by tax officials and Mr Treyer's continued assertions had been extremely beneficial to his clients if not to the nerves of Income Tax officials. Lockhart's arson deprived him of the ability to start letters beginning 'Your letter of the 5th refers . . .' with any confidence that one didn't.

'For all I know there may well have been half a dozen bloody letters of the 5th and all of them referring to some vital piece of information I know nothing about,' he shouted at Lockhart who promptly suggested that he try the 6th instead. Mr Treyer regarded him with starting eyes.

'Which since you burnt those too is a bloody useless suggestion,' he bawled.

'Well, you told me it was our business to protect our clients' interests and to be positive,' said Lockhart, 'and that's what I was doing.'

'How the hell can we protect clients' interests when we don't know what they are?' Mr Treyer demanded.

'But we do,' said Lockhart. 'It's all there in their files. I mean take Mr Gypsum, the architect. I was looking in his file the other day and he made £80,000 the year before last and all he paid in income tax was £1,758. The rest went in expenses. Let

29

me see. He spent £16,000 in the Bahamas in May and . . .'

'Stop,' yelled Mr Treyer, on the verge of apoplexy, 'I don't want to hear what he spent . . . Dear Christ!'

'Well, that's what he said he did,' objected Lockhart. 'It's there in his letter to you. £16,000 in four days. Whatever do you think he did with all that money in only four days?'

Mr Treyer leant forward and clutched his head with a hand. To be lumbered with a mentally deficient creature with a photographic memory who went around burning Her Majesty's Official correspondence with a disregard that bordered on the insane was shortening his life.

'Look,' he said as patiently as he could, 'from now on I don't want you to go anywhere near those files, you or anyone else, do you understand?'

'Yes,' said Lockhart. 'What I don't understand is why the richer you are the less tax you pay. There's Gypsum earning a whacking £80,000 and paying £1,758.40 pence while Mrs Ponsonby who only got £6,315.32 pence in income had to shell out £2,472. I mean . . .'

'Shut up,' screamed Mr Treyer, 'I don't want to hear any more of your questions and I don't want to catch you within ten yards of a filing cabinet. Is that clear?'

'If you say so,' said Lockhart.

'I do say so,' said Mr Treyer. 'If I so much as see you glancing towards the files . . . Oh get out.'

Lockhart got out and Mr Treyer tried to restore his shattered nerves by taking a pink pill and a paper cup of whisky. Two days later he had cause to regret his instructions. A series of terrible screams from the room which contained the Value Added Tax records sent him scurrying through to find an officer of the Customs and Excise VAT department trying to extricate his fingers from the drawer of a filing cabinet which Lockhart had slammed shut just as he was reaching for a file.

'Well, you told me not to let anyone go near those files,' Lockhart explained as the VAT man was led away to have four broken fingers attended to by a doctor. Mr Treyer stared at him frenziedly and tried to think of an adequate phrase to describe his detestation.

'I mean,' continued Lockhart, 'if he had laid a hand on Mr Fixstein's VAT records . . .'

'Laid a hand!' screamed Mr Treyer almost as loudly as the VAT man. 'The poor sod won't have a hand to lay after what you've just been and done to him. And what's worse we'll have a hundred Excise men descend on us tonight and go through our books with a fine-tooth comb.' He paused and tried to think of a way out of the ghastly mess. 'Now you just go through and apologize and tell him it was an accident and perhaps ...'

'I won't,' said Lockhart. 'It wasn't.'

'I know it bloody wasn't,' yelled Mr Treyer. 'I suppose if he had stuck his fucking head inside you'd have done the same.'

'I doubt it,' said Lockhart.

'I don't. Still it's a relief to know ...' Mr Treyer began but Lockhart ended what little relief he had known.

'I would have kicked the door shut,' he said.

'Christ,' said Mr Treyer, 'it's like living with a murderer.'

That night the staff at Sandicott & Partner worked late transferring records to a Rent-A-Van to be taken to a barn in the country until the VAT storm was over. And next day Lockhart was taken off all accounting and given an office of his own.

'From now on you will stay in there and if there is anything I think I can trust you not to make a hash of I'll give it to you,' said Mr Treyer. Lockhart sat at his desk and waited but it was four days before Mr Treyer could think of anything for him to do.

'I've got to go to Hatfield,' he said, 'and there's a Mr Stoppard coming in at twelve-thirty. I'll be back by two so all I want you to do is to take him out and give him an expense-account lunch until I get back. That should be easy enough. Just buy him lunch. Right?'

'Buy him lunch?' said Lockhart. 'Who pays?'

'The firm pays, you fool. I said an expense-account lunch, didn't I?' He went away dejectedly but with the feeling that Lockhart could hardly make a total cock-up of a lunch with one of the firm's oldest clients. Mr Stoppard was a reticent man at the best of times and, being a gourmet, seldom spoke during a meal. When Mr Treyer returned Mr Stoppard was voluble to a degree. Mr Treyer tried to appease him and having finally got rid of him sent for Lockhart.

'What in the name of heaven made you take that bloody man

to a fish and chip shop?' he asked trying to control his blood pressure.

'Well, you said it was an expense-account lunch and we'd got to pay and I thought there was no point in wasting money so—'

'Thought?' yelled Mr Treyer letting his blood pressure go to hell and gone. 'Thought? And wasting money? What the hell do you think an expense-account lunch is for if it isn't to waste money? The meal is tax-deductible.'

'You mean the more a lunch costs the less we pay?' said Lockhart.

'Yes,' sighed Mr Treyer, 'that is precisely what I mean. Now the next time ...'

The next time Lockhart took a Leicester shoe manufacturer to the Savoy Grill and wined and dined him to the tune of one hundred and fifty pounds, only to refuse to pay more than five when the bill was presented. It had taken the combined efforts of the shoe manufacturer and Mr Treyer, hastily summoned from a bout of flu, to persuade Lockhart to pay the one hundred and forty-five pounds' difference and make good the damage done to three tables and four waiters in the altercation that had ensued. After that Mr Treyer wrote to Mrs Flawse threatening to resign unless Lockhart was removed from the firm, and while waiting for a reply he barred Lockhart from leaving his office except to relieve himself.

But if Lockhart, to put it as mildly as modern parlance will allow, was having a job adjustment problem in Wheedle Street, his marriage proceeded as sweetly as it had started. And as chastely. What was lacking was not love – Lockhart and Jessica were passionlessly in love – but sex. The anatomical differences between males and females he had detected while gutting rabbits proved accurate in humans. He had balls and Jessica didn't. Jessica had breasts, large ones at that, and he didn't – or only of the most rudimentary kind. To further complicate matters, when they went to bed at night and lay in one another's arms he had an erection and Jessica didn't. The fact that he also had what are crudely termed 'lovers' balls' and spent part of the night in agony he was too brave and gentlemanly to mention. They simply lay in one another's arms and kissed. What happened after that he had no idea and Jessica had no idea either. Her mother's determination to retard her age of maturity had succeeded as completely as had Mr Flawse's equal determination that his grandson should inherit none of his mother's sexual vices. To compound this ignorance Lockhart's education, grounded in the most ancient of classical virtues, complemented Jessica's taste for the sickliest of historical romances in which sex was never mentioned. Taken together this fearful combination led them to idealize one another to the extent that it was impossible for Lockhart to conceive of doing anything more positive than worship Jessica and for Jessica to conceive at all. In brief, their marriage was never consummated and when after six weeks Jessica had her period rather more publicly than before, Lockhart's first impulse was to phone for an ambulance. Jessica in some distress managed to deter him.

'It happens once a month,' she said clutching a sanitary napkin to her with one hand while holding the phone down with the other.

'It doesn't,' said Lockhart, 'I've never bled like that in my life.'

'To girls,' said Jessica, 'not to boys.'

'I still say you ought to see a doctor,' insisted Lockhart.

'But it's been going on for ever so long.'

'All the more reason for seeing the doctor. It's obviously something chronic.'

'Well, if you insist,' said Jessica. Lockhart did. And so one morning when Lockhart had gone to his lonely vigil in the office, Jessica visited the doctor.

'My husband is worried about my bleeding,' she said. 'I told him not to be silly but he would insist.'

'Your husband?' said the doctor five minutes later, having discovered that Mrs Flawse was still a virgin. 'You did say "your husband"?'

'Yes,' said Jessica proudly, 'his name is Lockhart. I think that's a wonderful name, don't you?'

Dr Mannet considered the name, Jessica's manifest attractions, and the possibility that Mr Flawse, far from having a locked heart, must have a padlocked penis not to have been driven sexually berserk by the proximity of such a beautiful wife. Having run through this sequence he assumed the air of a counsellor and leant on the desk to conceal his own physical reaction.

'Tell me, Mrs Flawse,' he said with an urgency that was impelled by the almost certain feeling that he was about to have a spontaneous emission, 'has your husband never . . .' He stopped and shuddered violently in his chair. Dr Mannet had. 'I mean,' he began again when the convulsion was over, 'well . . . let me put it this way, have you refused to let him . . . er . . . touch you?'

'Of course not,' said Jessica who had watched the doctor's throes with some concern, 'we're always kissing and cuddling.'

'Kissing and cuddling,' said Dr Mannet with a whimper, 'Just kissing and . . . er . . . cuddling? Nothing more?'

'More?' said Jessica. 'What more?'

Dr Mannet looked despairingly into her angelic face. In a long career as a General Practitioner he had never been faced by such a beautiful woman who did not know that there was more to marriage than kissing and cuddling.

'You don't do anything else in bed?'

'Well, we go to sleep of course,' said Jessica.

'Dear Lord,' murmured the doctor, 'you go to sleep! And you do absolutely nothing else?'

'Lockhart snores,' said Jessica, thinking hard, 'but I can't think of anything else in particular.'

Across the desk Dr Mannet could and did his damnedest not to.

'And has no one ever explained where babies come from?' he asked, lapsing into that nursery whimsy that seemed to emanate from Mrs Flawse.

'Storks,' said Jessica bluntly.

'Stalks?' echoed the doctor, whose own stalk was playing him up again.

'Or herons. I forget which. They bring them in their beaks.'

'Beaks?' gurgled the doctor, now definitely back in the nursery.

'In little cradles of cloth,' continued Jessica, oblivious of the effect she was having. 'They have these little cradles of cloth and they carry them in their beaks. Surely you've seen pictures of them. And their mummies are ever so pleased. Is something the matter?'

But Dr Mannet was holding his head in his hands and staring at a prescription pad. He had shot his bolt again.

'Mrs Flawse, dear Mrs Flawse,' he whimpered when the crisis was past, 'if you'll just leave your telephone number ... Better still, would you mind if I had a word with your husband, Lock-prick ...'

'Hart,' said Jessica, 'Lockhart. You want him to come and see you?'

Dr Mannet nodded feebly. He had always previously disapproved of the permissive society but just at that moment he had to admit that there were things to be said in its favour.

'Just ask him to come and see me, will you? Excuse me for not rising. You know the way out.'

Jessica went out and made an appointment for Lockhart. In the consulting-room Dr Mannet worked feverishly on his trousers and donned a white lab coat to cover the havoc Jessica had provoked.

But if Mrs Flawse had been a disturbing if pleasurable patient, her husband was even more disturbing and definitely not pleasurable. From the start he had eyed the doctor with danger-ous suspicion brought on by Jessica's account of Dr Mannet's poking and prodding and general gynaecological curiosity. By the time Dr Mannet had spoken for five minutes the suspicion had gone and the danger doubled.

'Are you suggesting,' said Lockhart with a grimness that made one of the more awful Aztec gods look positively amiable, 'that I should intrude what you have chosen to call my penis into the person of my wife and that this intrusion should take place through the orifice between her legs?'

Dr Mannet nodded. 'More or less,' he muttered, 'though I wouldn't put it quite like that.'

'Which orifice,' continued Lockhart more ferociously than ever, 'being too small will then split and cause her pain and suffering and ...'

'Only temporarily,' said Dr Mannet, 'and if you object I can always make a slight incision myself.'

'Object?' snarled Lockhart and grabbed the doctor by the tie. 'If you think for one moment I'm going to let you touch my wife with your foul John Willie—'

'Not my John Willie, Mr Flawse,' gurgled the strangulated doctor, 'with a scalpel.'

It was an unwise suggestion. As Lockhart's grip tightened Dr Mannet turned from puce to purple and was passing to black when Lockhart released his grip and hurled him back into his chair.

'You come near my wife with a scalpel,' he said, 'and I'll gut you like a dead rabbit and have your balls for breakfast.'

Dr Mannet tried to get his voice back while considering this awful end. 'Mr Flawse,' he whispered finally, 'if you will just bear with me a moment. The purpose of what I call your penis and what you prefer to regard as your John Willie is not solely to pass water. I hope I make myself plain.'

'You do,' said Lockhart. 'Very plain, not to say downright ugly.'

'That's as may be,' continued the doctor. 'Now in the course of your adolescence you must at one time or another have noticed that your pen . . . John Willie gave you pleasurable sensations.'

'I suppose you could say that,' said Lockhart grudgingly. 'At night.'

'Precisely,' said the doctor. 'At night you had wet dreams.'

Lockhart admitted that he had had dreams and that the results had sometimes been wet.

'Good,' said the doctor, 'now we're getting somewhere. And in those dreams were you not conscious of an overwhelming desire for women?'

'No,' said Lockhart, 'I most certainly wasn't.'

Dr Mannet shook his head carefully to rid himself of the feeling that he was dealing with some violent and wholly unconscious homosexual who having turned nasty once might turn murderous a second time. He trod warily.

'Would you mind telling me what you did dream about?'

Lockhart consulted his memory for a moment. 'Sheep,' he said finally.

'Sheep?' said Dr Mannet faintly. 'You had wet dreams about sheep?'

'Well, I don't know about the wet part,' said Lockhart, 'but I certainly dreamt about sheep a lot.'

'And did you do anything to these sheep you dreamt about?'

'Shot them,' said Lockhart bluntly.

Dr Mannet's sense of unreality grew alarmingly. 'You shot sheep in your sleep,' he said with involuntary alliteration. 'Is that what you're slaying ... saying?'

'I shot them anyway,' said Lockhart. 'Wasn't anything much else to shoot so I took to potting them at fifteen hundred yards.'

'Potting them?' said the doctor slipping paediatrically. 'You potted sheep at fifteen hundred yards? Isn't that a bit difficult?'

'Well, you've got to aim up and off a bit, but at that range they've got a running chance.'

'Yes, I suppose they do,' said the doctor, who wished he had. 'And having potted them you then had spontaneous emissions about them?'

Lockhart studied him with concern now mixed with his disgust. 'I don't know what the hell you're talking about,' he said. 'First you fiddle with my wife and then you ask me here and start talking about fucking sheep ...'

Dr Mannet seized on the expression. 'Ah,' he said, heading for bestiality, 'so having shot sheep you fucked them?'

'Did I?' said Lockhart who had picked up the six-letter word from Mr Treyer who used it frequently in its seven-letter variety when speaking to or about Lockhart. It was usually suffixed by idiot.

'Well, you should know,' said Dr Mannet.

'I may have done,' said Lockhart, who didn't. 'Anyway afterwards we had them for dinner.'

Dr Mannet shuddered. Much more of these appalling revelations and he would be in need of therapy himself.

'Mr Flawse,' he said determined to change the subject, 'what you did or did not do with sheep is beside the point. Your wife consulted me because she said you were concerned about her menstrual discharge ...'

'I was concerned about her bleeding,' said Lockhart.

'Quite so, her monthly period. We call it menstruation.'

'I call it bloody horrible,' said Lockhart. 'And worrying.'

So did Dr Mannet but he took pains not to say so. 'Now the facts are simply these. Every woman—'

'Lady,' said Lockhart irritably.

'Lady what?'

'Don't call my wife a woman. She is a lady, a radiant, beautiful, angelic—'

Dr Mannet forgot himself. More particularly he forgot Lockhart's propensity for violence. 'Never mind all that,' he snapped. 'Any woman who can bring herself to live with a man who openly admits a preference for fucking sheep has got to be an angel, never mind the radiant or beautiful . . .'

'I mind,' said Lockhart and brought the outburst to a sudden end.

Dr Mannet remembered himself. 'All right, given that Mrs Flawse is a lady it is nevertheless true that as a lady she naturally produces an ovum every month and this ovum descends her Fallopian tubes and unless it is fertilized it passes out in the form of . . .'

He ground to a halt. Lockhart had gone Aztec again.

'What do you mean fertilized?' he snarled.

Dr Mannet tried to think of some way of explaining the process of fertilizing an ovum without causing further offence. 'What you do,' he said with an unnatural calm, 'is you put your pen . . . Jesus . . . your John Willie into her vagina and . . . Dear God.' He gave up in despair and rose from his chair.

So did Lockhart. 'There you go again,' he shouted. 'First you talk about dunging my wife and now you're on about shoving my John Willie—'

'Dung?' screamed the doctor backing into a corner. 'Who said anything about dung?'

'Dung's fertilizer,' bawled Lockhart. 'Dig it and dung it. That is what we do in our kitchen garden and if you think . . .'

But Dr Mannet was past thought. All he wanted to do was obey his instincts and get the hell out of his consulting-room before this sheep-obsessed maniac laid hands on him again. 'Nurse, nurse,' he screamed as Lockhart strode towards him. 'For God's sake . . .' But Lockhart's fury had abated.

'Call yourself a doctor,' he snapped and went out the door. Dr Mannet sank back into his chair and called his partner. By the time he had prescribed himself thirty milligrams of Valium washed down with vodka and was able to put his words into coherent order he was determined to strike Mr and Mrs Flawse off his books for ever.

'Don't let either of them into the waiting-room ever again,' he told the nurse. 'On pain of death.'

'But isn't there something we can do for poor Mrs Flawse?' said the nurse. 'She seemed such a sweet girl.'

'My advice to her would be to get a divorce as quickly as possible,' said Dr Mannet fervently. 'Failing that, a hysterectomy would be the only thing. The thought of that man breeding ...'

Outside in the street Lockhart slowly unclenched his jaw and fists. Coming at the end of a day in which he had been confined to an otherwise empty office with nothing whatsoever to do, the doctor's advice had been the last straw. He loathed London, Mr Treyer, Dr Mannet, East Pursley and everything about this insane rotten world into which he had been launched by his marriage. Every single thing about it conflicted absolutely with what he had been brought up to believe. In place of thrift there were expense-account lunches and rates of inflationary interest that were downright usury; instead of courage and beauty he found arrant cowardice in men – the doctor's squeals for help had made him too contemptible to hit – and in every building he saw only ugliness and a sordid obeisance to utility; and finally to cap it all there was this omnipresent concern with something called sex which grubby little cowards like Dr Mannet wanted to substitute for love. Lockhart walked along the street thinking of his love for Jessica. It was pure and holy and wonderful. He saw himself as her protector and the notion that he must hurt her to prove himself a dutiful husband was utterly repellent to him. He passed a newsagent's shop on whose racks were magazines displaying largely nude girls, dressed in the briefest of briefs or plastic macintoshes, and his gorge rose with disgust at their supposed appeal. The world was rotten and corrupt and he longed to be back on Flawse Fell with his rifle in his hands and some identifiable target between his sights while his darling Jessica sat in the stone-flagged kitchen by the black iron range waiting for him to come home with their supper. And with that longing there came the determination to make it come true.

One of these days he would take on the whole rotten world and impose his will on it, come hell or high water, and then people would learn what it meant to cross Lockhart Flawse. In the meantime he had to get home. For a moment he thought of catching the bus but it was only six miles to Sandicott Crescent and Lockhart was used to covering thirty in a day across the grassy fells of the Border country. With rage against everyone except Jessica and his grandfather and Mr Dodd, Lockhart strode off down the street.

Chapter five

At Flawse Hall the ex-Mrs Sandicott shared none of Lockhart's feelings. She would have given anything, most specifically strychnine, to old Mr Flawse, to be back in the cosy confines of Sandicott Crescent and the company of her acquaintances. Instead she was trapped in a large cold house on an empty wasteland, where the snow lay deep and the wind howled incessantly, with a horrid old man and his even more horrid gamekeeper-cum-handyman, Mr Dodd. Her husband's horridness had manifested itself almost as soon as they had taken their seats on the train from Southampton, and with each mile north it had increased while Mrs Flawse's conviction that she had made a terrible mistake grew into a certainty.

Old Mr Flawse on land had none of that old-world charm that had so affected her at sea. From being an eccentric and outspoken old man in his dotage, he had relapsed into an eccentric and outspoken old man with more faculties at his command than his age warranted. Porters scurried with their luggage, ticket collectors cringed, and even hardened taxi-drivers notorious for their rudeness when given an inadequate tip held their tongues while Mr Flawse disputed the fare and grudgingly gave them an extra penny. Mrs Flawse had been left speechless by his authority which flaunted a disregard for every tenet of her suburban creed and treated the world as his oyster.

Since Mrs Flawse had already been treated, almost literally, as his sexual oyster to be prised open on their honeymoon, she should not have been surprised. It had been bad enough to discover on their first night that Mr Flawse wore a red flannel nightgown with an odour all his own and that he failed three times to distinguish between the washbasin and the lavatory bowl. Mrs Flawse had put these failings down to his age and deficient eyesight and sense of smell. She had been similarly dismayed when he knelt by the bed and implored the good Lord to forgive him in advance the carnal excesses he was about to inflict 'upon this the person of my wedded wife'. Little suspecting what he had in mind, Mrs Flawse found this prayer rather complimentary. It confirmed her belief that she was still at fifty-six an attractive woman and that her husband was a deeply religious man. Ten minutes later she knew better. Whatever the good Lord might feel about the matter of forgiveness, Mrs Flawse's feelings were implacable. She would never forgive or forget the old man's carnal excesses and any notion that he was at all religious had gone by the board. Smelling like a old fox, Mr Flawse had behaved like a young one, and had roamed about her body with as little discrimination between points of entry, or as she more delicately put it, 'her orifices', as he did between the washbasin and the toilet and with much the same intent. Feeling like a cross between a sexual colander and a cesspit, Mrs Flawse had endured the ordeal by consoling herself that such goings-on, and the old man had indeed gone on and on and on, must end abruptly in his having either a heart attack or a hernia. Mr Flawse obliged her on neither count and when she awoke next morning it was to find him sitting up smoking a foul old pipe and regarding her with undisguised relish. For the rest of the voyage Mrs Flawse had waddled the deck by day and straddled the bed by night in the dwindling hope that the wages of his sin would leave her shortly a rich and well-endowed widow.

And so she had travelled north with him determined to see the ordeal out to the end and not to be deterred by his behaviour. By the time they reached Hexham her determination had begun to sag. The grey stone town depressed her and she was only briefly revived by the spectacle outside the station of an immaculate brougham drawn by two black horses with a gaitered and tunicked Mr Dodd holding the door open for her. Mrs Flawse climbed in and felt better. This was what she called riding in style and smacked of a world far removed from any-thing she had known before, an aristocratic world with uni-formed servants and smart equipages. But as the carriage rattled through the streets of the little market town Mrs Flawse began to have second thoughts. The carriage bounced and wobbled and shook and when after crossing the Tyne they took the road to Wark by way of Chollerford she was well into her third and fourth thoughts about the advantages of broughams. Outside the country varied by the mile. At times they passed along roads lined with trees and at others climbed bleak hills where the snow still lay in drifts against dry-stone walls. And all the time the carriage swayed and bounced horribly while beside her Mr Flawse was savouring her discomfort.

'A splendid prospect,' he commented as they crossed a par-ticularly unpleasant piece of open ground without a tree in sight. Mrs Flawse kept her thoughts to herself. Let the old man relish her misery while there was breath left in him but once she was firmly ensconced in Flawse Hall he would learn just how uncomfortable she could make his remaining days. There would be no more sex for one thing. Mrs Flawse had deter-mined on that, and being a vigorous woman, was capable of giving as good as she got. And so the two of them sat side by side contemplating the other's discomfiture. It was Mrs Flawse who got the first shock. Shortly after Wark they turned down a half-metalled track that led along a nicely wooded valley towards a large and handsome house set in a spacious garden. Mrs Flawse's hopes rose prematurely.

'Is that the Hall?' she asked as they rattled towards the gates.

'It is not,' said Mr Flawse. 'That's the Cleydons.'

For a moment his spirits seemed to sink. Young Cleydon had been an early candidate for Lockhart's paternity and only the certainty that he had been in Australia during the months that covered Lockhart's conception had saved him from being flogged within an inch of his life.

'It seems a nice house,' said Mrs Flawse, noting her husband's change of mood.

'Aye, 'tis better than the occupants, God rot their souls,' said the old man. Mrs Flawse added the Cleydons to the imaginary list of neighbours he disliked whose friendship she would cul-tivate. That the list seemed likely to be imaginary dawned on her a short time later. Past the house the road wound out of the woods and climbed the steep bank of a bare hillside; a mile beyond the rise they came to the first of many gates in drystone walls. Mr Dodd climbed down and opened the gate. Then he led the carriage through and shut it. Mrs Flawse searched the horizon for a sign of her new home but there was not a house in sight. Here and there a few dirty sheep showed up against the snow but for the rest there was emptiness. Mrs Flawse shivered.

'We've another ten miles yet,' said Mr Flawse cheerfully. For the next hour they bumped along the broken road with nothing more enchanting to view than an abandoned farmhouse standing within a garden wall and surrounded by fireweed and stinging nettles. Finally they arrived at another gate and beyond it Mrs Flawse could see a church standing on a knoll and around it several houses.

'That's Black Pockrington,' said Mr Flawse. 'You'll do your shopping there.'

'There?' said Mrs Flawse tartly. 'I most certainly won't. It doesn't look big enough to have shops.'

'It has a wee store and the cholera explains its size.'

'Cholera?' said Mrs Flawse, somewhat alarmed.

'The epidemic of 1842 or thereabouts,' said the old man, 'wiped out nine-tenths of the population. You'll find them buried in the graveyard. A terrible thing, the cholera, but without it I doubt we Flawses would be where we are today.'

He gave a nasty chuckle that found no echo in his wife. She had not the least desire to be where she was today.

'We bought the land around for a song,' continued Mr Flawse. 'Dead Man's Moor they call it now.'

In the distance there came the sound of an explosion.

'That'll be the artillery wasting good taxpayers' money on the firing-range. You'll get used to the noise. It's either that or they're blasting over Tombstone Law in the quarries.'

Mrs Flawse hugged her travelling rug to her. The very names were filled with dread.

'And when are we getting to Flawse Hall?' she asked, to drive away her fear. The old man consulted a large gold Hunter.

'About another half an hour,' he said, 'by half past four.'

Mrs Flawse stared out the window even more intently looking for the houses of neighbours but there were none to be seen only the unbroken expanse of open moor and the occasional outcrop of rock that topped the hills. As they drove on the wind rose. Finally they came to another gated wall and Mr Dodd climbed down again.

'The Hall is over yonder. You'll not get a better view,' said the old man as they drove through. Mrs Flawse wiped the mist from the window and peered out. What she could see of the home she had set such store by had nothing to recommend it now. Flawse Hall on Flawse Fell close under Flawse Rigg lived up to its name. A large grey granite building with a tower at one end, it reminded her of Dartmoor Prison in a miniature way. The high stone wall that surrounded three sides of the house had the same air of deliberate containment as that of the prison and the gated archway in the wall was large and ominous. A few stunted and wind-bent trees huddled beside the wall and far away to the west she caught sight of dark pinewoods.

'That's the reservoir over there,' said Mr Flawse. 'Ye'll see the dam below.'

Mrs Flawse saw the dam. It was built of blocks of granite that filled the valley and from its base there ran a stone-sided stream that followed the valley floor, passed under a gated bridge, wound on another quarter of a mile and disappeared into a dark hole in the hillside. All in all the prospect ahead was as grim as nature and nineteenth-century waterworks could make it. Even the iron gate on to the little bridge was spiked and locked. Again Mr Dodd had to climb down and open it before the carriage moved through. Mr Flawse looked up the hill proudly and rubbed his hands with glee. 'It's good to be home again,' he said as the horses began the slow ascent to the house.

Mrs Flawse could see nothing good about it. 'What's that tower at the end?' she asked.

'That's the old peel tower. Much restored by my grandfather but the house is structurally much as it was in the sixteenth century.'

Mrs Flawse had few doubts about that. 'A peel tower?' she murmured.

'A refuge for man and beast when the Scots raided. The walls are ten feet thick and it took more than a passel of marauding Scotsmen or moss troopers to break their way in where they weren't wanted.'

'And what are moss troopers?' Mrs Flawse inquired.

'They aren't any more, ma'am,' said the old man, 'but they were in the old days. Border raiders and cattle thieves from Redesdale and North Tynedale. The king's writ didn't run in the Middle Marches until well into the seventeenth century and, some say, later. It would have taken a brave law officer to come into these wild parts much before 1700.'

'But why moss troopers?' Mrs Flawse continued to take her mind off the looming granite house.

'Because they rode the moss and built their strongholds of great oak trunks and covered them with moss to hide them away and stop them being fired. It must have been a difficult thing to find them in among the bogs and swamps. Aye, and it needed a courageous man with no fear of death in his heart.'

'I should have thought that anyone who chose to live up here must have had a positive longing for death,' said Mrs Flawse.

But the old man was not to be diverted by the Great Certainty from the great past. 'You may well say so, ma'am, but we Flawses have been here since God alone knows when and there were Flawses with Percy at the Battle of Otterburn so celebrated in song.'

As if to emphasize the point another shell exploded to the west on the firing-range and as its boom died away there came another even more sinister sound. Dogs were baying.

'My God, what on earth is that?' said Mrs Flawse, now thoroughly alarmed.

Mr Flawse beamed. 'The Flawse Pack, ma'am,' he said and rapped on the window with his silver-headed stick. Mr Dodd peered down between his legs and for the first time Mrs Flawse saw that he had a cast in one eye. Upside-down, it gave his face a terrible leering look. 'Dodd, we'll gan in the yard. Mrs Flawse would like to see the hounds.'

Mr Dodd's topsy-turvy smile was horrible to behold. So too were the hounds when he climbed down and opened the heavy wooden gates under the archway. They swarmed out in a great seething mass and surrounded the brougham. Mrs Flawse stared down at them in horror. 'What sort of hounds are they? They're certainly not foxhounds,' she said to the old man's delight.

'Those are Flawse hounds,' he said as one great beast leapt up

45

and slobbered at the window with lolling tongue. 'Bred them myself from the finest stock. The hounds of spring are on winter's traces as the great Swinburne has it, and ye'll not find hounds that'll spring so fierce on anything's traces as these beasts. Two-thirds Pyrenean Mountain Dog for their ferocity and size. One-third Labrador for the keenness of scent and the ability to swim and retrieve. And finally one-third Greyhound for their speed. What do ye make of that, ma'am?'

'Four-thirds,' said Mrs Flawse, 'which is an absurdity. You can't make four-thirds of anything.'

'Can ye not?' said Mr Flawse, the gleam in his eye turning from pride to irritation that he should be so disproved. 'Then we'll have one in for your inspection.'

He opened the door and one of the great hybrids vaulted in and slavered in his face before turning its oral attentions to its new mistress.

'Take the horrid thing away. Get off, you brute,' shouted Mrs Flawse, 'stop that at once. Oh my God . . .'

Mr Flawse, satisfied that he had made his point, cuffed the dog out of the coach and slammed the door. Then he turned to his wife. 'I think ye'll agree that there's more than three-thirds of savage hound in him, my dear,' he said grimly, 'or would you care for another closer look?'

Mrs Flawse gave him a very close look indeed and said she would not.

'Then ye'll not contradict me on the matter of eugenics, ma'am,' he said, and shouted to Mr Dodd to drive on. 'I have made a study of the subject and I'll not be told I am wrong.'

Mrs Flawse kept her thoughts to herself. They were not nice ones. But they would keep. The carriage drew up at the back door and stopped. Mr Dodd came round through a sea of hounds.

'Get them out the way, man,' shouted Mr Flawse above the barks. 'The wife is afraid of the creatures.'

The next moment Mr Dodd, flailing around him with the horsewhip, had cowed the hounds back across the yard. Mr Flawse got out and held his hand for Mrs Flawse. 'You'll not expect a man of my age to carry you across the door-stone,' he said gallantly, 'but Dodd will be my proxy. Dodd, carry your mistress.'

'There's absolutely no need ...' Mrs Flawse began but Mr Dodd had obeyed orders, and she found herself staring too closely for her peace of mind into his leering face as he clutched her to him and carried her into the house.

'Thank you, Dodd,' said Mr Flawse, following them in. 'Ceremony has been observed. Put her down.'

For a horrid moment Mrs Flawse was clutched even tighter and Dodd's face came closer to her own, but then he relaxed and set her on her feet in the kitchen. Mrs Flawse adjusted her dress before looking round.

'I trust it meets with your approbation, my dear.'

It didn't but Mrs Flawse said nothing. If the outside of Flawse Hall had looked bleak, bare and infinitely forbidding, the kitchen, flagged with great stones, was authentically medieval. True there was a stone sink with a tap above it, which signified running if cold water, and the iron range had been made in the later stages of the Industrial Revolution; there was little else that was even vaguely modern. A bare wooden table stood in the middle of the room with benches on either side, and there were upright wooden seats with backs beside the range.

'Settles,' said Mr Flawse when Mrs Flawse looked inquiringly at them. 'Dodd and the bastard use them of an evening.'

'The bastard?' said Mrs Flawse. 'What bastard?' But for once it was Mr Flawse's turn to keep silent.

'I'll show ye the rest of the house,' he said and led the way out down a passage.

'If it's anything like the kitchen ...' Mrs Flawse began but it wasn't. Where the kitchen had been bleak and bare, the rest of the Hall lived up to her expectations and was packed with fine furniture, tapestries, great portraits and the contributions of many generations and as many marriages. Mrs Flawse breathed a sigh of relief as she stood below the curved staircase and looked around her. In marrying old Mr Flawse she had done more than marry a man in his dotage, she had wedded herself to a fortune in antique furniture and fine silver. And from every wall a Flawse face looked down from old portraits, wigged Flawses, Flawses in uniform and Flawses in fancy waistcoats, but the Flawse face was ever the same. Only in one corner did she find a small dark portrait that was not clearly identifiable as a Flawse.

'Murkett Flawse, painted posthumously, I'm afraid,' said the old man. Mrs Flawse studied the portrait more closely.

'He must have died a peculiar death from the look of him,' she said. Mr Flawse nodded.

'Beheaded, ma'am, and I have an idea the executioner had a bad head that morning from over-indulgence the night before and took more chops than were rightly called for.'

Mrs Flawse withdrew from the horrid portrayal of Murkett Flawse's head, and together they went from room to room. In each there was something to admire and in Mrs Flawse's case to value. By the time they returned to the entrance hall she was satisfied that she had done well to marry the old fool after all.

'And this is my inner sanctum,' said Mr Flawse opening a door to the left of the entrance. Mrs Flawse went inside. A huge coal fire blazed in the hearth and, in contrast to the rest of the house which had seemed decidedly damp and musty, the study was warm and smelt of book-leather and tobacco. An old cat basked on the carpet in front of the fire and from every wall books gleamed in the firelight. In the centre of the room stood a kneehole desk with a greenshaded lamp and an inkstand of silver. Mrs Flawse went to the lamp to switch it on and found a handle.

'You'll need a match,' said Mr Flawse, 'we're not on the electricity.'

'You're not ...' Mrs Flawse began and stopped as the full significance of the remark dawned on her. Whatever treasures in the way of old silver and fine furniture Flawse Hall might hold, without electricity it held only transitory attractions for Mrs Flawse. No electricity meant presumably no central heating, and the single tap above the stone sink had signified only cold water. Mrs Flawse, safe from the hounds and in the inner sanctum of her husband's study, decided the time had come to strike. She sat down heavily in a large high-backed leather chair beside the fire and glared at him.

'The very idea of bringing me here and expecting me to live in a house without electricity or hot water or any mod cons ...' she began stridently as the old man bent to light a spill from the fire. Mr Flawse turned his face towards her and she saw it was suffused with rage. In his hand the spill burnt lower. Mr Flawse ignored it.

'Woman,' he said with a soft and steely emphasis, 'ye'll learn never to address me in that tone of voice again.' He straightened up but Mrs Flawse was not to be cowed.

'And you'll learn never to call me "woman" again,' she said defiantly, 'and don't think that you can bully me because you can't. I'm perfectly capable ...'

They were interrupted by the entrance of Mr Dodd bearing a silver tray on which a teapot stood under a cosy. Mr Flawse signalled to him to put it on the low table beside her chair and it was only when Mr Dodd had left the room closing the door quietly behind him that the storm broke once again. It did so simultaneously.

'I said I'm—' Mrs Flawse began.

'Woman,' roared Mr Flawse, 'I'll not—'

But their unison silenced them both and they sat glowering at one another by the fire. It was Mrs Flawse who first broke the truce. She did so with guile.

'It's perfectly simple,' she said, 'we need not argue about it. We can install an electrical generator. You'll find it will make a tremendous improvement to your life.'

But Mr Flawse shook his head. 'I have lived without it for ninety years and I'll die without it.'

'I shouldn't be at all surprised,' said Mrs Flawse, 'but I see no reason why you should take me with you. I am used to hot water and my home comforts and—'

'Ma'am,' said Mr Flawse, 'I have washed in cold water ...'

'Seldom,' said Mrs Flawse.

'As I was saying ...'

'We can have Calor gas if you won't have electricity ...'

'I'll have no modern contraption ...'

They wrangled on until it was time for dinner and in the kitchen Mr Dodd listened with an interested ear while he stirred the stewed mutton in the pot.

'The auld divil's bitten off a sight more than he's teeth in his heid to chew,' he thought to himself, and tossed a bone to his old collie by the door. 'And if the mither's so rigid what's the lassie like?' With this on his mind he moved about the kitchen which had seen so many centuries of Flawse womenfolk come and go and where the smells of those centuries which Lockhart pined for still clung. Mr Dodd had no nose for them, that musk

49

of unwashed humanity, of old boots and dirty socks, wet dogs and mangy cats, of soap and polish, fresh milk and warm blood, baked bread and hung pheasant, all those necessities of the harsh life the Flawses had led since the house first was built. He was part of that musk and shared its ancestry. But now there was a new ingredient come to the house and one he had no mind to like.

Nor after a glum dinner had Mr Flawse when he and Mrs Flawse retired to a cold bedroom and a featherbed redolent of damp and too recently plucked chicken. Outside the wind whistled in the chimneys and from the kitchen there came the faint wail of Mr Dodd's Northumbrian pipes as he played 'Edward, Edward'. It seemed an appropriate ballad for the evil hour. Upstairs Mr Flawse knelt by the bed.

'Oh Lord . . .' he began, only to be interrupted by his wife.

'There's no point in your asking forgiveness,' she said. 'You're not coming near me until we've first come to an understanding.'

The old man regarded her balefully from the floor, 'Understanding? What understanding, ma'am?'

'A clear understanding that you will have this house modernized as quickly as possible and that until such time I shall return to my own home and the comforts to which I have been accustomed. I didn't marry you to catch my death of pneumonia.'

Mr Flawse lumbered to his feet. 'And I didn't marry you,' he thundered, 'to have my household arrangements dictated to me by a chit of a woman.'

Mrs Flawse pulled the sheet up round her neck defiantly. 'And I won't be shouted at,' she snapped back. 'I am not a shit of a woman. I happen to be a respectable . . .'

A fresh wail of wind in the chimney and the fact that Mr Flawse had picked up a poker from the grate stopped her.

'Respectable are ye? And what sort of respectable woman is it that marries an old man for his money?'

'Money?' said Mrs Flawse, alarmed at this fresh evidence that the old fool wasn't such an old fool after all. 'Who said anything about money?'

'I did,' roared Mr Flawse, 'You proposed and I disposed and

if you imagine for one moment that I didn't know what you were after you're sadly misguided.'

Mrs Flawse resorted to the stratagem of tears. 'At least I thought you were a gentleman,' she whimpered.

'Aye, you did that. And more fool you,' said the old man as livid as his red flannel gown. 'And tears will get you nowhere. You made it a condition of the bastard's marrying your numb-skull daughter that you were to be my wife. Well, you have made your bed, now you must lie in it.'

'Not with you,' said Mrs Flawse. 'I'd rather die.'

'And well you may, ma'am, well you may. Is that your last word?'

Mrs Flawse hesitated and made a mental calculation between the threat, the poker and her last word. But there was still stubbornness in her Sandicott soul.

'Yes,' she said defiantly.

Mr Flawse hurled the poker into the grate and went to the door. 'Ye'll live to rue the day you said that, ma'am,' he muttered malevolently and left.

Mrs Flawse lay back exhausted by her defiance and then with a final effort got out of bed and locked the door.

Chapter six

Next morning after a fitful night Mrs Flawse came downstairs to find the old man closeted in his sanctum and a note on the kitchen table telling her to make her own breakfast. A large pot of porridge belched glutinously on the stove and having sampled its contents she contented herself with a pot of tea and some bread and marmalade. There was no sign of Mr Dodd. Outside in the yard the grey products of Mr Flawse's experiments in canine eugenics lolled about in the wintry sunshine. Avoiding them by going out of the kitchen door, Mrs Flawse made her way round the garden. Enclosed by the high wall against the wind and weather, it was not unattractive. Some earlier Flawse had built greenhouses and a kitchen garden and Capability Flawse, whose portrait hung on the landing wall, had created a miniature Southern landscape in the half-acre not devoted to vegetables. Stunted trees and sanded paths wound in and out of rockeries and a fountain played in an oval fishpond. In one corner there was a gazebo, a little belvedere of flint and sea shells embedded in cement with a tiny Gothic window paned with coloured glass. Mrs Flawse climbed the steps to the door, found it unlocked and went inside to discover the first signs of comfort at the Hall. Lined with oak panels and faded velvet plush seats the little room had an ornately carved ceiling and a view out across the fell to the reservoir.

Mrs Flawse seated herself there and wondered again at the strangeness of the family into which she had so unwisely married. That it was of ancient lineage she had already gathered and that it had money she still suspected. Flawse Hall might not be an attractive building but it was filled with treasures filched from long-lost colonies by those intrepid younger sons who had risked malaria and scurvy and yellow fever to make their fortunes or meet untimely deaths in far-flung corners of the Empire. Mrs Flawse envied and understood their enterprise. They had gone south and east (and in many cases west) to escape the bleakness and boredom of home. Mrs Flawse yearned to follow their example. Anything would be preferable to the intolerable isolation of the Hall and she was just trying to think of some way of making her own departure when the tall gaunt figure of her husband emerged from the kitchen garden and made its way between the rockeries and miniature trees to the gazebo. Mrs Flawse steeled herself for this encounter. She need not have bothered. The old man was evidently in a genial mood. He strode up the steps and knocked on the door. 'May I come in?'

'I suppose so,' said Mrs Flawse.

Mr Flawse stood in the doorway. 'I see you have found your way to Perkin's Lookout,' he said. 'A charming folly built in 1774 by Perkin Flawse, the family poet. It was here that he wrote his famous "Ode to Coal", inspired no doubt by the drift mine you see over yonder.'

He pointed through the little window at a mound on the

opposite hillside. There was a dark hole beside the mound and some remnants of rusting machinery.

' "By Nature formed by Nature felled
'Tis not by Nature now expelled.
But man's endeavour yet sets free
The charred remains of many a tree
And so by forests long since dead
We boil our eggs and bake our bread."

A fine poet, ma'am, if little recognized,' continued the old man when he had finished the recitation, 'but then we Flawses have unsuspected gifts.'

'So I have discovered,' said Mrs Flawse with some acerbity.

The old man bowed his head. He too had spent a wakeful night wrestling with his conscience and losing hands down.

'I have come to beg your pardon,' he said finally. 'My conduct as your husband was inexcusable. I trust you will accept my humble apologies.'

Mrs Sandicott hesitated. Her former marriage had not disposed her to forfeit her right to grievance too easily. There were advantages to be gained from it, among them power. 'You called me a shit of a woman,' she pointed out.

'A chit, ma'am, a chit,' said Mr Flawse. 'It means a young woman.'

'Not where I come from,' said Mrs Flawse. 'It has an altogether different meaning and a very nasty one.'

'I assure you I meant young, ma'am. The defecatory connotation which you attributed to the word was entirely absent from my intention.'

Mrs Flawse rather doubted that. What she had experienced of his intentions on their honeymoon gave her reason to think otherwise, but she had been prepared to suffer in a good cause. 'Whatever you intended, you still accused me of marrying you for your money. Now that I won't take from anyone.'

'Quite so, ma'am. It was said in the heat of the moment and in the humble consciousness that there had to be a more sufficient reason than my poor self. I retract the remark.'

'I'm glad to hear it. I married you because you were old and lonely and needed someone to look after you. The thought of money never entered my head.'

53

'Quite so,' said Mr Flawse, accepting these personally insulting attributes with some difficulty, 'as you say I am old and lonely and I need someone to look after me.'

'And I can't be expected to look after anyone with the present lack of amenities in the house. I want electricity and hot baths and television and central heating if I am to stay here.'

Mr Flawse nodded sadly. That it should have come to this, 'You shall have them, ma'am,' he said, 'you shall have them.'

'I didn't come here to catch my death of pneumonia. I want them installed at once.'

'I shall put the matter in hand immediately,' said Mr Flawse, 'and now let us adjourn to my study and the warmth of my fire to discuss the matter of my will.'

'Your will?' said Mrs Flawse. 'You did say "your will"?'

'Indeed I did, ma'am,' said the old man and escorted her down the steps of the gazebo and across the stunted garden to the house. There, sitting opposite one another in the great leather armchairs, with a mangy cat basking before the coal fire they continued their discussion.

'I will be frank with you,' said Mr Flawse, 'My grandson, your son-in-law, Lockhart is a bastard.'

'Really?' said Mrs Flawse, uncertain whether or not to give that word its literal meaning. The old man answered the question.

'The product of an illicit union between my late daughter and person or persons unknown, and I have made it my life's work to determine firstly his paternal ancestry and secondly to eradicate those propensities to which by virtue of his being partly a Flawse I have access. I trust you follow my line of reasoning.'

Mrs Flawse didn't but she nodded obediently.

'I am, as you may have surmised from a perusal of my library, a firm believer in the congenital inheritance of ancestral characteristics both physical and mental. To paraphrase the great William, there is a paternity that shapes our ends roughhew them how we will. Paternity, ma'am. Not maternity. The mating of dogs, of which I have considerable experience, is a pointer to this end.'

Mrs Flawse shivered and stared wildly at him. If her ears did not deceive her, she had married a man with perversions beyond belief.

Mr Flawse ignored her stunned look and continued. 'The female bitch when on heat,' he said, adding, 'I trust this somewhat indelicate subject does not offend you?' and taking Mrs Flawse's shaking head as an assurance that she wasn't in the least put out, went on, 'the female bitch on heat attracts the attention of a pack of males, which pack pursues her up hill and down dale fighting among themselves for the privilege accorded to the fiercest and strongest dog of fecundating her *prima nocte*. She is thus impregnated by the finest specimen first but to assure conception she is then served by all the other dogs in the pack down to the smallest and weakest. The result is the survival of the species, ma'am, and of the fittest. Darwin said it, ma'am, and Darwin was right. Now I am an hereditarist. The Flawse nose and the Flawse chin are physical proof of the inheritance over the centuries of physical attributes evolved from our Flawse forefathers and it is my firm conviction that we not only inherit physical characteristics by way of paternal ancestry but also mental ones. To put it another way, the dog is father to the man, and a dog's temperament is determined by his progenitors. But I see that you doubt me.'

He paused and studied Mrs Flawse closely; there was certainly doubt on her face. But it was doubt as to the sanity of the man she had married rather than an intellectual doubt of his argument.

'You say,' continued the old man, 'as well you may, if inheritance determines temperament what has education to do with what we are? Is that not what you are thinking?'

Again Mrs Flawse nodded involuntarily. Her own education had been so pasteurized by permissive parents and progressive teachers that she found it impossible to follow his argument at all. Beyond the fact that he seemed obsessed with the sexual habits and reproductive processes of dogs and had openly admitted that in the Flawse family a dog was evidently the father to the man, she had no idea what he was talking about.

'The answer is this, ma'am, and here again the dog is our determinant, a dog is a domestic animal not by nature but by social symbiosis. Dog and man, ma'am, live together by virtue of mutual necessity. We hunt together, we eat together, we live together and we sleep together, but above all we educate one another. I have learnt more from the constant companionship of dogs than ever I have from men or books. Carlyle is the exception but I will come to that later. First let me say that a dog can be trained. Up to a point, ma'am, only up to a point. I defy the finest shepherd in the world to take a terrier and turn him into a sheepdog. It can't be done. A terrier is an earth dog. Your Latin will have acquainted you with that. Terra, earth; terrier, earth dog. And no amount of herding will eradicate his propensity for digging. Train him how you will he will remain a digger of holes at heart. He may not dig but the instinct is there. and so it is with man, ma'am. Which said, it remains only to say that I have done with Lockhart my utmost to eradicate those instincts which we Flawses to our cost possess.'

'I'm glad to hear it,' muttered Mrs Flawse, who knew to her cost those instincts the Flawses possessed. The old man raised an admonitory finger. 'But, ma'am, lacking a knowledge of his father's ancestry I have been handicapped. Aye, sorely handicapped. The vein of vice that runs in Lockhart's paternal line I know not and knowing not can but deduce. My daughter could by no stretch of the imagination be described as a discriminating girl. The manner of her death suffices to prove that. She died, ma'am, behind a dyke giving birth to her son. And she refused to name the father.'

Mr Flawse paused to savour his frustration and to expel that nagging suspicion that his daughter's obstinacy in the matter of Lockhart's paternity was a final gesture of filial generosity designed to spare him the ignominy of incest. While he stared into the depths of the fire as into hell itself, Mrs Flawse contented herself with the realization that Lockhart's illegitimacy was one more arrow to the bow of her domestic power. The old fool would suffer for the admission. Mrs Flawse had garnered a fresh grievance.

'When I think that my Jessica is married to an illegitimate man, I must say I find your behaviour inexcusable and dishonourable, I do indeed,' she said taking advantage of Mr Flawse's mood of submission. 'If I had known I would never have given consent to the marriage.'

Mr Flawse nodded humbly. 'You must forgive me,' he said, 'but needs must when the devil drives and your daughter's saintliness will dilute the evil of Lockhart's paternal line.'

'I sincerely hope so,' said Mrs Flawse, 'And talking about

inheritance I believe you mentioned remaking your will.' And so from things theoretical they moved to practicalities. 'I will send for my solicitor, Mr Bullstrode, and have him draw up the new will. You will be the beneficiary, ma'am. I assure you of that. Within the limits imposed by my obligations to my employees, of course, and with the proviso that on your demise the estate will go to Lockhart and his offspring.'

Mrs Flawse smiled contentedly. She foresaw a comfortable future. 'And in the meantime you will see to it that the Hall is modernized?' she said. And again Mr Flawse nodded.

'In that case I shall stay,' said Mrs Flawse graciously. This time there was the flicker of a smile on Mr Flawse's face but it died instantly. There was no point in giving his game away. He would buy time by affecting submission.

That afternoon Mrs Flawse sat down and wrote to Jessica. It was less a letter than an inventory of her possessions to be forwarded by road haulage to Flawse Hall. When she had finished she gave the letter to Mr Dodd to post in Black Pockrington. It was still unposted that night when she went up to bed. In the kitchen Mr Flawse boiled a kettle and steamed the envelope open and read its contents.

'You can post it,' he told Mr Dodd as he resealed the envelope. 'The auld trout has taken the bait. It just remains to play her.'

And so for the next few months he did. The amenities of Flawse Hall remained unimproved. The central heating firm was always coming next week and never did. The electricity remained in abeyance and the Post Office refused to connect the telephone except at a cost that even Mrs Flawse found prohibitive. There were hitches everywhere. The arrival of her private possessions was delayed by the inability of the furniture removal van to negotiate the bridge at the bottom of the valley and the refusal of the removal men to carry boxes and trunks half a mile uphill. In the end they unloaded the van and went away, leaving it to Mrs Flawse and Mr Dodd to bring the pieces up one by one, a slow process made slower by Mr Dodd's other multifarious occupations. It was late spring by the time every knick-knack and gewgaw from 12 Sandicott Crescent had been installed in the drawing-room where they competed in vain with the antique plunder of the Empire. Worst of all Mrs Flawse's Rover was dispatched by rail, and thanks to Mr Dodd's intervention with the stationmaster, in which transaction money passed hands, was rerouted back to East Pursley by way of Glasgow, and delivered to Lockhart and Jessica mechanically inoperable and with a label attached saying 'Addressee unknown'. Without her car Mrs Flawse was lost. She could accompany Mr Dodd in the dog-cart as far as Black Pockrington, but no one in Pockrington had a telephone and farther he refused to go.

After three months of discomfort, uncertainty, and procrastination on Mr Flawse's part in the matter of the will, she had had enough. Mrs Flawse delivered her ultimatum.

'You will either do the things you promised to do or I will leave,' she said.

'But, ma'am, I have done my best,' said Mr Flawse. 'The matter is in hand and . . .'

'It were better it were afoot,' said Mrs Flawse who had adapted her speech to that of her husband. 'I mean what I say. Mr Bullstrode, the solicitor, must draw up your will in my favour or I will up sticks and return to where I am appreciated.'

'Where there's a will there's a way,' said the old man, musing on the possible permutations implied in the maxim and thinking of Schopenhauer. 'As the great Carlyle said . . .'

'And that's another thing. I'll have no more sermonizing. I have heard enough of Mr Carlyle to last me a lifetime. He may be the great man you say he was but enough's as good as a feast and I've had my fill of Heroes and Hero Worship.'

'And is that your last word?' asked Mr Flawse hopefully.

'Yes,' said Mrs Flawse, and contradicted herself, 'I have endured your company and the inconveniences of this house long enough. Mr Bullstrode will put in an appearance within the week or I shall make myself absent.'

'Then Mr Bullstrode will be here tomorrow,' said Mr Flawse. 'I give you my word.'

'He'd better be,' said Mrs Flawse and flounced out of the room leaving the old man to regret that he had ever urged her to read Samuel Smiles on Self Help.

*

That night Mr Dodd was dispatched with a sealed envelope bearing the Flawse crest, a moss trooper pendant, imprinted in wax on the back. It contained precise instructions as to the contents of Mr Flawse's new will, and when Mrs Flawse came down to breakfast next morning it was to learn that for once her husband had lived up to his word.

'There you are, ma'am,' said Mr Flawse, handing her Mr Bullstrode's reply, 'he will be here this afternoon to draw up the will.'

'And just as well,' said Mrs Flawse. 'I meant what I said.'

'And I mean every word I say, ma'am. The will shall be drawn and I have summoned Lockhart to be present next week when it is to be read.'

'I can see no good reason why he should be present until after your death,' said Mrs Flawse. 'That's the usual time for reading wills.'

'Not this will, ma'am,' said Mr Flawse. 'Forewarned is fore-armed as the old saying has it. And the boy needs a spur to his flank.'

He retired to his sanctum leaving Mrs Flawse to puzzle this riddle, and that afternoon Mr Bullstrode arrived at the bridge over The Cut and was admitted by Mr Dodd. For the next three hours there came the sound of muted voices from the study, but though she listened at the keyhole Mrs Flawse could gain nothing from the conversation. She was back in the drawing-room when the solicitor came to pay his respects before leaving.

'One question before you go, Mr Bullstrode,' she said. 'I would like your assurance that I am the chief beneficiary of my husband's will.'

'You may rest assured on that point, Mrs Flawse. You are indeed the chief beneficiary. Let me go further, the conditions of Mr Flawse's new will leave his entire estate to you until your death.'

Mrs Flawse sighed with relief. It had been an uphill battle but she had won the first round. All that remained was to insist on modern conveniences being installed in the house. She was sick to death of using the earth closet.

Chapter seven

Lockhart and Jessica were sick, period. The Curse, as Jessica had been brought up to call it, blighted what little physical bond there was between them. Lockhart steadfastly refused to impose his unworthy person on his bleeding angel and, even when not bleeding, his angel refused to insist on her right as his wife to be imposed upon. But if they lived in a state of sexual stalemate, their love grew in the fertile soil of their frustration. In short, they adored one another and loathed the world in which they found themselves. Lockhart no longer spent his days at Sandicott & Partner in Wheedle Street. Mr Treyer, forced to decide whether to implement his threat to resign if Lockhart didn't leave, a decision thrust upon him by Mr Dodd who hadn't delivered his letter to Mrs Flawse, finally resorted to more subtle tactics and paid Lockhart his full salary plus a bonus to stay away from the office before he brought ruin to the business by killing a Tax Inspector or alienating all their clients. Lockhart accepted this arrangement without regret. What he had seen of Mr Treyer, VAT men, the contradictions between income and income tax and the wiles and ways of both tax collectors and tax evaders, only confirmed his view that the modern world was a sordid and corrupt place. Brought up by his grandfather to believe what he was told and to tell what he believed, the transition to a world in which the opposites held true had had a traumatic effect.

Left fully paid to his own devices Lockhart had remained at home and learnt to drive.

'It will help to kill time,' he told Jessica, and had promptly done his best to kill two driving instructors and a great many other road users. More accustomed to the ways of horses and buggies than to the sudden surges and stops of motor cars, Lockhart's driving consisted of putting his foot flat down on the accelerator before letting out the clutch and then putting his foot flat down on the brake before smashing into whatever stood in his path. The effect of this repeated sequence had been to leave his instructors speechless with panic and in no position to communicate an alternative procedure to their pupil. Having wrecked the front ends of three Driving School cars and the back ends of two parked cars plus a lamp-post, Lockhart had found it difficult to get anyone to instruct him.

'I just don't understand it,' he told Jessica. 'With a horse you climb into the saddle and away she goes. You don't keep bumping into things. A horse has got more sense.'

'Perhaps if you listened to what the instructors say you'd get on better, darling. I mean they must know what you ought to do.'

'According to the last one,' said Lockhart, 'what I ought to do is have my bloody head examined and I wasn't even bleeding. He was the one with the fractured skull.'

'Yes, dear, but you had just knocked down the lamp-post. You know you had.'

'I don't know anything of the sort,' said Lockhart indignantly. 'The car knocked it down. All I did was to take my foot off the clutch. It wasn't my fault the car shot off the road like a scalded cat.'

In the end, by paying one of the instructors danger money and allowing him to sit in the back seat with a crash helmet and two safety belts, Lockhart had got the hang of driving. The fact that the instructor had insisted on Lockhart providing his own vehicle had led him to buy a Land-Rover. It had been the instructor who installed a governor on the accelerator and together they had practised on an abandoned airfield where there were few obstacles and no other cars. Even in these unobstructed circumstances Lockhart had managed to puncture two hangars in ten places by driving straight through their corrugated walls at forty miles an hour and it was testimony to the Land-Rover that it took so well.

Not so the instructor. He had taken it extremely badly and had only been persuaded to come out again by being offered even more money and half a bottle of Scotch before he got into the back seat. After six weeks Lockhart had overcome his manifest desire to drive at things rather than round them and had graduated to side roads and finally to main ones. By that time the instructor pronounced him ready to take the test. The examiner thought otherwise and demanded to be let out of the car half-way through. But on his third attempt Lockhart had got his licence, largely because the examiner couldn't face the prospect of having to sit beside him a fourth time. By then the Land-

Rover had begun to suffer from metal fatigue and to celebrate the occasion Lockhart traded what remained of it in for a Range Rover which could do a hundred miles an hour on the open road and sixty cross-country. Lockhart proved the latter to his own satisfaction and the frenzied distraction of the Club Secretary by driving the thing at high speed across all eighteen holes of the Pursley Golf Course before plunging through the hedge at the end of Sandicott Crescent and into the garage.

'It's got four-wheel drive and goes through sand holes like anything,' he told Jessica, 'and it's great on grass. When we go to Northumberland we'll be able to drive right across the fells.'

He went back to the showroom to pay for the Range-Rover and it was left to Jessica to confront a partially demented Club Secretary who wanted to know what the hell her husband meant by driving a bloody great truck across all eighteen greens to the total destruction of their immaculate and painstakingly preserved surfaces.

Jessica denied that her husband had done any such thing. 'He's very fond of gardening,' she told the man, 'and he wouldn't dream of destroying your greens. And anyway I didn't know you grew vegetables on the golf course. I certainly haven't seen any.'

Faced by such radiant and disconcerting innocence the Secretary had retired muttering that some maniac had put paid to the Ladies Open, not to mention the Mixed Doubles.

Mr Flawse's letter summoning the couple to Flawse Hall to hear the contents of his will therefore came at an opportune moment.

'Oh, darling,' said Jessica, 'I've been dying to see your home. How marvellous.'

'It rather sounds as if grandfather were dying anyway,' said Lockhart studying the letter. 'Why does he want to read his will now?'

'He probably just wants you to know how generous he's going to be,' said Jessica, who always managed to put a nice interpretation on the nastiest actions.

Lockhart didn't. 'You don't know grandpa,' he said.

But next morning they left very early in the Range-Rover and managed to avoid the morning traffic into London. They were less fortunate at the traffic lights at the entrance to the motorway which happened to be red at the time. Here Lockhart slammed into the back of a Mini before reversing and driving on.

'Hadn't you better go back and say you're sorry?' asked Jessica.

But Lockhart wouldn't hear of it. 'He shouldn't have stopped so suddenly,' he said.

'But the lights were red, darling. They changed just as we came up behind him.'

'Well, the system lacks logic then,' said Lockhart. 'There wasn't anything coming on the other road. I looked.'

'There's something coming now,' said Jessica, turning to look out of the back window, 'and it's got a blue light flashing on the top. I think it must be the police.'

Lockhart put his foot hard down on the floor and they were doing a hundred in no time at all. Behind them the police car turned on its siren and went up to a hundred and ten.

'They're gaining on us, darling,' said Jessica, 'we'll never be able to get away.'

'Oh yes we will,' said Lockhart, and looked in the rear-view mirror. The police car was four hundred yards behind them and coming up fast. Lockhart switched up an overpass on to a side road, squealed round a corner into a country lane and putting his hunting instincts to good use charged a five-barred gate and bucketed across a ploughed field. Behind them the police car stopped at the gate and men got out. But by that time Lockhart had negotiated another hedge and had disappeared. Twenty miles and forty hedges farther on he doubled back across the motorway and, proceeding by back roads to the east, drove on.

'Oh, Lockhart, you're so manly,' said Jessica, 'you think of everything. You really do. But don't you suppose they'll have taken our licence number?'

'Won't do them much good if they have,' said Lockhart. 'I didn't like the one it had on it when I bought it so I changed it.'

'You didn't like it? Why not?'

'It said PEE 453 P so I had another one made up. It's much nicer. It's FLA 123.'

'But they'll still be looking for a Range-Rover with FLA 123,' Jessica pointed out, 'and they've got radios and things.'

Lockhart pulled into a lay-by. 'You really don't mind us being PEE 453 P?' he asked. Jessica shook her head.

'Of course not,' she said, 'you are silly.'

'If you're quite sure,' said Lockhart doubtfully, but in the end he got out and changed the number plates back again. When he climbed back into the car Jessica hugged him.

'Oh darling,' she said. 'I feel so safe with you. I don't know why it is but you always make things look so simple.'

'Most things are simple,' said Lockhart, 'if you go about them the right way. The trouble is that people never do what's obvious.'

'I suppose that's what it is,' said Jessica, and relapsed into the romantic dream of Flawse Hall on Flawse Fell close under Flawse Rigg. With each mile north her feelings, unlike those of her mother before her, grew mistier and more hazy with legend and the wild beauty she longed for.

Beside her Lockhart's feelings changed too. He was moving away from London and that low country he so detested and was returning, if only briefly, to those open rolling fells of his boyhood and to the music of guns firing in the distance or close at hand. A feeling of wildness and a strange surge of violence stirred in his blood and Mr Treyer assumed a new monstrosity in his mind, a vast question-mark to which there was never any answer. Ask Mr Treyer a question and the answer he gave was no answer at all; it was a balance sheet. On one side there were debits, on the other credits. You paid your money and took your choice, and Lockhart had been left none the wiser. The world he understood had no place for equivocation or those grey areas where everything was fudged and bets were hedged. If you aimed at a grouse it was hit or miss and a miss was as good as a mile. And if you built a dry-stone wall it stood or fell and in falling proved you wrong. But in the south it was all slipshod and cover-up. He was being paid not to work and other men who did no work were making fortunes out of buying and selling options on cocoa yet to be harvested and copper still unmined. And having made their money by swapping pieces of paper they had it taken away from them by Income Tax officials or had to lie to keep it. Finally there was the Government which in his simple way he had always thought was elected to govern and to maintain the value of the currency.

Instead it spent more money than was in the Exchequer and borrowed to make good the deficit. If a man did that he would go bankrupt and rightly so. But governments could borrow, beg, steal or simply print more money and there was no one to say them Nay. To Lockhart's arithmetical mind the world he had encountered was one of lunacy where two and two made five, or even eleven, and nothing added up to a true figure. It was not a world for him, with all its lying hypocrisy. 'Better a thief than a beggar,' he thought and drove on.

It was almost dark when they turned off the main road beyond Wark on to the half-metalled track that led to Black Pockrington. Above them a few stars speckled the sky and the headlamps picked out the gates and occasionally the eyes of a night animal, but everything else was dark and bare, a shape against the skyline. Jessica went into raptures.

'Oh, Lockhart, it's like another world.'

'It is another world,' said Lockhart.

When finally they breasted the rise of Tombstone Law and looked across the valley at the Hall, it was ablaze with lights in every window.

'Oh how beautiful!' said Jessica, 'Let's stop here for a moment. I want to savour it so.'

She got out and gazed ecstatically at the house. From its peel tower to its smoking chimneys and the lights gleaming from its windows it was everything she had hoped for. As if to celebrate this fulfilment the moon came out from behind a cloud and glinted on the surface of the reservoir and in the distance there came the baying of the Flawse hounds. The reading matter of Jessica's retarded adolescence was making itself manifest.

Chapter eight

It might be said that old Mr Flawse's reading matter made itself manifest next morning in the hall of the peel tower which his grandfather had restored to more than its former elegance. A contemporary of Sir Walter Scott and a voracious reader of his novels, he had turned what had been a fortified byre for cattle into a banqueting hall with plaster chasing and ornamental crests, while from the rafters there hung the tattered and entirely concocted battle-flags of half a dozen fictitious regiments. Time and moths had lent these standards a gauzelike authenticity while rust had etched a handiwork into the suited armour and armoury that they had never possessed when he had bought them. And armour and arms were everywhere. Helmeted figures stood against the walls and above them, interspersed with the stuffed heads of stags, moose, antelope and bear, and even one tiger, were the swords and battle-axes of bygone wars.

It was in this bellicose setting, with a great fire blazing in the hearth and smoke filtering up among the flags, that Mr Flawse chose to have his will read. Seated before him at a huge oak table were his nearest and supposedly dearest: Lockhart, Mrs Flawse, Jessica in a coma of romance, Mr Bullstrode the solicitor, who was to read the will, two tenant farmers to witness its signature, and Dr Magrew to certify that Mr Flawse was, as he proclaimed, of sound mind.

'The ceremony must be conducted under the most stringent of legal and jurisprudent conditions,' Mr Flawse had instructed, and so it was. He might just as well have added that the late and great Thomas Carlyle would lend the weight of his rhetorical authority to the proceedings, and certainly there were strains of the Sage of Ecchilfeccan in the old man's opening address. His words rang in the rafters and while for legal reasons the will contained few commas, Mr Flawse made good this deficiency by larding his speech with semi-colons.

'You are gathered here today,' he announced raising his coat-tails to the fire, 'to hear the last will and testament of Edwin Tyndale Flawse; once widowed and twice married; father of the late and partially lamented Clarissa Richardson Flawse; grandfather of her illegitimate offspring, Lockhart Flawse, whose father being unknown, I have out of no greatness of heart but that innate and incontrovertible practicality of mind which congenitally the family Flawse numbers most firmly among its features, adopted as my heir in the male line. But of the consequentiality of that anon; 'tis not of such low bestial matters that I speak; more lofty themes become my song, if song it be that old men sing out of their memories of what might have been; and I am old and near to death.'

He paused for breath and Mrs Flawse stirred expectantly in her seat. Mr Flawse regarded her with a gleaming predatory eye. 'Aye, ma'am, well may you squirm; your turn for dotage won't delay; death's bony finger beckons and we must obey; that black oblivion is our certain destination. Certain beyond all other certainties; the one fixed star in the firmament of man's experience; all else being loose and circumstantial and inco-ordinate, we can but set our sextant by that star of non-exist-ence, death, to measure what and where we are. Which I being ninety now see shining brighter and more darkly brilliant than before. And so towards the grave we move along the tramlines of our thoughts and deeds, those grooves of character which we, being born with them, are much beholden to and by, but which by virtue of their tiny flaws allow us unintentionally to exercise that little freedom which is man. Aye, is man, is. No animal knows freedom; only man; and that by fault of gene and chemi-cal congeneracy. The rest is all determined by our birth. So like an engine is a man, all steam and fire and pressure building up, he yet must move along predestined lines towards that end which is the end of all of us. Before you stands a semi-skeleton, all bones and skull with but a little spirit to ligature with life these odds and ends. And presently the parchment of my flesh shall break; all spirit flown; and shall my soul awake? I know not nor can ever know till death decides to answer yes or no. Which said I do not dis-esteem myself. I am yet here before you in this hall and you are gathered now to hear my will. My will? A strange word for the dead to claim; their will; when matters of decision are lost to those they leave behind. Their will; the supposition only of a wish. But I forestall that chance by setting forth before you now my will; and will it be in all the many meanings of that word. For I have laid conditions down which you will shortly hear and hearing do or forfeit all that fortune I have left to you.'

The old man paused and looked into their faces before con-tinuing. 'You wonder why I look?' he asked. 'To see one spark of some defiance in your eyes. One spark, that's all, one spark that yet might tell this partial skeleton to go to hell. Which it would at the least be ironical to conclude was indeed my destination. But I see it not; greed snuffs the candle of your courage out. You, ma'am,' he pointed a finger at Mrs Flawse, 'an undernourished vulture has more patience perched upon an upas tree than you with your squat backside on that bench.'

He paused but Mrs Flawse said nothing. Her little eyes narrowed with calculating hatred.

'Does nothing then provoke you to reply? No, but I know your thoughts; time runneth on; the metronome of heartbeats swings more slow and soon my threnody, a little premature perhaps, will cease. The grave I lie in will give you satisfaction. Let me forestall it for you, ma'am. And now the bastard Flawse. Have you defiance, sir, or did your education din it out of you?'

'Go to hell,' said Lockhart.

The old man smiled. 'Better, better, but prompted all the same. I told you what to say and you obeyed. But here's a better test.' Mr Flawse turned and took a battle-axe from the wall and held it out.

'Take it, bastard,' he said. 'Take the axe.'

Lockhart rose and took it.

'It was the custom of the Norsemen when a man grew old to cleave him headless with an axe,' continued Mr Flawse, 'it was the duty of his eldest son. Now having none but you, a ditch-born bastard grandson, take on the onus of this act and—'

'No,' said Jessica rising from her chair and grabbing the axe from Lockhart. 'I won't have it. You've got no right to put temptation in his way.'

The old man clapped his hands. 'Bravo. Now that's more like it. The bitch has better spirit than the dog. A flicker of spirit but spirit all the same. And I salute it. Mr Bullstrode, read the will.' And exhausted by his rhetoric old Mr Flawse sat down. Mr Bullstrode rose theatrically and opened the will.

'I, Edwin of Tyndale Flawse, being of sound mind and feeble yet sufficient body to sustain my mind, do hereby leave bequeath and devise all my worldly goods chattels property and land to my wife, Mrs Cynthia Flawse, for to have and to hold in trust and in use until her own death demise departure from this place which place being defined more closely is the radius of one mile from Flawse Hall and on condition that she do not sell mortgage rent borrow pledge or pawn a single or multiple of the possessions so bequeathed left and devised and in no way improves alters adds or amends the amenities of the said property possession chattels and house but subsists upon the income alone in recognition of which undertaking she signs herewith this will as being a binding contract to obey its strictures.'

Mr Bullstrode put down the will and looked at Mrs Flawse. 'Will you so sign?' he asked, but Mrs Flawse was in a flux of emotions. The old man had lived up to his word after all. He had left her his entire estate. Coming so shortly after being compared to a vulture this act of generosity had thrown her calculating compass off course. She needed time to think. It was denied her.

'Sign, ma'am,' said Mr Flawse, 'or the will becomes null and void in so far as it appertains to you.'

Mrs Flawse took the pen and signed and her signature was witnessed by the two tenant farmers.

'Continue, Mr Bullstrode,' said the old man almost gaily and Mr Bullstrode took up the will again.

'To my grandson Lockhart Flawse I leave nothing except my name until and unless he shall have produced in physical form the person of his natural father which father shall be proved to the satisfaction of my executor Mr Bullstrode or his successors to be the actual and admitted and undoubted father of the said Lockhart and shall have signed an affidavit to that effect which affidavit having been signed he shall be flogged by the said Lockhart to within an inch of his life. In the event of these aforestated conditions in regard to the proof of his paternity having been met the terms of the will in respect of my wife Cynthia Flawse as stated above her freely given signature shall and will become automatically null and void and the estate property chattels land and possessions pass *in toto* to my grandson Lockhart Flawse to do with whatsoever he chooses. To my servant Donald Robson Dodd I leave the use of my house and provender meat drink dogs and horse for as long as he shall live and they survive.'

Mr Bullstrode stopped and old Mr Flawse stepping up to the table picked up the pen. 'Am I in sound mind?' he asked Dr Magrew.

'Yes,' said the doctor, 'I attest that you are in sound mind.'

'Hear that,' said Mr Flawse to the two tenant farmers who nodded accordingly. 'You will witness that I am in sound mind when I sign this will.'

There was a sudden scream from Mrs Flawse. 'Sound mind? You're as mad as a hatter. You've cheated me. You said you would leave everything to me and now you've added a clause saying that I forfeit all right to inherit if . . . if . . . if that illegitimate creature finds his father.'

But Mr Flawse ignored her outburst and signed the will. 'Away with you, woman,' he said, handing the pen to one of the farmers, 'I kept my word and you'll keep mine or lose every penny I've left you.'

Mrs Flawse eyed the axe lying on the long table and then sat down defeated. She had been hoodwinked. 'There's nothing to say that I have to stay here while you are still alive. I shall leave first thing tomorrow.'

Mr Flawse laughed. 'Ma'am,' he said, 'you have signed a contract to remain here for the rest of your life or redress me for the loss of your presence to the tune of five thousand pounds a year.'

'I have done nothing of the sort,' screamed Mrs Flawse. 'I signed—'

But Mr Bullstrode handed her the will. 'You will find the clause on page one,' he said.

Mrs Flawse gaped at him incredulously and then followed his finger down the page. 'But you didn't read that out,' she said as the words swam before her eyes. 'You didn't read out "In the event of my wife Cynthia Flawse leaving . . ." Oh my God!' And she sank back into her chair. The clause was there in black on white.

'And now that the thing is signed, sealed and delivered,' said Mr Flawse as Bullstrode folded the extraordinary document and slipped it into his briefcase, 'let us drink a health to Death.'

'To Death?' said Jessica, still bemused by the bizarre romance of the scene.

Mr Flawse patted her radiant cheek fondly. 'To Death, my dear, the only thing we have in common,' he said, 'and the great leveller! Mr Dodd, the decanter of Northumbrian whisky.'

Mr Dodd disappeared through the door.

'I didn't know they made whisky in Northumberland,' said Jessica warming to the old man, 'I thought it was Scotch.'

'There are many things you don't know and Northumbrian whisky's among them. It used to be distilled in these parts by the gallon but Dodd's the only man with a still left. You see these walls? Ten feet thick. There used to be a saying hereabouts, "Six for the Scots and four for the Excise men." And it would be a canny man who would find the entrance but Dodd knows.'

In proof of this remark Mr Dodd reappeared with a decanter of whisky and a tray of glasses. When the glasses were all filled Mr Flawse rose and the others followed. Only Mrs Flawse remained seated.

'I refuse to drink to Death,' she muttered stubbornly. 'It's a wicked toast.'

'Aye, ma'am, and it's a wicked world,' said Mr Flawse, 'but you'll drink all the same. It's your only hope.'

Mrs Flawse got unsteadily to her feet and regarded him with loathing.

'To the Great Certainty,' said Mr Flawse and his voice rang among the battle-flags and armour.

Later after a lunch served in the dining-room Lockhart and Jessica walked across Flawse Fell. The afternoon sunlight shone down on the coarse grass and a few sheep stirred as they climbed Flawse Rigg.

'Oh, Lockhart, I wouldn't have missed today for all the world,' said Jessica when they reached the top. 'Your grandfather is the darlingest old man.'

It was not a superlative Lockhart would have applied to his grandfather and Mrs Flawse, white-faced in her room, would have used its opposite. But neither voiced their opinion. Lockhart because Jessica was his beloved angel and her opinion was not to be disputed and Mrs Flawse because she had no one to voice it to. Meanwhile Mr Bullstrode and Dr Magrew sat on with Mr Flawse at the mahogany table sipping port and engaged in that philosophical disputation to which their common background made them prone.

'I did not approve your toast to Death,' said Dr Magrew. 'It goes against my Hippocratic oath and besides it's a contradiction in terms to drink to the health of that which by its very nature cannot be called healthy.'

'Are you not confusing health with life?' said Mr Bullstrode. 'And by life I mean the vital element. Now the law of nature has it that every living thing shall die. That, sir, I think you will not deny.'

'I cannot,' said Dr Magrew, 'it is the truth. On the other hand I would question your right to call a dying man healthy. In all my experience as a practitioner of medicine I cannot recall being present at the deathbed of a healthy man.'

Mr Flawse rapped his glass to gain attention and the decanter. 'I think we are ignoring the factor of unnatural death,' he said refilling his glass. 'You doubtless know the conundrum of the fly and the locomotive. A perfectly healthy fly is travelling at twenty miles an hour in exactly the opposite direction to a locomotive travelling at sixty. The locomotive and the fly collide and the fly is instantaneously dead but in dying it stopped travelling forward at twenty miles per hour and reversed its motion at sixty. Now, sir, if the fly stopped and began reverse progress is it not also true that for it to do so the locomotive must also have stopped if for but the millionth of a second of the fly's stopping, and more germane to our argument is it not true that the fly died healthy?'

Mr Bullstrode poured himself more port and considered the problem but it was the doctor who took up the cudgels. 'If the locomotive stopped for a millionth of a second and about that, being no engineer, I cannot speak and must take your word for it, then it is also true that for that millionth of a second the fly was in an extremely unhealthy state. We have but to extend time in proportion to the life-expectancy of a fly to see that this is so. A fly's natural term of life is, I believe, limited to a single day, whereas the human term is three-score years and ten, present company excepted. In short a fly can look forward to approximately eighty-six thousand four hundred seconds of conscious existence whereas the human being can count on two billion one hundred and seven million five hundred and twenty seconds between birth and death. I leave it to you to discern the difference in lifetime of one millionth of a second for the fly and its equivalent length in a human's. At short notice I calculate the latter to be of the order of magnitude of five and a half

72

minutes. Certainly sufficient time in which to diagnose the patient as being unhealthy.'

Having disposed of the fly argument and the rest of the contents of his glass Dr Magrew sat back in his chair triumphantly.

It was Mr Bullstrode's turn to apply the methods of the law to the problem. 'Let us take the question of capital punishment,' he said. 'It was one of the proudest boasts of the penal system that no man went to the gallows unless he was fit to be hanged. Now a fit man is a healthy man and since death by hanging is instantaneous a murderer died healthy.'

But Dr Magrew was not to be put down so easily. 'Semantics, sir, semantics. You say that a murderer going to the gallows is fit to be hanged. Now I would have it that no man who murders is fit to live. We can turn these things on their heads. It all depends on one's viewpoint.'

'Aye, there's the rub,' said Mr Flawse, 'from what viewpoint should we look at things? Now, lacking any firmer ground than that afforded by my own experience, which has been largely confined to dogs and their habits, I would say we should start a little lower on the evolutionary scale than primates. It is a common saying that dog eats dog. The man who said it first did not know dogs. Dogs do not eat dogs. They work in packs and a pack animal is not a cannibal. It depends upon its fellows to bring down its prey and being dependent has the morality of a social being, an instinctive morality but morality for all that. Man on the other hand has no natural or instinctive morality. The process of history proves the contrary and the history of religion reinforces it. If there were any natural morality in man there would be no need for religion or indeed for law. And yet without morality man would not have survived. Another conundrum, gentlemen; science destroyed the belief in God upon which morality depended for its source; science has likewise substituted the means for man's destruction; in short we are without that moral sense that has saved us from extinction in the past and in possession of the means of extinguishing ourselves in the future. A bleak future, gentlemen, and one I trust I shall not be here to experience.'

'And what advice would you offer the future generation, sir?' inquired Mr Bullstrode.

'That which Cromwell gave his Roundheads,' said Mr

Flawse. 'To put their faith in God and keep their powder dry.'

'Which is to suppose that God exists,' said Dr Magrew.

'Which is to suppose no such thing,' said Mr Flawse. 'Faith is one thing; knowledge quite another. It were too easy otherwise.'

'Then you fall back on tradition, sir,' said Mr Bullstrode approvingly. 'As a lawyer I find much to commend your attitude.'

'I fall back on my family,' said Mr Flawse. 'The inheritance of characteristics is a fact of nature. It was Socrates who said "Know thyself." I would go further and say to know thyself one must first know thy ancestry. It is the key to my instructions to the bastard. Let him find out who his father was and then his grandfather and even further back and then he'll find himself.'

'And having found himself, what then?' asked Mr Bullstrode.

'Be himself,' said Mr Flawse, and promptly fell asleep.

Chapter nine

Upstairs in the solitude of her bedroom Mrs Flawse was beside herself. For the second time in her life a husband had cheated her and the occasion called for wailing and gnashing of teeth. But being a methodical woman and knowing the expense of a new pair of dentures, Mrs Flawse first removed her teeth and put them in a glass of water before gnashing her gums. Nor did she wail. To have done so would have afforded her husband too much satisfaction and Mrs Flawse was determined he should suffer for his sins. Instead she sat toothless and considered her revenge. It lay, she realized, in Lockhart. If in his will Mr Flawse had saddled her with the perpetual occupation of the Hall without amenities, he had likewise saddled his grandson with the task of finding his father. Only then could he deprive her of her inheritance and failing in his search and following the old man's death she would make what improvements she liked to the Hall. Better still, the income from the estate would be hers to do with as she pleased. She could accumulate it year by year and add it to her savings and one fine day she would have saved enough to leave and not return. But all this only if Lockhart failed to find his father. Deny Lockhart the means to search, and here Mrs Flawse's thoughts flew to money, and she would be secure. She would see that Lockhart had no means.

Reaching for her writing-case she put pen to paper and wrote a short, concise letter to Mr Treyer instructing him to dismiss Lockhart from Sandicott & Partner without notice. Then having sealed the envelope she put it away to give to Jessica to post or, more ironically, for Lockhart to deliver by hand. Mrs Flawse smiled a toothless smile and went on to consider other ways of taking her revenge, and by the time the afternoon had waned she was in a more cheerful mood. The old man had stipulated in his will that there should be no improvements to the Hall. She intended to stick to the letter of his instructions. There would be no improvements and for the rest of his unnatural life there would be the reverse. Windows would be opened, doors unlatched, food cold and damp beds damper still until with her assistance the infirmities of age had been accelerated to his end. And the old man had toasted Death. It was appropriate. Death would come sooner than he dreamt. Yes, that was it, delay Lockhart at all cost and hasten her husband's dying and she would be in a position to dispute the will and maybe, better still, bribe Mr Bullstrode to amend its dispositions. She would have to sound the man out. In the meantime she would put a fine face on things.

If Mrs Flawse had been disturbed by the reading of the will so had Lockhart. Sitting on Flawse Rigg with Jessica he did not share her romantic view of his bastardy.

'I didn't know it meant I had no father,' he told her. 'I thought it was just another word he used for me. He's always calling people bastards.'

'But don't you see how exciting it all is,' said Jessica. 'It's like a paper chase, or Hunt the Father. And when you find him you'll inherit the whole estate and we can come and live up here.'

'It isn't going to be easy to find a father who's got to be flogged within an inch of his life the moment he admits it,' said

Lockhart practically, 'and anyway I don't know where to start.'

'Well, at least you know when you were born and all you've got to find out then is who your mother was in love with.'

'And how do I find out when I was born?'

'By looking at your birth certificate, silly,' said Jessica.

'I haven't got one,' said Lockhart, 'grandpa wouldn't let me be registered. It's awfully inconvenient and Mr Treyer wasn't able to pay my National Insurance stamps or anything. That's one of the reasons he wouldn't let me go to work. He said that for all practical purposes I don't exist and wished I didn't for impractical ones. I can't vote or serve on a jury or get a passport.'

'Oh, darling, there must be something you can do,' said Jessica, 'I mean once you do find your father he'll let you have a birth certificate. Why don't you have a word with Mr Bullstrode about it? He seems the sweetest old gentleman.'

'Seems,' said Lockhart gloomily, 'just seems.'

But when as the sun began to set over the firing-range they walked hand-in-hand back to the house they found Mr Bullstrode examining the front of the Range-Rover with a legal eye.

'It would appear that you have been in some sort of collision,' he said.

'Yes,' said Jessica, 'we hit a little car.'

'Indeed?' said Mr Bullstrode. 'A little car. I trust you reported the accident to the police.'

Lockhart shook his head. 'I didn't bother.'

'Indeed?' said Mr Bullstrode more legally still. 'You simply hit a little car and then continued on your way. And the owner of the other vehicle, did he have something to say about it?'

'I didn't wait to find out,' said Lockhart.

'And then the police chased us,' said Jessica, 'And Lockhart was ever so clever and drove though hedges and across fields where they couldn't follow us.'

'Hedges?' said Mr Bullstrode. 'Am I to understand that having been involved in an accident which you failed to stop and report you were then chased by the police and committed the further felony of driving this remarkable vehicle through hedges and across, by the look of the tyres, ploughed and doubtless planted fields thus damaging property and leaving yourselves liable to criminal prosecution on grounds of trespass?'

'Yes,' said Lockhart, 'that just about sums it up.'

'Good God,' said Mr Bullstrode and scratched his bald head. 'And did it never occur to you that the police must have taken your number and can trace you by it?'

'Ah, but it wasn't the right number,' said Lockhart and explained his reasons for changing it. By the time he had finished Mr Bullstrode's legal sensibilities were in tatters. 'I hesitate to add to the proscriptions attendant upon your grandfather's will by describing your actions as wholly criminal and without the law but I must say . . .' He broke off unable to give words to his feelings.

'What?' said Lockhart.

Mr Bullstrode consulted commonsense. 'My advice is to leave the vehicle here,' he said finally, 'and to travel home by train.'

'And what about finding my father?' said Lockhart. 'Have you any opinion to offer on that?'

'I was not alerted to your mother's death or your delivery until some months had passed,' said Mr Bullstrode. 'I can only advise you to consult Dr Magrew. Not, of course, that I impute any interest other than the professional to his concern for your dear mother's condition at the time of her demise, but he may be able to help in the matter of timing your conception.'

But Dr Magrew when they found him in the study warming his feet at the fire could add little.

'As I remember the occasion,' he said, 'you were, to put it mildly, a premature baby distinguished largely by the fact that you appeared to be born with measles. A wrong diagnosis, I have to confess, but understandable in that I have seldom if ever been confronted by a baby born in a stinging-nettle patch. But definitely premature and I would therefore put your conception no earlier than February 1956 and no later than March. I must therefore conclude that your father was in close proximity to these parts and those of your mother during these two months. I am glad to be able to say that I do not qualify as a candidate for your paternity by the good fortune of being out of the country at that time.'

'But didn't he look like anyone you knew when he was born?' asked Jessica.

'My dear,' said Dr Magrew, 'a premature infant expelled from the womb into a stinging-nettle patch as a result of his mother's fall from her horse can only be said to look like nothing on earth. I would hesitate to defame any man by saying that Lockhart at birth looked like him. An orang-outang possibly, but an unsightly one at that. No, I am afraid your search will have to proceed along other lines than family likeness.'

'But what about my mother?' said Lockhart. 'Surely she must have had friends who would be able to tell me something.'

Dr Magrew nodded. 'Your presence here today would seem conclusive evidence of the former proposition,' he said. 'Unfortunately your grandfather's will makes the second highly unlikely.'

'Can you tell us what Lockhart's mother was like?' asked Jessica.

Dr Magrew's face grew solemn. 'Let's just say she was a wild lassie with a tendency to rush her fences,' he said. 'Aye, and a beauty too in her day.'

But that was as much as they could get out of him. And next morning, accepting a lift from Mr Bullstrode, who had stayed overnight, they left the Hall carrying Mrs Flawse's letter to Mr Treyer.

'My dear,' said old Mr Flawse patting Jessica's hand rather more pruriently than their relationship called for, 'you have married a numbskull but you'll make a man of him yet. Come and see me again before I die. I like a woman of spirit.'

It was a tearful Jessica who got into the car. 'You must think me awfully sentimental,' she said.

'Of course ye are, hinnie,' said the old man, 'which is what I admire about you. Where there's mush there's grit beneath. You must have got it from your father. Your mother's grit all over and as soft as a slug at the core.'

And with these parting words they left the Hall. In the background old Mrs Flawse added slugs to the menu of her revenge.

Two days later Lockhart presented himself for the last time at Sandicott & Partner and handed Mr Treyer the envelope containing Mrs Flawse's instructions. Half an hour later he left again while behind him Mr Treyer praised whatever Gods there be, and in particular Janus, in the environs of Wheedle Street that he had at long last been instructed to fire, sack, dismiss and generally send packing the ghastly liability to the firm of Sandicott & Partner that marched under the name of Lockhart Flawse. His mother-in-law's letter had been couched in much the same terms as the old man's will and for once Mr Treyer had no need to equivocate. Lockhart left the office with his head ringing with Mr Treyer's opinions and returned home to explain this strange turn of events to Jessica.

'But why should mummy have done such a horrid thing?' she asked. Lockhart could find no answer.

'Perhaps she doesn't like me,' he said.

'Of course she does, darling. She would never have let me marry you if she hadn't liked you.'

'Well, if you had seen what she wrote in that letter about me you'd have second thoughts about that,' said Lockhart. But Jessica had already summed her mother up.

'I think she's just an old cat and she's cross about the will. That's what I think. What are you going to do now?'

'Get another job, I suppose,' said Lockhart but the supposition came easier than the result. The Labour Exchange in East Pursley was already swamped with applications from ex-stockbrokers and Mr Treyer's refusal to grant that he had ever been employed at Sandicott, combined with his lack of any means of identification, made Lockhart's position hopeless. It was the same at the Social Security office. His non-entity in any bureaucratic sense became obvious when he admitted he had never paid any National Insurance stamps.

'As far as we are concerned you don't statistically speaking exist,' the clerk told him.

'But I do,' Lockhart insisted, 'I am here. You can see me. You can even touch me if you want to.'

The clerk didn't. 'Listen,' he said with all the politeness of a public servant addressing the public, 'you've admitted you aren't on the Voters' Roll, you haven't been included in any census count, you can't produce a passport or birth certificate, you haven't had a job . . . Yes, I know what you're going to say but I've a letter here from a Mr Treyer who states categorically you didn't work at Sandicott & Partner, you haven't paid a penny in National Insurance stamps, you haven't got a health card. Now then do you want to go your non-existent way or do I have to call the police?' Lockhart indicated that he didn't want the police to be called.

'Right then,' said the clerk, 'let me get on with some other applicants who've got a better claim on the Welfare State.'

Lockhart left him coping with an unemployed graduate in Moral Sciences who had for months been demanding to be treated rather more generously than an old-age pensioner while at the same time refusing any job that was not consistent with his qualifications.

By the time Lockhart got home he was utterly despondent.

'It's no use,' he said, 'I can't get anyone to employ me at any sort of job and I can't get social benefits because they won't admit I exist.'

'Oh dear,' said Jessica. 'If only we could sell all the houses daddy left me, we could invest the money and live off the income.'

'Well, we can't. You heard what the Estate Agent said. They're occupied, unfurnished and on long leases and we can't even raise the rent, let alone sell them.'

'I think it's jolly unfair. Why can't we just tell the tenants to go?'

'Because the law says they don't have to move.'

'Who cares what the law says?' said Jessica. 'There's a law which says unemployed people get free money, but when it comes to paying you they don't do it, and it isn't even as if you didn't want to work. I don't see why we have to obey a law which hurts us when the Government won't obey a law which helps us.'

'What's good for the goose is good for the gander,' Lockhart agreed and so was born the idea which, nurtured in Lockhart Flawse's mind, was to turn the quiet backwater of Sandicott Crescent into a maelstrom of misunderstandings.

That night, while Jessica racked her brains for some way to supplement their income, Lockhart left the house and, moving with all the silence and stealth he had acquired in pursuit of game on Flawse Fell, stole through the gorse bushes in the bird sanctuary with a pair of binoculars. He was not bird-watching in its true sense but by the time he returned at midnight the occupants of most of the houses had been observed and Lockhart had gained some little insight into their habits.

He sat up for a while making notes in a pocket book. It was carefully indexed and under P he put 'Pettigrew, man and wife aged fifty. Put dachshund named Little Willie out at eleven and make milk drink. Go to bed eleven-thirty.' Under G there was the information that the Grabbles watched television and went to bed at ten-forty-five. Mr and Mrs Raceme in Number 8 did something strange which involved tying Mr Raceme to the bed at nine-fifteen and untying him again at ten. At Number 4 the Misses Musgrove had entertained the Vicar before supper and had read the *Church Times* and knitted afterwards. Finally, next door to the Flawse house, Colonel Finch-Potter in Number 10 smoked a cigar after a solitary dinner, fulminated loudly at a Labour Party political broadcast on television, and then took a brisk walk with his bull-terrier before retiring.

Lockhart made notes of all these practices and went to bed himself. Something deep and devious was stirring in his mind. What exactly it was he couldn't say, but the instinct of the hunt was slowly edging its way towards consciousness and with it a barbarity and anger that knew nothing of the law or the social conventions of civilization.

Next morning Jessica announced that she was going to get a job.

'I can type and take shorthand and there's lots of firms wanting secretaries. I'm going to a bureau. They're advertising for temporary typists.'

'I don't like it,' said Lockhart. 'A man should provide for his wife, not the other way round.'

'I won't be providing for you. It's for us, and anyway I might even find you a job. I'll tell everyone I work for how clever you are.'

And in spite of Lockhart's opposition she caught the bus. Left to himself, he spent the day brooding about the house with a sullen look on his face and poking into places he hadn't been before. One of these was the attic and there in an old tin trunk he discovered the papers of the late Mr Sandicott. Among them he found the architect's drawings for the interiors of all the houses in the Crescent together with details of plumbing, sewers, and electrical connections. Lockhart took them downstairs and studied them carefully. They were extremely informative and by the time Jessica returned with the news that she was starting next day with a cement company, one of whose typists was away with flu, Lockhart had mapped in his head the exact location of all the mod cons the houses in Sandicott Crescent boasted. He greeted Jessica's news without enthusiasm.

'If anyone tries anything funny,' he said, remembering Mr Tryer's tendencies with temporary typists, 'I want you to tell me. I'll kill him.'

'Oh, Lockhart darling, you're so chivalrous,' said Jessica proudly. 'Let's have a kiss and cuddle tonight.'

But Lockhart had other plans for the evening and Jessica went to bed alone. Outside, Lockhart crawled through the undergrowth of the bird sanctuary to the foot of the Racemes' garden, climbed the fence and installed himself in a cherry tree that overlooked the Racemes' bedroom. He had decided that Mr Raceme's peculiar habit of allowing his wife to tie him to their double bed for three-quarters of an hour might provide him with information for future use. But he was disappointed. Mr and Mrs Raceme had supper and watched television before having an early and less restrained night. At eleven their lights went out and Lockhart descended the cherry tree and was making his way back over the fence when the Pettigrews at Number 6 put Little Willie out while they made Ovaltine. Attracted by Lockhart's passage through the gorse the dachshund dashed down the garden with a series of yelps and stood barking into the darkness. Lockhart moved away but the dog kept up its hullabaloo and presently Mr Pettigrew came down the lawn to investigate.

'Now, Willie, stop that noise,' he said. 'Good dog. There's nothing there.'

But Willie knew better and, emboldened by his master's presence, made further rushes in Lockhart's direction. Finally Mr Pettigrew picked the dog up and carried him back into the house leaving Lockhart with the resolution to do something about Willie as soon as possible. Barking dogs were a hazard he could do without.

He progressed by way of the Misses Musgrove's back garden

82

– their lights had gone out promptly at ten – and crossed into the Grabbles' where the downstairs lights were on and the living-room curtains partly open. Lockhart stationed himself beside the greenhouse and focused his binoculars on the gap in the curtains and was surprised to see Mrs Grabble on the sofa in the arms of someone who was quite clearly not the Mr Grabble he knew. As the couple writhed in ecstasy Lockhart's binoculars discovered the flushed face of Mr Simplon who lived at Number 5. Mrs Grabble and Mr Simplon? Then where was Mr Grabble and what was Mrs Simplon doing? Lockhart left the greenhouse and slipped across the road to the golf course, past the Rickenshaws at Number 1 and the Ogilvies at Number 3 to the Simplons' mock-Georgian mansion at Number 5. A light was on upstairs and since the curtains were drawn, the Simplons kept no dog and the garden was well endowed with shrubs, Lockhart ventured down a flowerbed until he was standing beneath the window. He stood as still as he had once stood on Flawse Fell when a rabbit had spotted him, and he was still as motionless when headlights illuminated the front of the house an hour later and Mr Simplon garaged his car. Lights went on in the house and a moment later voices issued from the bedroom, the acrimonious voice of Mrs Simplon and the placatory one of Mr Simplon.

'Working late at the office my foot,' said Mrs Simplon. 'That's what you keep telling me. Well, I phoned the office twice this evening and there was no one there.'

'I was out with Jerry Blond, the architect,' said Mr Simplon. 'He wanted me to meet a client from Cyprus who is thinking of building a hotel. If you don't believe me, phone Blond and see if he doesn't confirm what I say.'

But Mrs Simplon scorned the idea. 'I'm not going to advertise the fact that I have my own ideas about what you get up to,' she said. 'I've got more pride.'

Down in the bushes Lockhart admired her pride and was inspired by her reluctance. If she wasn't going to advertise what she correctly thought Mr Simplon was getting up to, namely Mrs Grabble, it might be to his own advantage to do it for her. And where was Mr Grabble? Lockhart decided to explore that gentleman's movements more closely before acting. Evidently there were nights when Mr Grabble stayed away from home.

He would have to find out when. In the meantime there was no more to be gained from the Simplons, and leaving them to their quarrel he returned to the golf course; passing the Lowrys who lived at Number 7 and Mr O'Brain, the gynaecologist, who inhabited the Bauhaus at Number 9 and was already in bed, he found himself at the bottom of the Wilsons' garden at Number 11. Here the lights were on, though dimly, in the downstairs lounge and the french windows open. Lockhart squatted in a bunker on the seventeenth hole and lifted his binoculars. There were three people in the room sitting round a small table with their fingers touching, and as he watched the table moved. Lockhart eyed it beadily and his keen ear detected the sound of knocking. The Wilsons and their friend were engaged in some strange ritual. Every now and again Mrs Wilson would put a question and the table would rock and knock. So the Wilsons were superstitious.

Lockhart crawled away and presently was adding this and all the other gleanings of the night's prowl to his notebook. By the time he went to bed, Jessica was fast asleep.

And so for the next fortnight Lockhart spent his evenings patrolling the bird sanctuary and the golf course and amassed dossiers on the habits, fads, foibles and indiscretions of all the tenants of the Crescent. By day he pottered about the house and spent a good many hours in his late father-in-law's workshop with lengths of wire, transistors and a Do-It-Yourself *Manual of Radio Construction*.

'I don't know what you do with yourself all day, darling,' said Jessica, who had moved from the cement company to a firm of lawyers who specialized in libel actions.

'I'm making provision for our future,' said Lockhart.

'With loudspeakers? What have loudspeakers got to do with our future?'

'More than you know.'

'And this transmitter thing. Is that part of our future too?'

'Our future and the Wilsons' next door,' said Lockhart. 'Where did your mother keep the keys to the houses?'

'You mean the houses daddy left me?'

Lockhart nodded and Jessica rummaged in a kitchen drawer.

'Here they are,' she said and hesitated. 'You're not thinking of stealing things, are you?'

'Certainly not,' said Lockhart firmly, 'if anything I intend to add to their possessions.'

'Oh, well, that's all right then,' said Jessica and handed him the bundle of Yale keys. 'I wouldn't want to think you were doing anything that wasn't legal. Working at Gibling and Gibling I've learnt just how easy it is to get into terrible trouble. Did you know that if you write a book and say nasty things in it about somebody they can sue you for thousands of pounds? It's called libel.'

'I wish someone would write nasty things about us then,' said Lockhart. 'We've got to get thousands of pounds if I'm ever going to start looking for my father.'

'Yes, a libel case would help, wouldn't it?' said Jessica dreamily. 'But you do promise you aren't doing anything that can get us into trouble, don't you?'

Lockhart promised. Fervently. What he had in mind was going to get other people into trouble.

In the meantime he had to wait. It was three days before the Wilsons went out for the evening and Lockhart was able to slip over the fence into their garden and let himself into Number 11. Under his arm he carried a box. He spent an hour in the attic before returning empty-handed.

'Jessica, my sweet,' he said, 'I want you to go into the workshop and wait five minutes. Then say "Testing. Testing. Testing" into that little transmitter. You press the red button first.'

Lockhart slipped back into the Wilsons' house and climbed to the attic and waited. A short time later the three loudspeakers hidden under the glass-fibre insulation and connected to the receiver concealed in a corner resounded eerily to Jessica's voice. One loudspeaker was placed over the Wilsons' main bedroom, a second over the bathroom and a third above the spare room. Lockhart listened and then climbed down and went home.

'You go up to bed,' he told Jessica, 'I shouldn't be long.' Then he stationed himself at the front window and waited for the Wilsons to return. They had had a good evening and were in an intensely spiritual state. Lochart watched the lights come on in their bedroom and bathroom before contributing his share to their belief in the supernatural. Holding his nose between finger and thumb and speaking adenoidally into the microphone he whispered, 'I speak from beyond the grave. Hear me. There will be a death in your house and you will join me.' Then he switched the transmitter off and went out into the night the better to observe the result.

It was, to put it mildly, electrifying. Lights flashed on in every room in the house next door and Mrs Wilson, more used to the gentler messages of the ouija board, could be heard screaming hysterically at this authentic voice of doom. Lockhart, squatting in an azalea bush next to the gateway, listened to Mr Wilson trying to pacify his wife, a process made more difficult by his evident alarm and the impossibility of denying that he too had heard there was going to be a death in the house.

'There's no use saying you didn't,' wailed Mrs Wilson, 'you heard it as clearly as I did and you were in the bathroom and look at the mess you made on the floor.'

Mr Wilson had to agree that his aim had been put off and, by way of Mrs Wilson's infallible logic, that the mess was in consequence of his having learnt that death was so close at hand.

'I told you we should never have started fooling with that damned table-rapping!' he shouted. 'Now look what you've been and let loose.'

'That's right, blame me,' screamed Mrs Wilson, 'that's all you ever do. All I did was ask Mrs Saphegie round to see if she really had psychic gifts and could get answers from our dear departed.'

'Well, now you bloody know,' shouted Mr Wilson. 'And that wasn't the voice of any of my dear departed, that's for sure. No one on our side of the family suffered from such an awful nasal condition. Mind you, I don't suppose being decomposed in a coffin does anything for sinusitis.'

'There you go again,' whined Mrs Wilson, 'one of us going to die and you have to go on about coffins. And don't hog all the brandy. I want some.'

'I didn't know you drank,' said Mr Wilson.

'I do now,' said his wife and evidently poured herself a stiff one. Lockhart left them consoling themselves somewhat unsuccessfully that at least the terrible prophecy proved that there was life after death. It didn't seem to comfort Mrs Wilson very much,

But while the Wilsons speculated on this imminent question about the afterlife and its existence, Little Willie, the Pettigrews' dachshund, went still further and found out. At precisely eleven o'clock Mr Pettigrew put him out and just as precisely Lockhart, lurking in the bird sanctuary, tugged on the nylon fishing-line that stretched under the fence and down the lawn. At the end of the line a lump of liver purchased that morning from the butcher pursued its erratic course across the grass. Behind it, for once unwisely soundless, came Willie in hot pursuit. He didn't come far. As the liver slid past the snare Lockhart had set at the end of the lawn, Willie stopped and, after a brief struggle, gave up both the pursuit and his life. Lockhart buried him under a rose bush at the bottom of his own garden where he would do most good and having accomplished his first two intentions went to bed in a thoroughly cheerful mood, made all the more lively by the fact that the lights were still on in every room of the Wilsons' house when he turned over at three in the morning, and from the house there could be heard the sound of drunken sobbing.

Chapter ten

While Lockhart began to make life uncomfortable for the tenants of his wife's houses, her mother was doing her damnedest to make life unbearable for Mr Flawse. The weather was not on her side. From a bright spring they passed into a hot summer and Flawse Hall showed itself to advantage. Its thick walls had more functions than the keeping out of the Scots and the keeping in of the whisky; they soothed the summer's heat. Outside, the hybrid hounds might slobber and loll in the dung-dry dust of the yard; inside, Mr Flawse could sit contentedly upright at his desk poring over the parish registers and ancient enclosure deeds to which he had lately become so addicted. Knowing that in the fullness of time he was about due to join his ancestors he thought it as well to acquaint himself with the faults and failings of his family.

That he looked only on the worst side of things came from his natural pessimism and knowledge of himself. He was therefore surprised to find that the Flawses were not all unconscionably bad. There were Flawse saints as well as Flawse sinners and if as he expected the latter predominated there was still a streak of generosity to their actions he could not but admire. The Flawse, one Quentin Flawse, who had murdered, or by the more polite usage of the time done to death in a duel, one Thomas Tidley in consequence of the latter implying at the sheep shearing at Otterburn that the name Flawse derived from the Faas, a notorious family of gipsies known best for their thieving, had yet had the generosity to marry his widow and provide for his children. Then again Bishop Flawse, burnt at the stake in the reign of Bloody Mary for his apostasy from Rome, had refused the bag of gunpowder which his brother had brought to tie round his neck on the sensible grounds of economy and its better use to fire muskets into the body of damned Papists when the time was ripe. It was this sort of practicality that Mr Flawse most admired in his forebears and showed that to whatever end they came they wasted no time on self-pity but sustained an indomitable will to do unto others as they were having done to them. Thus Headman Flawse, private executioner to the Duke of Durham in the fourteenth century, had, when his time came to lay his own head on the block, gallantly offered to sharpen the axe for his successor, a gesture so generous that it had been granted: to the extinction of the new headman, fifteen bodyguards, twenty-five bystanders and the Duke himself, all of whom lay headless while Headman Flawse put his expertise to private use and escaped on the Duke's own charger to spend his days as an outlaw among the moss troopers of Redesdale.

Old Mr Flawse thrilled to the account just as he thrilled to the verse that sang in the blood of the Flawse balladeers. Minstrel Flawse was renowned for his songs and Mr Flawse found himself almost unconsciously saying aloud the first stanza of 'The Ballad of Prick 'Em Dry' which the Minstrel was supposed by some authorities to have composed beneath the gibbet at Elsdon on the occasion of his hanging, drawing and quartering for misguidedly climbing into bed with Sir Oswald Capheughton's wife, Lady Fleur, when that noble lord was not only in it but in her at the same time. Minstrel Flawse's introduction of himself into Sir Oswald had met with that reaction known as dog-knotting on the part of all concerned, and it had taken the combined efforts of seven manservants to prise Sir Oswald from Lady Fleur and the sole resources of the local barber and surgeon to sever the connection between Sir Oswald and his Minstrel. The Eunuch Flawse had gone to his subsequent dismemberment relatively cheerfully and with a song in his heart.

I gan noo wha ma organs gan
　　When oft I lay abed
So rither hang me upside doon
　　Than by ma empty head.

I should ha' knoon 'twas never Fleur
　　That smelt so mooch of sweat
For she was iver sweet and pure
　　And iver her purse was wet.

But old Sir Oswald allus stank
　　Of horse and hound and dung
And when I chose to breech his rank
　　Was barrel to my bung.

So hang me noo fra' Elsdon Tree
　　And draw ma innards out
That all the warld around may see
　　What I have done without.

But ere ye come to draw ma heart
　　Na do it all so quick
But prise the arse of Oswald 'part
　　And bring me back ma prick.

So prick 'em wet or prick 'em dry
　　'Tis all the same to me
I canna wait for him to die
　　Afore I have a pee.

Mr Flawse found the poem heartening, if crude. He knew exactly how the Minstrel had felt: his prostate had lately been giving him trouble. But it was the dour gaiety of the ballads that gave him the greatest pleasure. The Flawses might, and indeed, had been thieves and robbers, cut-throats and moss troopers, even saints and bishops, but whatever their calling they had laughed the devil to scorn and made a mockery of misfortune, and their religion had been less Christian than that of personal honour. To call a Flawse a liar was to die or to defend yourself to the death and a Flawse who flinched in the face of adversity was an outcast without hame or name, as the old saying had it.

But there was more to old Mr Flawse's ancestral interest than mere curiosity concerning his own relations. There was still the great question-mark that haunted his nights as to the paternity of Lockhart. And behind it lay the horrifying feeling that Lockhart was as much his son as his grandson. It was with this in mind that he added the flagellant clause to the will in part-recognition that if his suspicions were true he deserved to be flogged within an inch of his life and more properly a yard beyond. The question had to be answered, if not in his own lifetime, in that of Lockhart and as he worked his way through ancient deeds and documents Mr Flawse continued to consider possible candidates. They all had this in common: that at the time of Lockhart's conception, which Mr Flawse calculated to be eight months before his birth, they had lived within riding distance of the Hall and had been between the ages of sixteen and sixty. He refused to believe that his daughter, whatever her vices, would willingly have taken to herself an old man. Much more likely the father had been in his twenties. Beside each name Mr Flawse put the age of the candidate, the colour of his eyes and hair, his features, height and, where possible, his cephalic index. Since the latter required the suspect to submit to Mr Flawse measuring his head both back to front and from side to side with a pair of unnecessarily pointed calipers, not everyone was willing to undergo the operation and those who didn't had registered against their names the letters VS, which signified Very Suspicious. Over the years the old man had collected an immense amount of anthropologically interesting information, but none of it fitted Lockhart's features. They were Flawsian in every particular from the Roman nose to the ice-blue eyes and the flaxen hair and thus increased the old man's sense of guilt and his determination to absolve himself even at the risk of failing and going down in the family history as Incest Flawse. So absorbed was he in his studies that he failed to notice the change that had occurred in his wife.

Mrs Flawse had, as part of her plan for his early death, decided to play the role of dutiful wife. Far from repulsing his advances she positively encouraged him to strain his heart by sleeping with her. Mr Flawse's prostate redressed the balance and prevented him from rising to these frequent occasions. Mrs Flawse took to bringing him his early-morning cup of tea in bed having first laced it with powdered paracetamol tablets which she had once read affected the kidneys adversely. Mr Flawse didn't drink tea in bed, but, not to hurt her feelings, emptied his cup into the chamber pot with the result that Mrs Flawse's hopes were aroused quite fortuitously by the colour of the contents when she emptied it later in the day. The fact that the potion contained tea leaves, and that she was too fastidious to examine it closely, led her to the vain hope that there was something seriously amiss with his bladder. Finally she put him on an even higher cholesterol diet than usual. Mr Flawse had eggs for breakfast, fried eggs with lamb chops for lunch, pork for dinner and zabaglione for dessert, and an eggnog before retiring. Mr Flawse thrived on eggs.

Mrs Flawse, following Professor Yudkin's advice in reverse, added sugar to her list of dietetic poisons and having pressed Mr Flawse to another egg or some more pork crackling, served sweets, cakes and biscuits that consisted almost entirely of sugar. Mr Flawse's energy increased enormously and when not sitting in his study he strode across the fell with renewed vigour. Mrs Flawse watched his progress in despair and her own increased weight with alarm. It was all very well trying to poison the old man by over-indulgence but she had to share the same diet and it didn't agree with her. Finally, in a last desperate effort, she encouraged him to hit the port bottle. Mr Flawse followed her advice cheerfully and felt all the better for it. Mrs Flawse fortified the port decanter with brandy and Mr Flawse, whose nose for a fine wine was acute, recognized the addition and congratulated her on her ingenuity. 'Gives it more body,' he declared. 'I wonder I hadn't thought of it before. Definitely more body.'

Mrs Flawse silently cursed but had to agree. Port with more than its normal quota of brandy did have more body. On the other hand so did she, and her dresses were beginning to look as though they belonged to another woman. Mr Flawse found her greater girth a source of amusement and made uncalled-for remarks to Mr Dodd about breasts, bottoms and bitches being all the better for bed when broad. And all the while Mrs Flawse was conscious that Mr Dodd kept his uncast eye upon her. She found it unnerving and Mr Dodd's collie had a nasty habit of snarling whenever she passed too close.

'I wish you'd keep the creature out of the kitchen,' she told Mr Dodd irritably.

'Aye and me with her I dare say,' said Mr Dodd. 'You'd be hard put to it to keep yoursel' warm without my going down the drift mine for coal. If you dinna want me in the kitchen, you'll have to gan dig it yoursel'.'

Mrs Flawse had no intention of going down the drift mine to dig coal and said so.

'Then the dawg stays,' said Mr Dodd.

Mrs Flawse promised herself to see that the collie didn't, but Mr Dodd's habit of feeding the beast himself prevented her from putting ground glass in the dog's food. All in all it was a trying summer for Mrs Flawse and she found herself un-characteristically yearning for the bleak winter ahead. She would have more opportunity for making things uncomfortable at the Hall.

Lockhart had already succeeded at Sandicott Crescent. Having dispatched Little Willie, the Pettigrews' dachshund, to that afterlife about which the Wilsons now had no doubts, he was able to move more easily about the gardens and the bird sanc-tuary on his solitary expeditions. Mr Grabble, whose wife he had seen in Mr Simplon's arms, was the European manager for a firm of electronics engineers and regularly went abroad. It was during his absences that Mrs Grabble and Mr Simplon kept what Lockhart called their trysts. Mr Simplon left his car two streets away and walked to the Grabble house; when he had finished trysting he went back to the car and drove home to Mrs Simplon at Number 5. Further investigation revealed that Mr Grabble had left an emergency number in Amsterdam where he could always be reached should need arise. Lockhart discovered this by the simple expedient of unlocking the front door to Number 2 with the late Mr Sandicott's key and consulting the Grabbles' bureau and telephone directory. Accordingly, on a hot afternoon in June, he went to the trouble of sending a telegram to Mr Grabble in Amsterdam recommending him to return home at once as his wife was dangerously ill, too ill in fact to be moved from the house. Having signed it in the name of a fictitious doctor Lockhart quietly shinned a telegraph pole in the bird sanctuary and neatly severed the line to the Grabbles' house. After that he went home and had tea before going out as dusk fell and making his way to the corner of the road in which Mr Simplon left his car. The car was there.

It was not there twenty-five minutes later when Mr Grabble, driving with more reckless concern for his wife than her behaviour justified and less for other road users, hurtled through East Pursley and into Sandicott Crescent. It was not there when Mr Simplon, naked and covering his previously private parts with both hands, scampered down the Grabbles' drive and shot frenziedly round the corner. It was sitting in the Simplons' garage where Lockhart had parked with a cheerful toot of the horn to alert Mrs Simplon that her husband was home, before crossing to the golf course and making his way sedately back to Jessica at Number 12. Behind him Numbers 5 and 2 were a holocaust of domestic understanding. The discovery that his wife, far from being dangerously ill, was copulating ardently with a neighbour he had never much liked anyway, and that he had been brought anxiously all the way back from Amsterdam to have this ugly fact thrust under his unsuspecting nose, was too much for Mr Grabble's temper. His shouts and Mrs Grabble's screams, as he used first his umbrella, and then, having broken it, an Anglepoise lamp that stood on the bedside table, to express his feelings, could be heard far down the street. They were particularly audible next door where the Misses Musgrove were entertaining the Vicar and his wife to dinner. They were also audible to Mrs Simplon. The fact that her husband, having just driven into the garage, figured so largely in Mr Grabble's invective provoked her to investigate how he could possibly be in two places at the same time. Mr Grabble's commentary supplied a third occupation, that of Mrs Grabble.

Mrs Simplon emerged from the front door at the very same moment as the Vicar, driven as much by the Misses Musgroves' curiosity as by any desire to interfere in a domestic disaster, came out of Number 4. His collision with a naked Mr Simplon who had taken his courage in both hands and was scampering back to his own house had at least the merit of explaining exactly what and whom her husband had been doing in the Grabble house. Not that she needed much telling. Mr Grabble was singularly lucid on the subject. The Rev. Truster was less well-informed. He had never met Mr Grabble in the flesh and naturally supposed that the naked man cowering on the ground at his feet was a sinner, and a wife-beater, come to repentance.

'My dear man,' said the Vicar, 'this is no way to conduct your domestic life.'

Mr Simplon was fully aware of the fact. He stared frantically up at the Rev. Truster and clutched his scrotum. Over the road his wife went indoors and slammed the front door.

'Your wife may have done all the things you say she's done but to beat a woman is the act of a cad.'

Mr Simplon thoroughly agreed but was spared the need to explain that he had never so much as laid a finger on Mrs Simplon by the crash of breaking french window and the emergence of a large and very heavy piece of Waterford glass. Mrs Grabble, in fear for her life, was fighting back to some effect. Mr Simplon took the opportunity to get to his feet and rush across the road to Number 5, a progress that took him past the Ogilvies, the Misses Musgrove and the Pettigrews, none of whom he knew at all intimately but who now knew him by rather more than the cut of his coat. As he stood under the mock-Georgian portico of his front door and beat on the Cupid-head knocker with one hand while pressing the bell with his elbow at the same time, Mr Simplon knew that his reputation as a consultant engineer was at an end. So was Mrs Simplon's tolerance. Her husband's constant absences and lame excuses had combined with her own sexual frustration to leave her a bitter woman. She had emerged to save what she could of her marriage but at the sight of her husband cowering naked in front of a clergyman had decided to end it. And not with a whimper.

'You can stay out there till hell freezes over,' she shouted through the letter box at her nearest, 'but if you think I'm letting you into my home ever again you've got another think coming.'

Mr Simplon had had enough thoughts coming without this additional one and he particularly disliked the use of the possessive adjective. 'What do you mean "my home"?' he yelled, momentarily forgetting his other lost possessions. 'I've as much right—'

'Not any more,' screamed Mrs Simplon adding an extra sting to the statement by squirting the contents of an aerosol can of De-Icing Fluid, which Mr Simplon kept on a shelf in the hall for quite other purposes, through the letter box on to those shrivelled organs Mrs Grabble had recently found so attractive. The screams that followed this remarkable initiative were music to her ears. They were certainly music to Lockhart, who had last heard their like at a pig-killing without use of a humane killer. He sat in the kitchen with Jessica and smiled over his Ovaltine.

'I wonder what can be going on,' said Jessica anxiously. 'It sounds as if someone is dying. Hadn't you better go and investigate? I mean perhaps you could do something.'

Lockhart shook his head. 'Strong fences make good neighbours,' he said complacently, a maxim that was in some dispute at the far end of the Crescent. There Mr Simplon's screams and Mr Grabble's denunciations and Mrs Grabble's absurd denials had been joined by the siren of a police car. The Pettigrews, already in communication with the police following the loss of Little Willie, had phoned again. This time the police took their complaint more seriously and, with that fine discrimination for anything vaguely homosexual, had taken both the Rev. Truster and Mr Simplon into custody, the former on the grounds that he was soliciting and the latter for indecent exposure, a charge Mr Simplon, who had been playing the garden sprinkler rather erratically on his inflamed penis when they arrived, was incapable of finding words to deny. It was left to the Rev. Truster to explain as best he could that far from soliciting Mr Simplon's sexual favours, such as they remained, he was simply doing his utmost to prevent him actually castrating himself with the revolving sprinkler. It didn't sound a likely explanation to the

Duty Sergeant, and Mr Simplon's inability to specify with any precision what he had got on his private parts to cause him to act in this peculiar manner didn't help matters.

'Put the sods in separate cells,' said the Duty Sergeant, and the Rev. Truster and Mr Simplon were dragged away.

With their going Sandicott Crescent resumed its interrupted routine. Mrs Simplon went unrepentantly to bed alone. Mr and Mrs Grabble went to bed separately and shouted abuse at one another. The Misses Musgrove did their best to console Mrs Truster who kept repeating hysterically that her husband wasn't queer.

'No, dear, of course he isn't,' they said in unison and without the slightest notion what Mrs Truster actually meant. 'He was taken queer when the policemen came but then who wouldn't be.'

Mrs Truster's attempt to explain by saying he wasn't gay either brought them no nearer to understanding what she was talking about.

But there were other less innocent reactions to the events of the evening. Mr and Mrs Raceme had been exhilarated by the sound of beating and for once forgetful of the curtains in the bedroom had allowed Lockhart a full view of their particular perversion. He had watched with interest first Mr Raceme tying his wife to the bed and beating her lightly with a cane and then allowing her to repeat the performance on himself. He went home and added the details to their dossier and finally to round the evening off had gone into the garage and promised the Wilsons next door an imminent death to such effect that once again their lights remained on all night. All in all, he thought, as he climbed into bed beside his radiant angel, Jessica, it had been a most rewarding and informative day, and if he could keep the impetus of his campaign up the For Sale boards would shortly be in evidence in Sandicott Crescent. He cuddled up to Jessica and presently they were engaged in that chaste lovemaking that characterized their marriage.

Chapter eleven

It was Jessica, returning from her work as a temporary typist next day, who brought a further development.

'You'll never guess who lives in Green End,' she said excitedly.

'I never will,' Lockhart agreed with that apparent and literal frankness that masked the devious depths of his mind. Green End was not his concern, and lay a mile away beyond the golf course in West Pursley, an even more substantial suburb with larger houses, larger gardens and older trees.

'Genevieve Goldring,' said Jessica.

'Never heard of her,' said Lockhart swishing the air with a riding crop he had constructed out of a length of garden hose bound with twine and thonged at the end with a number of leather strips.

'You must have,' said Jessica, 'she's just the most wonderful writer there ever was. I've got dozens of her books and they're ever so interesting.'

But Lockhart had his mind on other things, and whether or not to splice the leather strips with lead shot.

'A girl in our office had been working for her and she says she's really weird,' Jessica continued. 'She walks up and down the room and talks and Patsy just has to sit at the typewriter and write down everything she says.'

'Must be boring work,' said Lockhart, who had decided lead shot would be overdoing things a bit.

'And do you know what? Patsy's going to let me go and work over there in her place tomorrow. She wants the day off and they haven't found a job for me. Isn't that wonderful?'

'I suppose so,' said Lockhart.

'It's marvellous. I've always wanted to meet a real live author.'

'Won't this Goldring woman want to know why Patsy hasn't come?' asked Lockhart.

'She doesn't even know Patsy's name. She's so inspired she just starts talking as soon as Patsy comes and they work in a garden shed that revolves to catch the sun. I'm so excited. I can't wait.'

Nor could Mr Simplon and the Rev. Truster. Their appearance in court had been brief and they had been released on bail to await trial. Mr Simplon returned home in clothes borrowed from the body of a tramp who had died the previous week. He was almost unrecognizable and certainly not by Mrs Simplon, who not only refused him entry to her house but had locked the garage. Mr Simplon's subsequent action of breaking a back window in his own house had been met by the contents of a bottle of ammonia and a further visit to the police station on a charge of making a public nuisance of himself. The Rev. Truster's reception had been more gentle and understanding, Mrs Truster's understanding being that her husband was a homosexual and that far from being a crime homosexuality was simply a freak of nature. The Rev. Truster resented the imputation and said so. Mrs Truster pointed out that she was merely repeating his own words in a sermon on the subject. The Rev. Truster retorted that he wished to God he'd never given that damned sermon. Mrs Truster had asked why, if he felt so strongly on the matter of being a fag, he had ever ... The Rev. Truster told her to shut up. Mrs Truster didn't. In short, discord reigned almost as cruelly as it did in the Grabble household, where Mrs Grabble finally packed her bags and took a taxi to the station to go to her mother in Hendon. Next door the Misses Musgrove shook their heads sadly and spoke softly of the wickedness of the modern world while speculating separately on the size, shape and subsequent colour charge of Mr Simplon's genitalia. It was the first glimpse they had ever had of a naked man and those parts which played so large a role, they understood, in marital happiness. And having glimpsed, their appetite, though too late in life to lead them to hope it would be satisfied, was whetted. They need not have been so pessimistic. It was soon to be sated.

Lockhart, intrigued by what he had seen in the Racemes' bedroom, had decided to acquaint himself more fully with the sexual peccadilloes of the human race and, while Jessica went joyfully off next day to her rendezvous with literary fame in Miss Genevieve Goldring's garden hut, Lockhart took the train to London, spent several hours in Soho leafing through magazines and returned with a catalogue from a sex shop. It was full of the most alarming devices which buzzed, vibrated, bounced and ejaculated *ad nauseam*. Lockhart began to understand more fully the nature of sex and to recognize his own ignorance. He took the magazines and the catalogue up to the attic and hid them for future reference. The Wilsons next door were a more immediate target for his campaign of eviction and it had occurred to him that something more than the sound of a voice from beyond the grave might add urgency to their departure. He decided to include smell and taking a spade he dug up the putrefying body of Little Willie, dismembered it in the garage, and distributed its portions in the Wilsons' coal cellar while they were out drowning their memories of the previous night at the local pub. The effect, on their return later and drunker that evening to a house that not only prophesied death but now stank of it more eloquently than words, was immediate. Mrs Wilson had hysterics and was sick and Mr Wilson, invoking the curse of the ouija board and table-knocking, threatened to fulfil the prophecy that there would soon be a death in the house by strangling her if she didn't shut up. But the smell was too strong even for him and rather than spend another night in the house of death they drove to a motel.

Even Jessica noticed the stench and mentioned it to Lockhart.

'It's the Wilsons' drains,' he said impromptu, and having said it promptly began to wonder if he couldn't make use of the drains and the sewage system to introduce noxious matter into the houses of other unwanted tenants. It was worth thinking about. Meanwhile he was having his job cut out comforting Jessica. Her experience of acting as amanuensis to the literary heroine of her youth, Miss Genevieve Goldring, had filled her with a terrible sense of disillusionment.

'She's just the most horrible person you ever met,' she said almost sobbing, 'she's cynical and nasty and all she thinks about is money. She didn't even say "Good Morning" or offer me a cup of tea. She just walks up and down dictating what she calls "The verbal shit my public likes to lick its chops over". And I'm part of her public and you know I'd never . . .'

'Of course you wouldn't, darling,' said Lockhart soothingly.

'I could have killed her when she said that,' said Jessica, 'I

99

really could have. And she writes five books a year under different names.'

'How do you mean, under different names?'

'Well she is not even called Genevieve Goldring. She's Miss Magster and she drinks. After lunch she sat and drank crême de menthe and daddy always said people who drank crême de menthe were common and he was right. And then the golf ball went wrong and she blamed me.'

'Golf ball?' said Lockhart. 'What the hell was she doing with a golf ball?'

'It's a typewriter, a golf-ball typewriter,' Jessica explained. 'Instead of having separate letters on bars that hit the paper it has this golf ball with the alphabet on it that goes round and runs along the paper printing the letters. It's ever so modern and it wasn't my fault it went wrong.'

'I'm sure it wasn't,' said Lockhart intrigued by this mechanism, 'but what's the advantage of a golf ball?'

'Well, you can just take the golf ball with the alphabet on it off and put on another one when you want a different typeface.'

'You can? That's interesting. So if you took the golf ball off her typewriter and brought it home you could put it on your own typewriter and it would look exactly the same, the stuff you wrote I mean?'

'You couldn't do it with an ordinary typewriter,' said Jessica, 'but if you had the same sort as hers nobody could tell the difference. Anyway she was just beastly and I hate her.'

'Darling,' said Lockhart, 'you remember when you were working for those solicitors, Gibling and Gibling, and you told me about writing nasty things in books about people and libel and all that?'

'Yes,' said Jessica, 'I just wish that horrid woman would write something nasty about us ...'

The gleam in Lockhart's eye stopped her and she looked questioningly at him.

'Oh Lockhart!' she said. 'You are clever.'

Next day Lockhart went to London once again and came back with a golf-ball typewriter of exactly the same make as Miss Genevieve Goldring's. It had been a costly purchase but what he had in mind would make it cheap at the price. Miss Goldring, it appeared, never bothered to correct her proofs.

Jessica had learnt that from Patsy. 'Sometimes she has three books on the go at the same time,' said the innocent Patsy. 'She just dashes them off and forgets all about them.'

An additional advantage was that Miss Goldring's daily output remained in a drawer in the desk in the shed at the bottom of her garden and since she switched from crème de menthe to gin at six she was seldom sober by seven and almost always pooped by eight.

'Darling,' said Lockhart when Jessica came home with this news, 'I don't want you to go to work as a temporary typist any more. I want you to stay at home and work at night.'

'Yes, Lockhart,' said Jessica obediently, and as darkness fell over the golf course and East and West Pursley, Lockhart made his way to Green End and the shed at the bottom of the great authoress's garden. He returned with the first three chapters of her latest novel, *Song of the Heart*, plus the golf ball from her typewriter. And late into the night Jessica sat and retyped the chapters. The heroine, previously called Sally, was now called Jessica and the hero, such as he was, was transformed from David to Lockhart. Finally, the name Flawse figured largely in the revised version which at three in the morning Lockhart placed in the drawer in the shed. There were other changes, too, and none of them to the advantage of Miss Goldring's characters. Lockhart Flawse in the new version liked being tied to the bed and whipped by Jessica, and when not being whipped stole money from banks. All told, *Song of the Heart* had ingredients added that were extraordinarily libellous and were calculated to make a hole in Miss Goldring's purse and a dirge in her heart. Since she wrote her novels at top speed Lockhart was so busy fetching her daily output and replacing it by Jessica's nightly amendments that his campaign for the eviction of the tenants in Sandicott Crescent had to be temporarily suspended. It was only when the novel was finished a fortnight later that Lockhart could relax and put Phase Two into operation. This involved a further outlay of money and was aimed simultaneously at the mental stability of the Misses Musgrove, and the physical ill-health of either, or both, depending on the degree of recrimination they indulged in, Mr and Mrs Raceme. But first he made further use of Jessica's typewriter by purchasing a fresh golf ball with a different typeface and composing a letter to the manufacturers of those artifacts of sexual stimulation that had intrigued and disgusted him in the catalogue. The letter was addressed from 4 Sandicott Crescent, enclosed postal orders to the tune of eighty-nine pounds and was signed with a squiggle over the typed name of Mrs Musgrove. In it Mrs Musgrove ordered an ejaculatory and vibrating dildo of adjustable proportions, the bottom half of a plastic man complete with organs, and finally a studded rubber pad with battery attached which called itself a clitoral stimulator. Not to spoil the ship for a ha'porth of tar, Lockhart also subscribed to *Lesbian Lusts*, *Women Only*, and *Pussy Kiss*, which three magazines he had been so appalled by that their effect on the Misses Musgrove month after month would be devastating. But having sent the letter he had to wait for the postal delay before observing any result.

In the case of the Racemes results were more immediate. Lockhart's methodical observations compiled in their dossier showed that Wednesday was the night the couple favoured for their horseplay and that it was usually Mr Raceme's turn first. With that gallantry that his grandfather had observed in his ancestors, Lockhart decided that it would be ungentlemanly to strike a lady. He had also noted that Mrs Raceme was friendly with a Mrs Artoux who lived in a flat in the centre of East Pursley. Mrs Artoux was not in the phone book and therefore presumably had no phone. And so on Wednesday night Lockhart waited in the bird sanctuary with a stopwatch and gave Mrs Raceme ten minutes in which to attach her husband to the bed with the leather straps they seemed to favour before going to the phone box on the corner and dialling the Raceme number. Mrs Raceme took the call.

'Can you come at once?' said Lockhart through a handkerchief, 'Mrs Artoux has had a stroke and is asking for you.'

He emerged from the phone box in time to see the Racemes' Saab shoot out of the drive, and consulted his stopwatch. Two minutes had elapsed since he had made the call and two minutes would not have given Mrs Raceme time to untie her husband. Lockhart sauntered down the street to their house, unlocked the door and went quietly inside. He turned out the light in the hall, climbed the stairs and stood in silence on the landing. Finally he peered into the bedroom. Naked, hooded, bound and gagged,

Mr Raceme was in the grip of those obscure masochistic emotions which gave him so much peculiar satisfaction. He squirmed ecstatically on the bed. A second later he was still squirming but the ecstasy had gone. Used to the exquisite pain of Mrs Raceme's light birch, the application of Lockhart's patent horsewhip at maximum velocity to his rump produced a reflex that threatened to lift both his body off the bed and the bed off the floor. Mr Raceme spat the gag out of his mouth and tried to express his feelings vocally. Lockhart suppressed his yell by pushing his head into the pillow and applied his horsewhip to full advantage. By the time he had finished Mr Raceme had passed from masochism to sadism.

'I'll murder you, you fucking bitch,' he screamed as Lockhart shut the bedroom door and went downstairs, 'so help me God, I'll kill you if it's the last thing I do.'

Lockhart let himself out of the front door and went round to the garden. From inside the house Mr Raceme's screams and threats had begun to alternate with whimpers. Lockhart installed himself in the bushes and waited for Mrs Raceme to return. If half of the threats her husband was making were carried out he might well have to intervene once again to save her life. He debated the point but decided that whatever Mr Raceme might say the state of his backside would deter him from putting anything into practice. He was on the point of leaving when the Saab's headlights shone in the drive and Mrs Raceme let herself into the house.

The ensuing sounds surpassed even those that had enlivened Sandicott Crescent on the evening of the Grabbles' domestic tiff. Mrs Raceme's statement, even before she entered the bedroom and saw Mr Raceme's condition, that there was absolutely nothing the matter with Mrs Artoux and that she certainly hadn't had a stroke was greeted by a scream of rage that shook the curtains and was followed by a second scream of almost equal proportions from Mrs Raceme. Lacking Lockhart's clear understanding of what Mr Raceme had promised to do to her the moment he got free, she made the mistake of untying his legs. A second later, disproving Lockhart's supposition that he wasn't in any fit state to put theory into practice, Mr Raceme was on his feet and clearly raring to go. Unfortunately his hands were still lashed to the double bed and

Mrs Raceme, recognizing almost instantaneously her mistake in untying his feet, refused to undo his hands.

'What do you mean I did this to you?' she shrieked as the double bed wedded to Mr Raceme's feet blundered towards her. 'I got this phone call from someone saying Mrs Artoux had had a stroke.'

The word was too much for Mr Raceme. 'Stroke?' he yelled in a muffled sort of way through the pillow and the mattress that obstructed his view of things. 'What in the name of hell do you mean by stroke?'

In the garden Lockhart knew precisely. His patent horsewhip had needed no lead weights added to the leather thongs.

'Well all I'm telling you,' shrieked Mrs Raceme, 'is that if you think I did that to you, you're out of your mind.'

Mr Raceme was. Impeded by the bed and driven insane by the pain he hurtled across the room in the general direction of her voice, smashed through the dressing-table behind which Mrs Raceme was sheltering and carrying all before him, dressing-table, bed, bedside lamp and teamaker, not to mention Mrs Raceme, shot through the curtains of the patio window, smashed the double glazing and cascaded down into the flowerbed below. There his screams were combined with those of Mrs Raceme herself, lacerated in much the same part of her anatomy by the double glazing and a rose bush.

Lockhart hesitated and crossed into the bird sanctuary, and as he moved silently towards Number 12 the sound of sirens could be heard above the shouts and yells of the Racemes. The Pettigrews had exercised their social conscience once again and phoned for the police.

'What on earth was all that noise?' Jessica inquired as he came in from the garage where he had deposited his horsewhip. 'It sounded as if someone had fallen through a greenhouse roof.'

'Most peculiar tenants we've got,' said Lockhart, 'they seem to kick up such a rumpus.'

Certainly Mr and Mrs Raceme were kicking up a rumpus and the police found their predicament most peculiar. Mr Raceme's lacerated posterior and his hood made instant identification difficult but it was the fact that he was still tied to the bed that intrigued them.

'Tell me, sir,' said the sergeant who arrived and promptly phoned for an ambulance, 'do you make a habit of wearing hoods when you go to bed?'

'Mind your own bloody business,' said Mr Raceme inadvisedly. 'I don't ask you what you do in the privacy of your home and you've got no right to ask me.'

'Well, sir, if that's the line you're going to take, we'll take the line that you've used obscene language to a police officer in the execution of his duty and have issued menaces against the person of your wife.'

'And what about my person?' yelled Mr Raceme. 'You seem to have overlooked the fact that she thrashed me.'

'We haven't overlooked it, sir,' said the sergeant, 'the lady seems to have made a good job of it.'

The arrival of a constable who had been investigating the contents of the Racemes' bedroom and was now carrying a bundle of rods, whips, canes and cats-o'-nine tails merely confirmed the police in their suspicion that Mr Raceme had got what he asked for. Their sympathy was all for his wife and when Mr Raceme tried to renew his assault on her they dispensed with the need for handcuffs and carried him bed and all into the Black Maria. Mrs Raceme went away in an ambulance. The sergeant following in a police car was frankly puzzled.

'Something bloody odd going on down there,' he said to the driver. 'We'd better keep an eye on Sandicott Crescent from now on.'

From that night on a patrol car was stationed at the bottom of the Crescent and its presence there forced Lockhart to adopt new tactics. He had already given some thought to the use of the sewage system and the police lent him the incentive. Two days later he purchased a wet-suit for underwater diving and an oxygen mask and, making use of the late Mr Sandicott's detailed plans of the Crescent's amenities, lifted the cover of the main sewer opposite his house, descended the ladder and closed it behind him. In the darkness he switched on his torch and made his way along, noting the inlets from each house as he went. It was a large main sewer and afforded him fresh insight into the habits of his neighbours. Opposite Colonel Finch-Potter's subsidiary were deposited a number of white latex

105

objects which didn't accord with his supposedly bachelor status, while Mr O'Brain's meanness was proven by his use of a telephone directory for toilet paper. Lockhart returned from his potholing determined to concentrate his attention on these two bachelors. There was the problem of the Colonel's bull-terrier to be considered. It was an amiable beast but of as ferocious an aspect as that of its owner. Lockhart knew the Colonel's habits already, though the discovery of so many contraceptives in the vicinity of his drain came as something of a surprise. There was more to the Colonel than met the eye. He would have to observe him more closely. Mr O'Brain presented less of a problem. Being Irish, he was a relatively easy target, and when Lockhart had divested himself of his wet-suit and had washed it, he resorted to the telephone yet again.

'This is the Pursley Brigade of the Provisional IRA,' he said in a supposedly Irish voice. 'We'll be expecting your contribution in the next few days. The code-word is Killarney.'

Mr O'Brain's reply went unheard. A retired gynaecologist, he was sufficiently anglicized and wealthy to feel resentful of this call on his time and resources. He promptly phoned the police and asked for protection. Lockhart from the window of his bedroom saw the patrol car at the end of the street move forward and stop outside the O'Brain house. It would be as well not to use the telephone again, he decided, and went to bed with a different scheme in mind. It involved the use of the sewer and was likely to disprove Mr O'Brain's claim to have nothing to do with any organization that sought to achieve its ends by violence.

The following morning he was up early and on his way to the shopping centre when the mail van arrived and delivered several packets to the Misses Musgrove. Lockhart heard them express some surprise and the hope that these were fresh donations to the church jumble sale. Lockhart doubted the suitability of the contents for any church function, a view shared a moment or two later by the Misses Musgrove who, having glimpsed Mr Simplon's penis, recognized some awful similarity between it and the monstrous objects that they found inside the packets.

'There must be some mistake,' said Miss Mary, examining the address. 'We didn't order these frightful things.'

Her elder sister, Maud, looked at her sceptically.

'I didn't anyway. I can assure you of that,' she said icily.

'Well you don't supposed for one moment that I did, do you?' said Mary. Maud's silence was answer enough.

'How perfectly horrid of you to entertain such a suspicion,' continued the outraged Mary. 'For all I know you did and you're just trying to throw the blame on me.'

They threw the blame on one another for the next hour but finally curiosity prevailed.

'It says here,' said Maud, reading the instructions for the ejaculatory and vibrating dildo of adjustable proportions, 'that the testicles can be filled with the white of egg and double cream in equal proportions to attain the effect of a lifelike ejaculation. Which do you think the testicles are?'

Miss Mary correctly discovered them and presently the two spinsters were busy mixing the necessary ingredients, using the vibrating dildo to best advantage as an egg-beater. Having satisfied themselves that the texture was that recommended in the instructions, they had just filled the testicles to capacity and were arguing from their little observation of Mr Simplon's unobtrusive organ what proportion to adjust the dildo to, when the doorbell rang.

'I'll answer it,' said Mary and went to the front door. Mrs Truster was there.

'I've just dropped in to say that Henry's solicitor, Mr Watts, is confident that the charge will be dropped,' she said sweeping in her accustomed way down the passage and into the kitchen, 'I thought you'd be glad to know that .. '

Whatever the Misses Musgroves might be glad to know, Mrs Truster was horrified at the spectacle that greeted her. Maud Musgrove was holding an enormous and anatomically exact penis in one hand and what appeared to be an icing syringe in the other. Mrs Truster stared wildly at the thing. It had been bad enough to suspect that her husband was a homosexual; to discover with absolute certainty that the Misses Musgrove of all people were lesbians who mixed slight culinary gifts with gigantic sexual ones was too much for her poor mind. The room swam for a moment and she collapsed into a convenient chair.

'Dear God, oh Lord,' she whimpered, and opened her eyes. The beastly thing was still there and from its . ; . whatever you called a dildo's opening ... there dribbled ... 'Jesus,' she said calling on the Almighty yet again before reverting to more appropriate speech, 'what in hell's name is going on?'

It was this question that alerted the Misses Musgrove to their socially catastrophic predicament.

'We were just ...' they began in unison when the dildo answered for them. Triggered by Miss Maud's sitting on the mechanism that controlled its functions the dildo expanded, vibrated, jerked up and down and fulfilled the guarantee of its manufacturer to the letter. Mrs Truster stared at the terrible thing as it gyrated and expanded and the mock veins stood out on its trunk.

'Stop it, for hell's sake, stop the fucking thing,' she yelled, forgetting her own social position in the enormity of her horror. Miss Maud did her best. She grappled with the creature and tried desperately to stop it jerking. She succeeded all too well. The dildo lived up to its promise and shot half a pint of mixed egg white and double cream across the kitchen like some formidable fire extinguisher. Having achieved this remarkable feat it proceeded to go limp. So did Mrs Truster. She slid off her chair on to the floor and mingled with the dildo's recent contents.

'Oh dear, what do we do now?' asked Miss Mary. 'You don't think she's had a heart attack, do you?'

She knelt beside Mrs Truster and felt her pulse. It was extremely weak.

'She's dying,' Miss Mary moaned, 'We've killed her.'

'Nonsense,' said Miss Maud practically, and put the deflated dildo on the draining board. But when she knelt beside Mrs Truster she had to admit that her pulse was dangerously weak.

'We'll just have to give her the kiss of life,' she said and together they lifted the Vicar's wife on to the kitchen table.

'How?' said Mary.

'Like this,' said Maud, who had attended a first aid course, and applied her knowledge and her mouth to the resuscitation of Mrs Truster. It was immediately successful. From her swoon Mrs Truster regained consciousness to find Miss Maud Musgrove kissing her passionately, an activity that was entirely in sexual keeping with what she had already observed of the two spinsters' unnatural lusts. Her eyes bulging in her head and her breath reinforced by that of Miss Maud, Mrs Truster broke away and screamed at the very top of her voice. And once again Sandicott Crescent resounded to the shrieks of an hysterical woman.

This time there was no need for the Pettigrews to phone the police. The patrol car was at the front door almost immediately and, breaking the glass panel in the window beside it, the police unlocked the door and swarmed down the passage into the kitchen. Mrs Truster was still shrieking and crouching in the far corner, and, on the draining board beside her, motivated a second time by Miss Maud's slumping into the chair on which its mechanism stood, slowly swelling and oozing, the dreadful dildo.

'Don't let them come anywhere near me with that thing,' screamed Mrs Truster as she was helped out of the house, 'they tried to ... oh God ... and she was kissing me and ...'

'If you wouldn't mind just stepping this way,' said the sergeant to the Misses Musgrove in the kitchen.

'But can't we put that ...'

'The constable will take that and any other evidence he finds into possession,' said the sergeant, 'Just put your coats on and come quietly. A policewoman will come for your night clothes, etc.'

And following in the footsteps of Mr Simplon, the Rev. Truster and Mr and Mrs Raceme, the Misses Musgrove were taken to the police car and driven off at high speed to be charged.

'What with?' Lockhart asked as he passed the constable on duty outside the house.

'You name it, sir, you've got it. They'll throw the book at them and two nicer old ladies to meet you couldn't imagine.'

'Extraordinary,' said Lockhart and went on his way with a smile. Things were working remarkably well.

When he got home Jessica had prepared lunch.

'There was a phone message for you from Pritchetts, the ironmongers,' she told him as he sat down. 'They say they'll send round the two hundred yards of plastic piping you asked for some time later this afternoon.'

'Great,' said Lockhart. 'Just what I needed.'

'But, darling, the garden's only fifty yards long. What on

earth can you want with two hundred yards of hosepipe?'

'I wouldn't be surprised if I don't have to go and water the Misses Musgrove's garden at Number 4. I think they're going to be away for some considerable time.'

'The Misses Musgrove?' said Jessica. 'But they never go away.'

'They've gone this time,' said Lockhart. 'In a police car.'

Chapter twelve

That afternoon, on Lockhart's suggestion, Jessica went round to the Wilsons to ask if there was anything she could do as their landlady to rectify the state of their drains.

'There's a very nasty smell,' she said to the wild-eyed Mrs Wilson. 'It's really most offensive.'

'Smell? Drains,' said Mrs Wilson, who hadn't considered this practical reason for the stench of death in the house.

'Surely you can smell it?' said Jessica as Little Willie wafted from the coal cellar.

'The grave,' said Mrs Wilson, sticking firmly to first principles. 'It is the smell of afterlife.'

'It smells more like that of afterdeath,' said Jessica. 'Are you sure something hasn't died? I mean things do, don't they? We had a raf die once behind the fridge and it smelt just like this.'

But though they looked behind the fridge and under the oven, and even inside the Wilsons' tumbler drier, there was no sign of a rat.

'I'll ask my husband to come over,' Jessica said, 'and see if it isn't the drains. He's very practical.'

Mrs Wilson thanked her but doubted there was anything practical Mr Flawse could do. She was wrong. Lockhart arrived ten minutes later with two hundred yards of plastic piping, and proceeded to investigate the drainage system with a thoroughness that was entirely reassuring. His conversation wasn't. Lapsing into his broadest Northumbrian as he worked he spoke of ghosties and ghouls and things that went bump in the night.

'I ha' the gift of second sight,' he told a gibbering Mrs Wilson. ' 'Twas given me as ma birthright. 'Tis death I smell and not the drain, aye, not one death but e'en the twain.'

'Twain? Don't you mean two?' shuddered Mrs Wilson.

Lockhart nodded grimly. 'Aye twain it is depart this life, with blude red throats and bludier knife, so runs the rune my heart espied, 'tis murder first then suicide.'

'Murder first? Then suicide?' said Mrs Wilson in the grip of a terrible curiosity.

Lockhart glanced significantly at a carving knife hanging from a magnetic board. 'A woman screams without a tongue, and then from rafter man is hung. I see it all as I ha' said, ye both mun leave ere both be dead. The hoose it is that has the curse, I smell your death and soomat worse.'

His eyes lost their glazed look and he busied himself about the drains. Upstairs Mrs Wilson was packing frantically and when Mr Wilson returned she had already left. On the kitchen table there was a hardly legible note in her shaking hand to say that she had gone to her sister's and that if he was wise he'd leave at once too. Mr Wilson cursed his wife, the ouija board and the smell, but being of a more insensitive nature refused to be daunted.

'I'm damned if I'll be driven out of my own house,' he muttered, 'ghost or no ghost.' And went up to have a bath, only to find a rope with a noose on it hanging from the rafter in the mock-Tudor ceiling in the bedroom. Mr Wilson stared at it in horror and recalled his wife's message. The smell in the bedroom was equally alarming. Lockhart had retrieved portions of the putrefying Willie and distributed them in the wardrobe, and as Mr Wilson stood sickened by the bed the voice he had heard before spoke again, and this time closer and more convincingly. 'Hanged by your neck till ye be dead, the grave tonight shall be your bed.'

'It bloody well won't,' quavered Mr Wilson but he too packed and left the house, stopping briefly at Number 12 to hand Jessica the key and his notice. 'We're going and we're never coming back,' he said, 'that bloody house is haunted.'

'Oh surely not, Mr Wilson,' said Jessica, 'it's just got a nasty smell, but if you are leaving would you mind saying so in writing?'

'Tomorrow,' said Mr Wilson who didn't want to dally.

'Now,' said Lockhart emerging from the hall with a form.

Mr Wilson put down his suitcase and signed a formal statement to the effect that he renounced his tenant-right to Number 11 Sandicott Crescent immediately and without condition.

'But that's marvellous,' said Jessica when he had gone. 'Now we can sell the house and have some money.'

But Lockhart shook his head. 'Not yet,' he said. 'When we sell we sell them all. There's such a thing as Capital Gains Tax.'

'Oh dear, why are things always so complicated,' said Jessica, 'why can't they be simple?'

'They are, darling, they are,' said Lockhart. 'Now don't worry your sweet little head about anything.' And he crossed to the Wilsons' house and began to work again. His work involved the hosepipe, the drains and the gas system, and that night when he slipped down the manhole entrance to the sewer in his wet suit with a large lump of putty in one hand and his torch in the other there was murder in Lockhart's heart. Mr O'Brain was about to rue the day he ignored the threat of the Pursley Brigade of the IRA. Dragging the hosepipe behind him he crawled down to the outlet from Mr O'Brain's lavatories. There was one on the ground floor and one in the bathroom upstairs. Working swiftly Lockhart fed the pipe up the outlet and then cemented it in place with the putty. Then he crawled back, emerged from the manhole, replaced the cover and entered the Wilsons' empty house. There he switched on the gas main to which he had connected the pipe and waited. Outside all was quiet. The police car at the entrance to the Crescent burbled occasionally with radio messages but there was no criminal activity in East Pursley to warrant their attention, only a slight burbling, bubbling sound in the U bend of Mr O'Brain's downstairs toilet. Upstairs Mr O'Brain slept soundly, secure in the knowledge that he had police protection. Once during the night he got up for a pee and thought he smelt gas but, since he didn't use it himself but relied on electricity, imagined sleepily that he must be mistaken and went back to bed. Mr O'Brain slept more soundly still, but when he awoke in the morning and went downstairs the smell was overpowering. Mr O'Brain groped for the telephone and less wisely for a cigarette and, while dialling Emergency Services, struck a match.

The resulting explosion dwarfed all Sandicott Crescent's previous catastrophes. A ball of fire enveloped Mr O'Brain, billowed through the kitchen, blew out both front and back doors and every downstairs window, destroyed the conservatory, ripped plaster from the ceiling and turned to shrapnel the thick glazed porcelain of the downstairs lavatory pan which hurtled through the door and embedded itself in the wall of the hall outside. In an instant Number 9 was turned from British Bauhaus into Berlin bunker by a series of sequential explosions that ripped cupboards from walls, Mr O'Brain from the telephone, the telephone from its connection box, books on gynaecology from their shelves and finally sweeping upstairs lifted the flat roof off its moorings and deposited fragments of concrete in the road at the front and the garden at the back. By some extraordinary miracle Mr O'Brain survived the blast and was catapulted, still clutching the receiver, through the drawing-room window on to the gravel of his drive as naked as ever Mr Simpson had been but blackened beyond belief and with his moustache and fringe of hair scorched to a tinder. He was found there raving about the IRA and the ineffectuality of the British police force by Colonel Finch-Potter and his bull-terrier.

It was an unfortunate rendezvous. Colonel Finch-Potter held the firmest views about the Irish and had always regarded Mr O'Brain as a pussy-prying Paddy on account of the consultant's profession. Assuming, with some slight justification, that Mr O'Brain had brought this holocaust on himself by making bombs, Colonel Finch-Potter exercised his right as a citizen to make a citizen's arrest and Mr O'Brain's demented resistance only exacerbated matters. The bull-terrier, resenting his resistance and particularly the punch Colonel Finch-Potter had just received on the nose, turned from the amiable beast it had previously been into a ferocious one and sank its implacable teeth in Mr O'Brain's thigh. By the time the police car arrived, a matter of two minutes, Mr O'Brain had escaped the clutches of the Colonel and was climbing the lattice-work of his magnolia with an agility that was surprising for a man of his age and sedentary profession, but was to be explained by the bull-terrier's adherence to his backside. His screams, like those of Mr

Raceme, Mrs Truster and Mrs Grabble, could be heard beyond the bird sanctuary and below the surface of the road where Lockhart was busily removing the putty from the outlet and dragging the hosepipe back to the Wilsons' house. Ten minutes later, while more police cars sealed off the entrance to Sandicott Crescent and only allowed the ambulance through, Lockhart emerged from the sewer and crossing the Wilsons' back garden went home for a bath. Jessica met him in her dressing-gown.

'What was that awful bang?' she asked.

'I don't know,' said Lockhart, 'I thought it might have been the Wilson's drains.' And having explained his noisome odour he shut the bathroom door and undressed. He came out twenty minutes later and went down the street with Jessica to survey his handiwork. Mr O'Brain had still to be coaxed from the lattice-work, a process that required the cooperation of the bull-terrier, but which, having at long last got its teeth into something juicy, the dog seemed disinclined to give. Colonel Finch-Potter was likewise uncooperative. His loathing for Mr O'Brain and his admiration for his bull-terrier's British tenacity plus the punch he had received on the nose all combined to add weight to his opinion that the bloody Irishman had got what was coming to him and that if swine like him chose to make bombs they deserved to be hoist with their own petards. In the end it was the lattice-work which gave way. Mr O'Brain and the bull-terrier flaked off the wall and landed on the drive where the police tried to prise them apart. They failed. The bull-terrier seemed to have developed lock-jaw and Mr O'Brain rabies. He foamed at the mouth and shouted expletives with a fluency and particularity that came presumably from his professional interest in women's anatomy. By the time he had abused all ten policemen, who between them were holding his shoulders and the dog's hind legs, they were in no mood to exercise their renowned moderation.

'Put them both in the ambulance,' ordered the sergeant, ignoring the Colonel's claim to his pet, and Mr O'Brain and the bull-terrier were bundled into the ambulance and driven off at high speed. As they went forensic experts moved cautiously through the rubble of the house and sought the cause of the explosion.

'The IRA have been threatening him,' the sergeant told them,

'It looks as if they got him too.' But when the experts finally left they were still puzzled. No sign of explosives had been found and yet the house was a shambles.

'Must have been using something entirely new,' they told the Special Branch officers at the police station. 'See if you can get something out of the man himself.'

But Mr O'Brain was in no mood to be helpful. The vet who had been called to sedate the bull-terrier into relaxing his grip had found his job made all the more difficult by Mr O'Brain's refusal to lie still and having twice tried to inject the dog, the vet had finally lost his nerve and short-sightedly given Mr O'Brain a jab sufficient to placate a rhinoceros. In the event it was the gynaecologist who relaxed first and passed into a coma. The bull-terrier, convinced that his victim was dead, let go and was led away with a self-satisfied look on its muzzle.

At Number 12 Sandicott Crescent Lockhart had much the same look on his face.

'It's quite all right,' he told Jessica, who was worried that one of her houses had been largely destroyed. 'It's in the lease that the occupier has to make good any damage done during his tenancy. I've checked that out.'

'But whatever can have caused it to blow up like that? I mean it looked as if it had been hit by a bomb.'

Lockhart supported Colonel Finch-Potter's argument that Mr O'Brain had been making bombs and left it at that.

He also left his activities at that for the time being. The Crescent was swarming with police who had even invaded the bird sanctuary in search of hidden caches of IRA arms and besides he had other things to think about. A telegram had arrived from Mr Dodd. It said quite simply and with that economy of expression that was typical of the man, 'COME DODD'. Lockhart went, leaving a tearful Jessica with the promise that he would be back soon. He caught the train to Newcastle and on to Hexham and then took a bus to Wark. From there he walked in a straight line across the fells to Flawse Hall with the long stride of a shepherd, climbing the dry-stone walls nimbly and leaping across the boggy patches from one hard turf to another. And all the while his mind was busy pondering the urgency of Mr Dodd's message while at the same time he was glad of the excuse to be back in the land of his heart. It was not an idle expression. The isolation of his boyhood had bred in Lockhart a need for space and a love of the empty moorlands of his happy hunting. The havoc he was wreaking in Sandicott Crescent was as much an expression of his hatred for its closeness, its little snobberies and its stifling social atmosphere, as it was for the recovery of Jessica's right to sell her own property. The south was all hypocrisy and smiles that hid a sneer. Lockhart and the Flawses seldom smiled and when they did it was with due cause, either at some inner joke or at the absurdity of man and nature. For the rest they had long faces and hard eyes that measured man or the range of a target with an exactitude that was unerring. And when they spoke, as opposed to making speeches or arguing disputatiously at dinner, they used few words. Hence Mr Dodd's message was all the more urgent by its brevity and Lockhart came. He swung over the final wall, across the dam and down the path to the Hall. And, by that instinct that told him Mr Dodd had bad news, he knew better than to approach the Hall by the front door. He slipped round the back and through the gate into the garden shed where Dodd kept his tools and himself to himself. Mr Dodd was there whittling a stick and whistling softly some ancient tune.

'Well, Mr Dodd, I'm here,' said Lockhart.

Mr Dodd looked up and motioned to a three-legged milking stool. 'It's the auld bitch,' he said, not bothering with preliminaries, 'she's set hersel' to kill the man.'

'Kill grandfather?' said Lockhart recognizing the man for what he was. Mr Dodd always called Mr Flawse 'the man'.

'Aye, first she overfeeds him. Then she waters his drink with brandy and now she's taken to wetting his bed.'

Lockhart said nothing. Mr Dodd would explain.

'I was in the whisky wall the other night,' said Mr Dodd, 'and the auld bitch comes in with a pitcher of water and sprinkles it on his sheets afore he gan to bed.'

'Are you sure it was water?' said Lockhart who knew the cavity in the bedroom that Mr Dodd called the whisky wall. It was behind the panelling and Mr Dodd stored his privately distilled whisky there.

'It smelt like water. It touched like water and it tasted like water. It was water.'

'But why should she want to kill him?' said Lockhart.

'So she'll inherit afore ye find your father,' said Mr Dodd.

'But what good will that do her? Even after grandfather dies I've only to find my father and she loses her inheritance.'

'True,' said Mr Dodd, 'but who's to say ye'll find him, and even then she'll have possession and nine points of the law. You will have the devil's own job getting her out the place once the man dies and you've no father to your name. She'll gan to litigation and you've no money to fight her with.'

'I will have,' said Lockhart grimly. 'I'll have it by then.'

'By then's too late, man,' said Mr Dodd, 'you mun do something now.'

They sat in silence and considered possibilities. They were none of them nice.

'It was an evil day the man married hisself to a murderous wife,' said Mr Dodd, and sliced the stick in half to express his desire.

'What if we tell grandfather?' said Lockhart, but Mr Dodd shook his head.

'He's all consumed with guilt and fit to die,' he said. 'He'd laugh to leave the widow to dree her weird as the auld books have it. He does not care to live o'er long.'

'Guilt?' said Lockhart, 'What guilt?'

Mr Dodd gave him a quizzical look and said nothing.

'There's surely something we can do,' Lockhart said after a long silence. 'If she knows that we know . . .'

'She'll find another way,' said Mr Dodd. 'She's a canny old bitch but I have her measure.'

'Then what?' said Lockhart.

'My mind's been running to accidents,' said Mr Dodd. 'She should never go swimming in the reservoir.'

'I didn't know she did,' said Lockhart.

'But she yet might.'

Lockhart shook his head.

'Or she could have a fall,' said Mr Dodd looking across at the top of the peel tower, 'it's been known to happen.'

But Lockhart refused. 'She's family,' he said. 'I wouldn't want to kill my wife's mother before I had to.'

Mr Dodd nodded. He approved the sentiment. Having so little family himself he treasured what he had.

'You mun do something, else he'll not see the spring.'

Lockhart's finger drew a gibbet in the dust at his feet.

'I'll tell her the story of Elsdon Tree,' he said finally. 'She will think twice about hurrying grandfather to his grave after that.' He got to his feet and moved towards the door but Mr Dodd stopped him.

'There something you've forgotten,' he said. 'The finding of your father.'

Lockhart turned back. 'I haven't got the money yet, but when I have ...'

Dinner that night was a sombre affair. Mr Flawse was in a guilty mood and the sudden arrival of Lockhart had enhanced it. Mrs Flawse was effusively welcoming but her welcome died in the glower of Lockhart's scowl. It was only after dinner when Mr Flawse had retired to his study that Lockhart spoke to his mother-in-law.

'You'll take a walk with me,' he said as she dried her hands at the sink.

'A walk?' said Mrs Flawse, and found her arm gripped above the elbow.

'Aye, a walk,' said Lockhart and propelled her into the dusk and across the yard to the peel tower. Inside it was dark and gloomy. Lockhart shut the great door and bolted it and then lit a candle.

'What do you mean by this?' said Mrs Flawse. 'You've got no right ...'

But she was stopped by an unearthly sound that seemed to come from above, a shrill weird sound that echoed the wind and yet had a melody. In front of her Lockhart held the candle high and his eyes were gleaming as weirdly as the music. He set the candle down and taking a long sword from the wall leapt upon the thick oak table. Mrs Flawse shrank back against the wall and the candle flickered a great shadow among the tattered flags and as she stared at Lockhart he began to sing. It was no such song as she had ever heard before but it followed the tune above.

'From Wall to Wark you canna call
    Nor voice to heaven from hell
But follow the fell to old Flawse Hall
    And list the tale I tell.

118

For old Flawse Hall has tales anew
    And walls can sometimes see
The deeds that wicked women do
    And what their thoughts may be.

Aye silent stones can weep their woe
    With never a word between
But those that read their tears can know
    The murder that ye mean.

An old man's taken a wicked wife
    And the murd'ress to his bed
While all the while she'd take his life
    And see him shortly dead.

The grave's a place we all must gan
    When Time has rolled away
But finish the deed ye've just begun
    And you shall rue the day.

Take heed, take heed and keep your head
    For I your daughter doat
And would not want her mother dead
    Because I slit your throat.

So warm your husband's bed aright
    And see the sheets are dry
Or else I'll seek ye out the night
    Wherever ye may hie.

But slowly, slowly shall ye die
    Lest hell forgetful be
So e'en the devil himself shall cry
    Such tortures shall he see.

So Wife of Flawse remember well
    When next in bed you lie
The Widow Flawse will pray for hell
    Afore she comes to die.

Aye Wife of Flawse of Flawse's Fell
    Look straight upon this sword
For 'tis the honest truth I tell
    As honour is my word.

And I would die to see thee die
    Should any harm befall
The Flawse who heard my birthday cry
    Beneath a dry-stone wall.'

Outside in the darkness Mr Flawse called from his study by the sound of the pipes played on the battlements of the peel tower, stood by the door and listened intently as the ballad ended. Only the breeze rustling the leaves of the wind-bent trees and the sound of sobbing remained. He waited a moment and then shuffled back to the house, his mind swirling with a terrible series of new certainties. What he had just heard left no room in his mind for doubt. The bastard was a true Flawse and his ancestry was impeccably of the same line that had produced the Minstrel Flawse who had improvised beneath the Elsdon gibbet. And with that certainty there came a second. Lockhart was a throwback born by eugenic circumstances out of time, with gifts the old man had never suspected and could not but admire. And finally he was no bastard grandson. Mr Flawse went into his study and locked the door. Then sitting by the fire he gave way privately to his grief and pride. The grief was for himself; the pride for his son. For a moment he considered suicide, but only to reject it out of hand. He must dree his weird to the bitter end. The rest was left to providence.

Chapter thirteen

But on at least two points the old man was wrong. Lockhart was leaving nothing to providence. While Mrs Flawse cowered in the darkness of the banqueting hall and wondered at the remarkable insight he had shown into the workings of her own mind and hands, Lockhart climbed the stone turret to the first storey and then by way of wooden ladders up on to the battlements. There he found Mr Dodd casting his one good eye over the landscape with a fondness for its bleak and forbidding aspect that was somehow in keeping with his own character. A rugged man in a dark and rugged world, Mr Dodd was a servant without servility. He had no brief for fawning or the notion that the world owed him a living. He owed his living to hard work and a provoked cunning that was as far removed from Mrs Flawse's calculation as Sandicott Crescent was from Flawse Fell. And if any man had dared despise him for a servant he would have told him to his face that in his case the servant was master to the man before demonstrating with his fists the simple truth that he was a match for any man, be he master, servant or drunken braggart. In short Mr Dodd was his own man and went his own way. That his own way was that of old Mr Flawse sprang from their mutual disrespect. If Mr Dodd allowed the old man to call him Dodd, he did so in the knowledge that Mr Flawse was dependent on him and that for all his authority and theoretical intelligence he knew less about the real world and its ways than did Mr Dodd. It was thus with an air of condescension that he lay on his side in the drift mine and hewed coal from a two-foot seam and carried scuttles of it to the old man's study to keep him warm. It was with the same certainty of his own worth and superiority in all things that he and his dog herded sheep on the fells and saw to the lambing in the snow. He was there to protect them and he was there to protect Mr Flawse and if he fleeced the one of wool, he fed and housed himself upon the other and let no one come between them.

'You'll have scared the wits out of the woman,' he said when Lockhart climbed on to the roof, 'but it will not last. She'll have your inheritance if you do not act swift.'

'That's what I've come to ask you, Mr Dodd,' said Lockhart. 'Mr Bullstrode and Dr Magrew could remember none of my mother's friends. She must have had some.'

'Aye, she did,' said Mr Dodd stirring on the parapet.

'Then can you tell me who they were? I've got to start the search for my father somewhere.'

Mr Dodd said nothing for some moments.

'You might inquire of Miss Deyntry down over Farspring way,' he said at last. 'She was a good friend of your mother's. You'll find her at Divet Hall. She maybe could tell you something to your advantage. I canna think of anyone else.'

Lockhart climbed down the ladder and out of the peel tower. He went round to say goodbye to his grandfather but as he passed the study window he stopped. The old man was sitting by the fire and his cheeks were streaked with tears. Lockhart shook his head sadly. The time was not ripe for farewells. Instead he let himself out the gate and strode off along the path that led to the dam. As he crossed it he looked back at the house. The light was still burning in the study and his mother-in-law's bedroom was bright but otherwise Flawse Hall was in darkness. He went on into the pinewoods and turned off the path along the rocky shore. A light wind had risen and the water of the reservoir lapped on the stones at his feet. Lockhart picked a pebble up and hurled it out into the darkness. It fell with a plop and disappeared as completely as his own father had disappeared, and with as little chance of his ever finding it or him again. But he would try, and following the shoreline for another two miles he reached the old Roman military road that ran north. He crossed it on to more open country and the dark pinewoods round the reservoir dwindled behind him. Ahead lay Britherton Law and eighteen miles of empty countryside. He would have to sleep out but there was a long-abandoned farmhouse with hay in the byre. He would stay the night there and in the morning drop down into Farspring Valley to Divet Hall. And as he walked his mind filled with strange words that came from some hidden corner of himself that he had always known about but previously ignored. They came in snatches of song and rhyme and spoke of things he had never experienced. Lockhart let them come and did not bother to inquire the why or wherefore of their coming. It was enough to be alone at night striding across his own country again. At midnight he came to the farm called Hetchester and passing through the gap in the wall where the gate had hung made his bed in the hay in the old byre. The hay smelt musty and old but he was comfortable and in a short while fast asleep.

He was up again at dawn and on his way but it was half past seven before he crossed the Farspring Knowe and looked down into the wooded valley. Divet Hall stood a mile away and smoke was coming from a chimney. Miss Deyntry was up and about surrounded by dogs, cats, horses, parrots and a tame fox she had once waded through a pack of hounds to rescue while its vixen mother was being torn to pieces. In middle age Miss Deyntry disapproved of bloodsports as heartily as she had once pursued them in her wild youth. She also disapproved of the human species and was known for her misanthropy, a reversal of opinions that was generally explained by her having three times been jilted. Whatever the cause, she was known as a woman with a sharp tongue and people tended to avoid her. The only ones who didn't were tramps and the few wandering gipsies who still followed the ancient ways. Known as muggers in the past because they made pots and mugs during the winter and sold them in the summer, there were a few caravans left in the country and autumn would find them camped in the meadow behind Divet Hall. There was a caravan there now as Lockhart loped sideways down the steep hillside and their dog began to bark. Before long Miss Deyntry's menagerie had followed suit. Lockhart opened the gates to a cacophony of dogs but he was as mindless of them as he was of almost everything else and he walked past them and knocked on the door. After an interval Miss Deyntry appeared. Dressed in a smock she had designed without regard for appreciation but solely for convenience (it was fitted with pockets all down the front), she was more ornamental than attractive. She was also brusque.

'Who are you?' she asked as soon as she had taken stock of Lockhart and noted with imperceptible approval the straw in his hair and his unshaven chin. Miss Deyntry disapproved of too much cleanliness.

'Lockhart Flawse,' said Lockhart as bluntly as she had put the question. Miss Deyntry looked at him with more interest.

'So you're Lockhart Flawse,' she said and opened the door wider. 'Well, don't just stand there, boy. Come in. You look as if you could do with some breakfast.'

Lockhart followed her down the passage to the kitchen which was filled with the smell of home-cured bacon. Miss Deyntry sliced some thick rashers and put them in the pan.

'Slept out, I see,' she said. 'Heard you'd been and married. Walked out on her, eh?'

'Good Lord, no,' said Lockhart. 'I just felt like sleeping out last night. I've come to ask you a question.'

'Question? What question? Don't answer most people's questions. Don't know that I'll answer yours,' said Miss Deyntry staccato.

'Who was my father?' said Lockhart, who had learnt from Mr Dodd not to waste time on preliminaries. Even Miss Deyntry was taken by surprise.

'Your father? You're asking *me* who your father was?'

'Yes,' said Lockhart.

Miss Deyntry prodded a rasher. 'You don't know?' she said after a pause.

'Wouldn't be asking if I did.'

'Blunt too,' she commented, again with approval. 'And why do you think I know who your father was?'

'Mr Dodd said so.'

Miss Deyntry looked up from the pan. 'Oh, Mr Dodd did, did he now?'

'Aye, he said you were her friend. She'd be likely telling you.'

But Miss Deyntry shook her head 'She'd as soon have confessed to the priest at Chiphunt Castle, and he being a Papist and a Highlander to boot while she and your grandfather were ever godless Unitarians; it's as likely as spaniels laying eggs,' said Miss Deyntry, breaking eggs on the edge of the iron pan and dropping them into the fat.

'Unitarians?' said Lockhart. 'I never knew my grandfather was a Unitarian.'

'I doubt he does himself,' said Miss Deyntry, 'but he's forever reading Emerson and Darwin and the windbags of Chelsea and the ingredients of Unitarianism are all there, mix them in proper proportions.'

'So you don't know who my father was?' said Lockhart not wishing to be drawn into theology before he had had his fill of bacon and eggs. Miss Deyntry added mushrooms.

'I did not say that,' she said, 'I said she did not tell me. I have a mind who he was.'

'Who?' said Lockhart.

'I said I had a mind. I didna say I'd tell. There's many a slip 'twixt cup and lip as no better than I should know and I would not want to cast aspersions.'

She brought two plates across to the table and ladled eggs and bacon and mushrooms onto them. 'Eat and let me think,' she said and picked up her knife and fork. They ate in silence and drank from large cups of hot tea noisily. Miss Deyntry poured hers into a saucer and supped it that way. When they had finished and wiped their mouths, she got up and left the room, returning a few minutes later with a wooden box inlaid with mother-of-pearl.

'You'll not have known Miss Johnson,' she said laying the

box on the table. Lockhart shook his head. 'She was the post-mistress over Ryal Bank, and when I say postmistress I don't mean she had a wee shop. She carried the mail herself on an old bicycle and lived in a cottage before you reach the village. She gave me this before she died.'

Lockhart looked at the box curiously.

'The box is nothing,' said Miss Deyntry, 'It's what's in it that is pertinent. The old woman was a sentimental body though you'd not have thought it to hear her. She kept cats and when she had finished her round of a summer day she'd sit out beside her door in the sun with the cats and kittens around her. One day a shepherd called with his dog and the dog took a mind to kill one of these kittens. Miss Johnson never moved an eyelid. She just looked at the man and said, "Ye should feed your dawg." That was Miss Johnson. So you wouldn't credit her with o'ermuch sentiment.'

Lockhart laughed and Miss Deyntry studied him.

'You're afful like your mither. She had a bray like that but there's something more besides.' She pushed the box towards him and opened the lid. Inside, wrapped neatly in an elastic band, was a pile of envelopes.

'Take them,' she said but kept her hand on the box. 'I promised the old woman I'd never let the box fall into anyone else's hands but she said nothing of the contents.'

Lockhart picked the bundle out and looked at the envelopes. They were all addressed to Miss C. R. Flawse, c/o The Post-mistress, Ryal Bank, Northumberland, and they were still sealed.

'She wouldn't open them,' Miss Deyntry explained. 'She was an honest old soul and it would have been against her religion to meddle with the Royal Mail.'

'But why didn't my mother have them sent to Black Pock-rington and Flawse Hall?' Lockhart asked. 'Why have them care of The Postmistress, Ryal Bank?'

'And have your grandfather lay his hands on them and know what she was doing? Are ye so soft in the head? The old devil was so jealous of her he'd never have hesitated to censor them. No, your mother was too canny for him there.'

Lockhart looked at the postmark of one letter and saw that it came from America and was dated 1961.

'This was sent five years after she died. Why didn't Miss Johnson send it back?'

'It would have meant opening it to find the return address and she would never have done that,' said Miss Deyntry. 'I told you the Royal Mail was a sacred trust to her. Besides she did not care to have your mother's only friend to know that she was dead. "Better to live in hope than abide in sorrow," she used to say and she knew what she was talking about. The man she was affianced to went missing at Ypres but she would never admit that he was dead. Love and life eternal she believed in, more power to the old woman. I would that I believed in either but I have not the faith.'

'I suppose I have the right to open them,' said Lockhart. Miss Deyntry nodded.

'She did not leave you much else except your looks but I doubt you'll find your father's name in any of them.'

'I may get a clue.'

But Miss Deyntry would not have it. 'You'll not. I can tell you that now. You would be better advised to ask the old Romany woman in the caravan who claims she can tell fortunes. Your father never wrote a letter in his life.'

Lockhart looked at her suspiciously.

'You seem very sure of your facts,' he said, but Miss Deyntry was not to be drawn. 'You can at least tell me why you . . .'

'Begone with you,' she said rising from the table. ' 'Tis too much like looking at Clarissa to have you sitting there moping over letters from the long-dead past. Go ask the spaewife who your father was. She'll more likely tell you than I will.'

'Spaewife?' said Lockhart.

'The fortune-teller woman,' said Miss Deyntry, 'who would have it that she is a descendant of old Elspeth Faas of the old stories.' She led the way down the passage to the door and Lockhart followed with the bundle of letters and thanked her.

'Don't thank me,' she said gruffly. 'Thanks are words and I've had my fill of them. If you ever want help, come and ask me for it. That's the sort of thanks I can appreciate, being of some use. The rest is blathering. Now go and ask the old woman for your fortune. And don't forget to cross her palm with silver.'

Lockhart nodded and went round the back of the house into the meadow and presently he was squatting on his haunches some twenty yards from the caravan saying nothing but waiting, by some ancient instinct of etiquette, to be spoken to. The gipsies' dog barked and was silent. Smoke filtered up into the still morning air from the open fire and bees hummed in the honeysuckle of Miss Deyntry's garden wall. The Romanies went about their business as if Lockhart didn't exist but after half an hour an old woman came down the steps of the caravan towards him. She had a brown wind-burnt face and her skin was as wrinkled as the bark of an old oak. She squatted down in front of Lockhart and held out her hand.

'Ye'll cross my loof with silver,' she said. Lockhart reached in his pocket and brought out a ten-pence piece but the woman would not touch it.

'Na silver there,' she said.

'I have no other silver,' said Lockhart.

'Then better still gold,' said the old woman.

Lockhart tried to think of something gold and finally remembered his fountain pen. He took it out and uncovered the nib. 'It's all the gold I have.'

The gipsy's hand with standing veins like ivy took the pen and held it. 'You have the gift,' she said and as she said it the pen seemed to take on a life of its own and twitched and swung in her fingers like a water diviner's dowsing rod or hazel twig. Lockhart stared as it writhed and the gold nib pointed straight at him. 'Ye have the gift of words, aye, and a tongue for a song. The pen a compass point will be and yet ye'll get its message wrong.' She turned the pen away but the nib swung round again to him. Then she handed it back to him.

'Is there anything else you see?' asked Lockhart. The gipsy did not take his hand but stared at the ground between them.

'A death, twa deaths and maybe more. Three open graves and one unfilled. I see a hanged man on a tree and more that have been killed. No more. Be gone.'

'Nothing about my father?' asked Lockhart.

'Your father is it? Ye search him out and search him long. And all the time you'll find his name in song. I'll not say more.'

Lockhart put the pen back in his pocket and took out a pound note. The old woman spat on the ground as she took it. 'Paper,' she muttered, 'it would be paper as paper's wood but paper and ink will do you no good till ye come to your gift

127

again.' And with that she was up and away back to the caravan while Lockhart, hardly knowing that he was doing it, crossed the air where she had been with his two fingers. Then he too turned and set off down the valley towards the old military road and Hexham. That night he was back in Sandicott Crescent. He found Jessica in a state of alarm.

'The police have been,' she said as soon as he entered the house, 'they wanted to know if we'd seen or heard anything unusual lately.'

'What did you tell them?'

'The truth,' said Jessica. 'That we'd heard people screaming and Mr O'Brain's house explode and windows breaking and everything.'

'Did they ask about me?' said Lockhart.

'No,' said Jessica, 'I just said you were away at work.'

'They didn't search the house then?'

Jessica shook her head and looked at him fearfully. 'What has been going on, Lockhart? The Crescent used to be such a nice quiet place and now everything seems to have gone haywire. Did you know that someone cut the telephone wire to the Racemes' house?'

'I did,' said Lockhart both answering her question and stating the fact.

'It's all most peculiar, and they've had to put the Misses Musgrove in a mental home.'

'Well, that's one more house you can sell,' said Lockhart, 'and I don't suppose Mr O'Brain will be coming back.'

'Mr and Mrs Raceme aren't either. I had a letter from him this morning to say that they were moving.' Lockhart rubbed his hands happily. 'That only leaves the Colonel and the Pettigrews on this side of the street. What about the Grabbles and Mrs Simplon?'

'Mr Grabble has kicked his wife out and Mrs Simplon came round to ask if I'd accept no rent until her divorce comes through.'

'I hope you told her no,' said Lockhart.

'I said I'd have to ask you.'

'The answer is no. She can clear out with the others.'

Jessica looked at him uncertainly but decided not to ask any questions. Lockhart was her husband, and besides, there was a look on his face that did not invite questions. All the same she went to bed troubled that night. Beside her Lockhart slept as soundly as a child. He had already made up his mind to deal with Colonel Finch-Potter next, but first there was the problem of the bull-terrier to be overcome. Lockhart was fond of bull-terriers. His grandfather kept several at the Hall and like the Colonel's dog they were amiable beasts unless aroused. Lockhart decided to arouse the bull-terrier again but in the meantime he had a vigil to keep on Number 10. The quantity of contraceptives deposited in the sewer below the Colonel's outlet suggested that the old bachelor had private habits that were amenable to use.

And so for the next week Lockhart sat in a darkened room that overlooked Number 10 and watched from seven till midnight. It was on the Friday that he saw the Colonel's ancient Humber drive up and a woman step out and enter the house with him. She was rather younger than Colonel Finch-Potter and more gaudily dressed than most of the women who came to Sandicott Crescent. Ten minutes later a light shone in the Colonel's bedroom and Lockhart had a better look at the woman. She came into the category his grandfather had described as Scarlet Women. Then the Colonel drew the curtains. A few minutes later the kitchen door opened and the bull-terrier was hustled out into the garden. The Colonel evidently objected to its presence in the house at the same time as his Scarlet Woman.

Lockhart went downstairs and across to the fence and whistled quietly and the bull-terrier waddled over. Lockhart reached through and patted it and the bull-terrier wagged what there was of its tail. And so while the Colonel made love to his lady friend upstairs, Lockhart made friends with the dog in the garden. He was still sitting stroking the dog at midnight when the front door opened and the couple came out and got into the Humber. Lockhart noted the time and made his plans accordingly.

Next day he travelled to London and hung around Soho. He sat in coffee bars and even strip shows which disgusted him and finally by dint of striking up acquaintance with a sickly young man he managed to buy what he had come to look for. He came home with several tiny tablets in his pocket and hid them in the garage. Then he waited until the following Wednesday before making his next move. On Wednesdays Colonel Finch-Potter played eighteen holes of golf and was absent all morning. Lockhart slipped next door into Number 10 carrying a tin of oven cleaner. The label on the tin advised the use of rubber gloves. Lockhart wore them. For two reasons; one that he had no intention of leaving fingerprints in the house with so many police in the vicinity; two because what he had come to do had nothing whatsoever to do with oven cleaning. The bull-terrier welcomed him amiably and together they went upstairs to the Colonel's bedroom and through the drawers of his dressing-table until Lockhart found what he was after. Then with a pat on the head of the dog he slipped out of the house and back over the fence.

That night, to while away the time, he blew all the lights in the Pettigrews' house. His procedure was quite simple. Using a piece of nylon cord he attached some stiff wire from a coat-hanger to the end and lobbed it over the twin electric cables that led from the post into the house. There was a flash and the Pettigrews spent the night in darkness. Lockhart spent it telling Jessica the story of the old gipsy woman and Miss Deyntry.

'But haven't you looked at the letters?' Jessica asked.

Lockhart hadn't. The gipsy's prophecy had driven all thought of them out of his mind and besides her final prophecy that paper was wood and paper and ink would do no good till he came to his gift again had startled him superstitiously. What had she meant by his gift of tongue and song and three graves open and one unfilled? And a hanged man on a tree? All auguries of some frightening future. Lockhart's mind was too engrossed in the present and the gift he foresaw was to come from the sale of all twelve houses in Sandicott Crescent, which he had already calculated would gross Jessica over six hundred thousand pounds at present-day prices.

'But we'll have to pay taxes on them, won't we?' said Jessica when he explained that she would shortly be a rich woman. 'And anyway we don't know that everyone is going to leave . . .'

She left the question open but Lockhart didn't answer it. He knew.

'Least said soonest mended,' he said cryptically and waited

for his preparations for Colonel Finch-Potter's self-eviction to take effect.

'I still think you should see what is inside those letters,' Jessica said as they went to bed that night. 'They might contain proof of your father's identity.'

'There's time enough for that,' said Lockhart. 'What's in those letters will keep.'

What was in the French letter that Colonel Finch-Potter nudged over his penis at half past eight the following night had certainly kept. He was vaguely aware that the contraceptive felt more slippery than usual when he took it out of the box but the full effect of the oven cleaner made itself felt when he had got it three-quarters on and was nursing the rubber ring right down to achieve maximum protection from syphilis. The next moment all fear of that contagious disease had fled his mind and far from trying to get the thing on he was struggling to get the fucking thing off as quickly as possible and before irremediable damage had been done. He was unsuccessful. Not only was the contraceptive slippery but the oven cleaner was living up to its maker's claim to be able to remove grease baked on to the interior of a stove like lightning. With a scream of agony Colonel Finch-Potter gave up his manual efforts to get the contraceptive off before what felt like galloping leprosy took its fearful toll and dashed towards the bathroom in search of a pair of scissors. Behind him the Scarlet Woman watched with growing apprehension and when, after demonically hurling the contents of the medicine cabinet on to the floor, the Colonel still screaming found his nail scissors she intervened.

'No, no, you mustn't,' she cried in the mistaken belief that the Colonel's guilt had got the better of him and that he was about to castrate himself, 'for my sake you mustn't.' She dragged the scissors from his hand while the Colonel had he been able to speak would have explained that for her sake he must. Instead, gyrating like some demented dervish, he dragged at the contraceptive and its contents with a mania that suggested he was trying to disembowel himself. Next door but one the Pettigrews, now quite accustomed to things that went bump in the night, ignored his pleas for help before he burst. That they were mingled with the screams of the Scarlet Woman didn't surprise them in the least. After the Racemes' disgusting display of perversion they were prepared for anything. Not so the police at the end of the road. As their car screeched to a halt outside Number 10 and they were bundled out to the scene of the latest crime they were met by the bull-terrier.

It was not the amiable beast it had been previously; it was not even the ferocious beast that had bitten Mr O'Brain and clung to him up his lattice-work; it was an entirely new species of beast, one filled to the brim with LSD by Lockhart and harbouring psychedelic vision of primeval ferocity in which policemen were panthers and even fence posts held a menace. Certainly the bull-terrier did. Gnashing its teeth, it bit the first three policemen out of the Panda car before they could get back into it, then the gatepost, broke a tooth on the Colonel's Humber, sank its fangs into the police car's front radial tyre to such effect that it was knocked off its own feet by the blow-out while simultaneously rendering their escape impossible, and went snarling off into the night in search of fresh victims.

It found them aplenty. Mr and Mrs Lowry had taken to sleeping downstairs since the explosion of Mr O'Brain's Bauhaus next door and the new explosion of the blown-out tyre brought them into the garden. Colonel Finch-Potter's illuminated bull-terrier found them there and, having bitten them both to the bone and driven them back into the house, had severed three rose bushes at the stem with total disregard for their thorns. If anything it felt provoked by creatures that bit back and was in no mood to trifle when the ambulance summoned by Jessica finally arrived. The bull-terrier had once travelled in that ambulance with Mr O'Brain and residual memories flickered in its flaming head. It regarded that ambulance as an offence against Nature and with all the impulsion of a dwarf rhinoceros put its head down and charged across the road. In the mistaken belief that it was the Pettigrews at Number 6 who needed their attention the ambulance men had stopped outside their house. They didn't stop long. The pink-eyed creature that knocked the first attendant over, bit the second and hurled itself at the throat of the third, fortunately missing and disappearing over the man's shoulder, drove them to take shelter in their vehicle, and ignoring the plight of Mr and Mrs Lowry, three policemen and the Colonel whose screams had somewhat subsided as he slashed at his penis with a breadknife in the kitchen, the ambulance men drove themselves as rapidly as possible to hospital.

They should have waited. Mr Pettigrew had just opened the front door and was explaining that for once he didn't know who was making such a fuss in the Crescent to the ambulance man who had rung the bell when something shot between his legs and up the stairs. Mr Pettigrew misguidedly shut the door, for once acting with a degree of social conscience he hadn't intended. For the next twenty minutes Colonel Finch-Potter's bull-terrier ravaged the Pettigrew house. What it saw in tasselled lampshades and velvet curtains, not to mention fur-belowed dressing-tables and the mahogany legs of the Pettigrews' dining suite, it alone knew, but they had evidently taken on some new and fearful meaning for it. Acting with impeccable good taste and unbelievable savagery it tore its way through these furnishings and dug holes in a Persian rug in search of some psychedelic bone while the Pettigrews cowered in the cupboard under the stairs. Finally it leapt at its own reflection in the french windows and crashed through into the night. After that its howls could be heard horrifically from the bird sanctuary. Colonel Finch-Potter's howls had long since ceased. He lay on the kitchen floor with a cheese-grater and worked assiduously and with consummate courage on the thing that had been his penis. That the corrosive contraceptive had long since disintegrated under the striations of the breadknife he neither knew nor cared. It was sufficient to know that the rubber ring remained and that his penis had swollen to three times its normal size. It was in an insane effort to grate it down from a phallic gargoyle to something more precise that the Colonel worked. And besides, the pain of the cheese-grater was positively homeopathic compared to oven cleaner and came as something of a relief albeit a minor one. Behind him garnished in suspender belt and bra the Scarlet Woman had hysterics in a kitchen chair and it was her shrieks that finally drove the three policemen in the patrol car to their duty. Bloody and bowed they broke the front door down in a wild rush provoked as much by fear of the bull-terrier as by any desire to enter the house. Once in they were in half a dozen minds whether to stay or go. The sight of a puce-faced old gentleman sitting naked on the kitchen floor using a cheese-grater on what looked like a pumpkin with high blood pressure while a woman wearing only a suspender belt shrieked and gibbered and in between whiles helped herself to a bottle of neat brandy, was not one to reassure them as to anyone's sanity. Finally to add to the pandemonium and panic the lights failed and the house was plunged into darkness. So were all the other houses in Sandicott Crescent. Lockhart, under cover of the concentration of police and ambulance men on Number 6 and 10, had slipped on to the golf course and hooked his patent fuseblower over the main power lines. By the time he got back to the house even Jessica was in a state of shock.

'Oh, Lockhart, darling,' she wailed, 'what on earth is happening to us?'

'Nothing,' said Lockhart, 'it's happening to them.' In the pitch darkness of the kitchen Jessica shuddered in his arms.

'Them?' she said. 'Who's them?'

'Them's the warld that is not us,' he said involuntarily slipping into the brogue of his native fells, 'For arl that's them the good Lord curse. And if ma prayer he doesna heed, It's up to me to do the deed.'

'Oh, Lockhart, you are wonderful,' said Jessica, 'I didn't know you could recite poetry.'

Chapter fourteen

No more did anyone else in Sandicott Crescent. Poetry was the last thing on their minds. Colonel Finch-Potter had no mind to have anything on, and it was doubtful if his Scarlet Woman would ever be the same again. Certainly the Pettigrews' house wouldn't. Torn to shreds by the bull-terrier, the house was in a state of total chaos. The Pettigrews, emerging finally from the closet under the stairs just after the lights had failed, supposed that they alone had suffered this misfortune and it was only when Mr Pettigrew, trying to reach the phone in the living-room, tripped over the hole in the Persian carpet and landed on a savaged lampshade that the true extent of the damage began to dawn on them. By the light of a torch they surveyed the remnants of their furniture and wept.

'There's some terrible curse on the street,' wailed Mrs Pettigrew, echoing Lockhart's prayer, 'I won't stay here a moment longer.' Mr Pettigrew tried in vain to adopt a more rational approach but he wasn't helped by the demented howls of the bull-terrier in the bird sanctuary. Having lost a tooth it had fortunately lost its way as well and after gnawing several large trees in the archetypal belief that they were mammoths' legs had given up to wail at five multi-coloured moons that squirmed in the sky above its imagination. Mr and Mrs Lowry were busily trying to bandage one another in portions of anatomy least amenable to bandaging and were considering suing Colonel Finch-Potter for his dog's damage when they too were plunged into darkness. Next door, Mrs Simplon, convinced that her husband had deliberately fused the lights so that he could the more easily break in to retrieve his belongings, proceeded to warn him off by loading the shotgun he kept in the cupboard in the bedroom and firing it out of the window twice at nothing in particular. Not being the best shot in the world and lacking the light of the bull-terrier's imaginary moons, she managed with the first shot to blast the greenhouse in the garden of the Ogilvies at Number 3 and with the second, fired from the front, to add to the Pettigrews' problems by peppering those windows the bull-terrier had left unscathed. Only then did she realize her mistake and the fact that the entire street was in darkness. Not to be dissuaded but rather encouraged by the screams and yells of the Scarlet Woman, who was being dragged into the police car, and convinced now that the IRA had struck again, she reloaded and loosed off two more barrels in the general direction of Mr O'Brain's former house. This time she missed the house and fired point-blank into the Lowrys' bedroom which happened to intervene between the Simplons' and Mr O'Brain's residence. Outside Colonel Finch-Potter's the policemen hastily dropped their burden, took cover and radioed for armed assistance.

It was no time at all coming. Sirens sounded, police cars converged and under covering fire a dozen men surrounded

Mrs Simplon's mock-Georgian mansion and ordered everyone inside to come out with their hands up. But Mrs Simplon had finally discovered her mistake. The volley of revolver shots that seemed to come from all quarters and through every window, and the winking lights of the police cars, not to mention the voice on the loudhailer, persuaded her that absence was the best defence. Dressing as swiftly as she could and grabbing her jewels and what money she had, she went through the connecting door in the garage and hid in the sump pit which Mr Simplon, who liked tinkering with the underbodies of cars as well as Mrs Grabble's, had thoughtfully constructed. There, with the wood pulled over her head, she waited. Through the wood and the garage door she could hear the loudhailer declare that the house was surrounded and there was no point in further resistance. Mrs Simplon had no intention of resisting. She cursed herself for her stupidity and tried to think of an excuse. She was still trying in vain when dawn finally broke over the Crescent and fifteen policemen broke cover, the front and back door, four windows and found the house to be empty.

'There's no one there,' they told the Superintendent who had come to take charge. 'Searched the attic but there's not a soul.'

Mr Pettigrew protested that there must be. 'I saw the flash of the guns myself,' he said, 'and you've only got to look at my house to see what they did.'

The Superintendent looked and expressed some doubt that gunshot had ripped lampshades from their stands, cushions from sofas and curtains from windows, and had sunk what looked like fangs into the mahogany dining-tables.

'That was the dog,' said Mr Pettigrew, 'the dog the ambulance men brought with them.'

The Superintendent looked even more doubtful 'Are you trying to tell me that all this devastation was caused by a dog and that the aforesaid dog was introduced into your house by ambulance men?' he asked.

Mr Pettigrew hesitated. The Superintendent's scepticism was contagious.

'I know it doesn't sound likely,' he admitted, 'but it looked like a dog.'

'I certainly find it hard to believe that a dog can have created this degree of havoc on its own,' said the Superintendent, 'and if you're suggesting that the ambulance men ...' He was interrupted by a howl from the bird sanctuary. 'What in God's name is that?'

'That's the thing that wrecked my house,' said Mr Pettigrew. 'It's coming from the bird sanctuary.'

'Bird sanctuary my foot,' said the Superintendent. 'More like a banshee sanctuary by the sound of things.'

'I didn't think banshees wailed,' said Mr Pettigrew inconsequentially. A sleepless night, most of it spent in a broom cupboard, and the rest in the darkness of his devastated house, had not helped to make him clear-headed and Mrs Pettigrew was wailing too. She had discovered the remnants of her underwear shredded in the bedroom.

'I tell you it wasn't a dog,' she screamed, 'some sex maniac's been chewing my undies.'

The Superintendent looked at Mrs Pettigrew dubiously. 'Anyone who chewed your undies, madam, would have to be ...' he began before checking himself. Mrs Pettigrew had only her vanity left and there was no good to be done by removing that too. 'You've got no idea who might have a grudge against you?' he asked instead. But the Pettigrews shook their heads in unison. 'We've always lived such quiet lives,' they said. It was the same in every other occupied house the Superintendent visited. There were only four. At Number 1 Mr and Mrs Rickenshaw had nothing to add except gratitude that the police car was always parked outside their house. 'It makes us feel much safer,' they said.

The Ogilvies didn't share their opinion. The blast of the shotgun that had smashed every pane of glass in their greenhouse had given them a sense of grievance they voiced to the Superintendent. 'What's the world coming to when peaceful citizens can't rest easy in their beds, that's what I want to know,' said Mr Ogilvie indignantly. 'I shall complain to my MP, sir. The country is going to the dogs.'

'So it would appear,' said the Superintendent soothingly, 'but you're not suggesting that a dog destroyed your greenhouse?'

'Certainly not,' said Mr Ogilvie, 'some damned swine with a shotgun did.'

The Superintendent breathed a sigh of relief. He was getting sick of hearing all the blame put on dogs. Mrs Simplon wasn't.

Cowering beneath the wooden beams in the inspection pit under her car her nerves, like Mrs Pettigrew's undies, were in tatters. She fumbled in her bag for her cigarettes, found one and was in the process of striking a match to light it when the Superintendent, thanking the Ogilvies for their cooperation and being trounced by Mr Ogilvie for the lack of police protection made his way past the garage door.

In fact the garage door made its way past him. Mrs Simplon had discovered to her cost that inspection pits filled with oil waste and petrol fumes were not the best place to light cigarettes. With several explosions, first of the fume-laden air in the pit, second of the petrol tank of the car above, and third of the half-empty oil tanks that had served to provide Number 5 Sandicott Crescent with hot water and central heating, Mrs Simplon's hopes of calming her nerves succeeded beyond her wildest dreams. She was no longer conscious after the first explosion and by the time the oil tanks exploded she had passed into the great beyond. With her went portions of the garage, the car and the oil tanks. A ball of flame containing elements of all three billowed out where the garage door had been and hurtled round the head of the Superintendent before pocking still more the Pettigrews' already-acned façade. In the middle of this holocaust the Superintendent kept his head. He kept little else. What the blast hadn't stripped from his little authority the flames did. His moustache crinkled and turned black under his nose. His eyebrows streaked, flaming, past the top of his ears, themselves sufficiently hot to suggest that several million people were thinking about him at the same time, and he was left standing in his boots and leather belt, a blackened, scorched and thoroughly disenchanted copper.

Once again the sirens sounded on the approaches to Sandicott Crescent but this time it was the fire brigade. As they worked frantically to extinguish the flames, which flames had already extinguished Mrs Simplon so thoroughly that she was in no need of a more ceremonial cremation, the bull-terrier made its last sortie. The flames that had flickered in its head had been dying down when the Simplons' garage revived them. With blood-red eyes and lolling tongue it lumbered out of the bird sanctuary, through the Misses Musgroves' herb garden, and having whetted its appetite on the calf of a fireman, proceeded to engage one of the fire brigade's hosepipes in mortal combat in the belief that it was wrestling with an anaconda in the ancestral forest of its dreams. The hosepipe fought back. Punctured in a dozen places, it shot water into the air with enormous pressure, and carried the bull-terrier several feet off the ground where it hung a moment snarling ravenously. By the time the dog hit the ground again the Superintendent no longer disbelieved the Pettigrews. He had seen it with his own two scorched eyes, a dog that wailed, snarled, slobbered and snapped like a crocodile with St Vitus' dance. Convinced that the animal had rabies the Superintendent stood still according to instructions. He would have been better advised to move. Baffled by the liquid resistance of the writhing hosepipe the bull-terrier sank its teeth into the Superintendent's leg, let go momentarily to re-engage the hose which it savaged in several more places and then hurled itself at the Superintendent's throat. This time the Superintendent moved and his juniors, twenty firemen, the Ogilvies and Mr and Mrs Rickenshaw were privileged to see a naked (and badly scorched) policeman in boots and belt cover one hundred metres in under ten seconds from a standing start. Behind him with starting eyes and scrabbling paws came, bullet-like, the bull-terrier. The Superintendent hurdled the Grabbles' gate, clobbered across their lawn and into the bird sanctuary. And presently in harmony with the dog he too could be heard howling for help.

'Well, at least he knows we were telling the truth,' said Mr Pettigrew and told his wife to shut up wailing like some woman for her demon lover, a remark hardly calculated to restore domestic peace to their sufficiently demented lives.

From their bedroom at the end of the street Lockhart and Jessica watched the chaotic scene. The Simplons' garage still blazed, largely thanks to the intervention of the dog, the hosepipe still writhed and spouted water from a score of holes high into the air like a lawn sprinkler with megalomania, firemen huddled on their engines and policemen in their cars. Only the armed men, brought in to deal with whoever had fired from the house, were still abroad. Convinced that the blazing garage was a diversion to allow the gunmen inside the house, who had eluded their search, to make good their escape under cover of the smoke, they lurked in the adjacent gardens and in the foliage of the bushes by the golf course. It was in consequence of this and of the smoke that obscured their view and that of an early foursome, one of whom had an incurable slice, that a ball hit an armed constable on the head.

'They're coming at us from the rear,' he yelled and emptied his revolver into the drifting smoke, hitting the man with the now terminal slice and the Club House. He was followed by several other policemen who fired in the general direction of the screams. As the bullets ricocheted round the East Pursley Golf Course and punctured the windows of the bar, the Secretary lay on the floor and dialled the police.

'We're under attack,' he screamed, 'bullets are coming from every direction.' So were other golfers. As they dashed through the smoke they were met by a hail of bullets from the Simplons' back garden. Four fell on the eighteenth, two on the first, while on the ninth a number of women clustered together in a bunker they had previously done their best to avoid. And with each fresh volley the police, unable to observe who was firing from where, engaged in warfare among themselves. Even the Rickenshaws at Number 1 who had only an hour before been congratulating themselves on the presence of police protection came to regret their premature gratitude. The contingent of police who arrived at the Club House armed now with rifles as well as revolvers and stationed themselves in the bar, the Secretary's office and the changing-room, answered their comrades' desultory fire with a positive barrage of their own. A hail of bullets screamed across the heads of the women cowering in the sandtrap on the ninth and through the smoke into the Rickenshaws' sitting-room. In the sandtrap the women screamed, in the sitting-room Mrs Rickenshaw shot through the thigh screamed and the fire engine driver, mindless of his extended ladder, decided the time had come to get out while the going was good. The going was not good.

'Never mind that fucking fire,' he yelled at the men huddled on the back, 'it's gunfire we've got now.' At the top of the ladder a fireman didn't share his point of view. Clutching his dribbling hose he suddenly found himself moving backwards. 'Stop,' he yelled, 'for God's sake stop!' But the roar of the flames and the rifles drowned his protest and the next moment the fire engine was off at top speed down Sandicott Crescent. Fifty feet above it the fireman clung to the ladder. He was still clinging when having cut a swathe through half a dozen telephone wires and a overhead electric cable the fire engine, travelling at seventy miles an hour, shot under the main railway line to London. The fireman on the ladder didn't. He shot over and landed in the path of an oncoming petrol tanker, missing the London to Brighton express by inches on the way. The tanker driver, already unnerved by the careering fire engine, now ladder-less, swerved to avoid the catapulting fireman, and the tanker ploughed into the railway embankment and exploded in time to shower flaming petrol over the last five coaches of the express above. In the guards van, now engulfed in flames, the guard did his duty. He applied the emergency brake and the express's wheels locked at eighty miles an hour. The subsequent screech of scored metal drowned even the sound of gunfire and the Police Superintendent's howls in the bird sanctuary. Inside every compartment passengers sitting with their fronts to the engine shot into the laps of those with their backs to it and in the dining-car, where breakfast was being served, coffee and waiters mingled with diners to shoot everywhere. Meanwhile the last five coaches blazed away.

So did the police in the golf club. The sight of the burning train emerging from what appeared to be a napalm bomb exploded in the centre of East Pursley only lent weight to their conviction that they were dealing with an outbreak of urban and golf-course terrorism unprecedented in the annals of British history. They radioed for army help and explained that they were pinned down in the East Pursley Club House by suburban guerrillas firing from the houses in Sandicott Crescent who had just exploded a bomb under the London to Brighton express. Five minutes later helicopter gunships were hovering over the golf course searching for the enemy. But the policemen in the Simplons' garden had had their fill. Three lay wounded, one was dead and the rest were out of ammunition. Dragging their wounded they wormed their way across the lawn and round the side of the house. and ran for the police cars.

'Get the hell out of here,' they yelled as they scrambled in, 'there's a fucking army out there.' A minute later, their sirens receding into the distance, the patrol cars had left the Crescent and were heading towards the police station. They didn't reach it. The tanker that had exploded on to the express had doused the road beneath and the tunnel was an inferno. Behind them Sandicott Crescent was in little better shape. The fire in the Simplons' garage had spread to the fence and from the fence to the Ogilvies' potting shed. It was well named. Riddled with bullet holes it added its flames and smoke to the general pall that hung over Jessica's inheritance and lent a grisly light to the scene. The Ogilvies clung to one another in the cellar listening to the whine of bullets ricocheting round their kitchen, and at Number 1 Mr Rickenshaw, tightening a tourniquet round his wife's leg, promised her that if they ever get out of this alive they'd get out of the house.

It was the same at the Pettigrews'. 'Promise me we'll move,' whined Mrs Pettigrew. 'Another night in this awful house and I'll go mad.'

Mr Pettigrew needed no urging. The series of events that had swept through Sandicott Crescent, and in particular their house, like the plagues that had affected Egypt inclined him to renounce his rationalism and return to religion. His social conscience had certainly deserted him and when Mr Rickenshaw, unable to phone for medical assistance thanks to the scythe-like activities of the fire engine's ladder, crawled across the street to ring the Pettigrews' doorbell to ask for help, Mr Pettigrew refused to open the door on the reasonable grounds that the last time anyone had asked for medical help, namely the ambulance men, of all people, they had introduced a mad dog into the house and that as far as he was concerned Mrs Rickenshaw could bleed to death before he opened his door again.

'You can think yourself lucky,' he shouted, 'your fucking wife's only got a hole in her leg, mine's got one in her head.' Mr Rickenshaw cursed him for his bad neighbourliness and, wholly unaware that Colonel Finch-Potter, having been relieved of his penis-grater, was now in intensive care at the Pursley Hospital, tried to knock him up. It was Jessica who finally came to his aid, and braving the slackening gun-fire from the Club House went down to Number 1 and applied her knowledge of first aid to Mrs Rickenshaw's wound. Lockhart took advantage of her absence to make a last sally into the sewer. Donning his wet-suit he crawled along to the outlet of Mr Grabble's house with a bucket and a World War II stirrup pump that Mr Sandicott had kept in his workshop for watering plants. Lockhart had another purpose in mind, and having introduced the nozzle into the discharge pipe and cemented it there with putty, filled the bucket from the sewer and began to pump vigorously. He worked steadily for an hour and then undid his apparatus and crawled home. By that time Mr Grabble's ground floor was awash with the effluent from every other house in the street and all his attempts to get his ground-floor lavatory to behave in the normal manner and discharge excreta out of the house rather than pump it in had failed disastrously. Driven to desperate measures and wading through sewage with his trousers rolled up, Mr Grabble had seized on the idea of using caustic soda. It was not a good idea. Instead of going down the pipe to unblock whatever infernal thing was blocking it, the caustic soda erupted from the pan in an extremely vindictive fashion. Fortunately Mr Grabble had had the good sense to foresee this possibility and was out of the tiny room when it happened. He was less sensible in resorting to an ordinary lavatory cleanser and when that failed, adding to it a liquid bleach. The two combined to produce chlorine and Mr Grabble was driven from his house by the poisonous gas. Standing on the back lawn he watched his living-room carpet lap up the foul liquid and the caustic soda eat into his best armchair. Mr Grabble took the unwise step of trying to dam the flood and the caustic soda dissuaded him. He sat on the edge of the fishpond bathing his feet and cursing.

In the bird sanctuary the Superintendent was still shouting for help, though less loudly, and at the far end the bull-terrier was sleeping it off on the mat outside his master's back door.

Lockhart, divesting himself of the wet-suit, ran himself a bath and lay in it contentedly. On the whole he thought he had done rather well. There could be no doubting now that Jessica would be in full possession of her inheritance and with the right to sell every house whenever she chose. He lay thinking about the tax problem. His experience at Sandicott & Partners had told him that Capital Gains Tax was levied on every extra house an individual owned. There had to be some way round it. The tax on twelve houses would be enormous. By the time he got out of the bath he had found a simple solution.

Chapter fifteen

Nobody else could find a simple solution to the problem of what had occurred in East Pursley. The discovery by an army helicopter of the Superintendent of Police hanging to the upper branches of a monkey-puzzle tree which would have defied the efforts of any but the most insane men to climb it didn't help to clarify matters. He kept screaming about mad dogs being loose in the neighbourhood and his statement was supported by Mr Pettigrew and the Lowrys who had wounds to prove it.

'It hardly explains how six golfers and five of my own men came to be shot,' said the Commissioner of Police. 'Mad dogs and Englishmen may go out in the midday sun but the former don't carry side-arms. And what the hell do we say about that fire engine and the petrol tanker, not to mention the London to Brighton express? How many passengers went west in that inferno?'

'Ten,' said the Assistant Commissioner, 'though accurately speaking they were going south. The Southern Region caters . . .'

'Shut up,' snarled the Commissioner, 'I've got to explain this to the Home Secretary and it's got to sound good.'

'Well, I suppose we could divide the two incidents into separate areas,' suggested the Assistant Commissioner, but the Commissioner only looked at him the more lividly.

'Two? Two?' he yelled rattling the windows of his office. 'One, we have an utterly insane half-pay colonel whittling his prick with a cheese-grater in the company of a high-class whore. Two, we have a mad dog roaming the district biting everything in sight. Three, someone looses off firearms into several houses and then explodes a fucking garage with an unidentifiable woman in the inspection pit. Do I have to spell it *all* out for you?'

'I take your point,' said the Assistant Commissioner, 'which according to Miss Gigi Lamont is what Colonel Finch-Potter . . .'

'Shut up,' said the Commissioner savagely and crossed his legs. They sat in silence and considered a convincing explanation.

'At least the TV people and the press weren't present,' said the Assistant Commissioner, and his superior nodded thankfully.

'What about blaming the IRA?'

'And give them something else to boast about? You must be out of your tiny mind.'

'Well, they did blow up Mr O'Brain's house,' said the AC.

'Nonsense. The sod blew himself up. There wasn't a trace of explosive in the house,' said the Commissioner, 'he was fiddling with the gas stove ...'

'But he wasn't connected to the gas main ...' the AC began.

'And I won't be connected to my job unless we come up with something before noon,' shouted the Commissioner. 'First of all we've got to stop the press going in there and asking questions. Got any ideas on the subject?'

The Assistant Commissioner considered the problem. 'I don't suppose we could say the mad dogs had rabies,' he said finally. 'I mean we could put the area in quarantine and shoot anything ...'

'We've already shot half the police in that patch,' said the Commissioner, 'and while I'm inclined to agree that they were mad you still don't go round shooting people who've contracted rabies. You inoculate the brutes. Still, it would serve to keep the press and the media out. And how do you explain the six bleeding golfers? Just because some fool slices his drive you don't have a drive to slice him and five others with multiple gunshot wounds. We've got to come up with some logical explanation.'

'Sticking to the rabies theory,' said the Assistant Commissioner, 'if one of our men contracted rabies and went berserk ...'

'You can't contract rabies instantaneously. It takes weeks to come out.'

'But if there were a special sort of rabies, a new variety like swine fever,' persisted the Assistant. 'The dog bites the Colonel ...'

'That's out for a start. There's no evidence that anybody bit Colonel Finch-Fucking-Potter except himself and that in an anatomically impossible place unless the bastard was a contortionist as well as a pervert.'

'But he's not in a fit condition to deny the rabies theory,' said

145

the Assistant Commissioner. 'He's clean off his rocker.'

'Not the only thing he's off,' muttered the Commissioner, 'but all right, go on.'

'We start with galloping rabies and the dog and everything follows quite logically. The armed squad go off their heads and start shooting . . .'

'That's going to sound great on the nine o'clock news. "Five officers of the Special Squad, organized to protect foreign diplomats, this morning went mad and shot six golfers on the East Pursley Golf Course." I know there's no such thing as bad publicity but in this case I have my doubts.'

'But it doesn't have to be announced on the news,' said the Assistant Commissioner. 'In a case of this sort we invoke the Official Secrets Act.'

The Commissioner nodded approvingly. 'We'd need the co-operation of the War Office for that,' he said.

'Well, those helicopters could have come from Porton Down and the Biological Warfare Research Station is there.'

'They just happen to have come from somewhere else, and anyway they came after the show was over.'

'But they don't know that,' said the Assistant Commissioner, 'and you know how dim the Army Command is. The main thing is that we can threaten to put the blame on them and . . .'

In the end it was agreed at a Joint Meeting of the Home Secretary, the Minister of Defence and the Commissioner of Police that the happenings at Sandicott Crescent were subject to official silence and, invoking the Defence of The Realm Act together with the Official Secrets Act, the editors of all papers were ordered not to publicize the tragedy. The BBC and ITV were similarly warned and the news that night contained only the story of the petrol tanker that had exploded and set the London to Brighton express on fire in the process. Sandicott Crescent was sealed off and army marksmen went through the bird sanctuary with rifles killing anything that moved as an exercise in stopping the spread of rabies. They found only birds and from a sanctuary the wood became a mortuary. Fortunately for the bull-terrier it didn't move. It slept on and on outside the Colonel's kitchen door. It was about the only creature apart from Lockhart and Jessica who didn't move. Mr

Grabble, driven from his house by the upsurge of the sewer, handed in his notice that afternoon wearing a pair of bedroom slippers over his chemically cauterized feet. Mr Rickenshaw finally managed to get his wife to hospital and the Pettigrews spent the afternoon packing. They too left before dark. The Lowrys had already left and were being given rabies inoculations in the company of several firemen, the Police Superintendent and a number of his men at the local isolation hospital. Even Mrs Simplon had gone, in a small sinister plastic bag which so upset Mrs Ogilvie that she had to be sedated.

'There's only us left,' she moaned, 'everyone else has gone. I want to go too. All those dead men lying out there ... I'll never be able to look out at the golf course without seeing them on the dogleg ninth.'

This remark put Mr Ogilvie in mind of both dogs and legs. He too would never feel the same about Sandicott Crescent. A week later they too left and Lockhart and Jessica could look out their bedroom window at eleven empty houses, each standing (with the exception of Mr O'Brain's Bauhaus, which had slumped somewhat) in substantial and well-kept grounds in an apparently desirable neighbourhood within easy reach of London and adjoining an excellent golf club whose waiting list had been conveniently shortened by recent events. As the builders moved in to restore the houses to their pristine state, and in the case of Mr Grabble's to a sanitary one, Lockhart had time to turn his attention to other things.

There was, for instance, the little matter of Miss Genevieve Goldring's forthcoming novel, *Song of the Heart*, to be considered. Lockhart took to buying the *Bookseller* to check when it was due to be published. Since Miss Goldring managed to write five books a year under various pseudonyms, her publishers were forced by the impetus of her output to bring out two Goldring books in the same period. There was a Spring List Goldring novel and an Autumn one. *Song of the Heart* appeared in the Autumn List and came out in October. Lockhart and Jessica watched it climb from nine on the best-sellers list to two within three weeks and finally to Top. It was then that Lockhart struck. He travelled to London with a copy of the novel and spent part of an afternoon in the office of the younger of the two Giblings, and the rest of it in the office of the older with young Mr Gibling in attendance. By the time he left, the Giblings were in transports of legal rhapsody. Never in all their experience, and old Mr Gibling had had a great deal of experience in matters concerning libel; never had they come across a more blatant and outrageously wicked libel. Better still, Miss Genevieve Goldring's publishers were immensely rich, thanks in large part to her popularity, and now they were going to be immensely generous out of court in their settlement, thanks to Miss Goldring's wicked libel, or best of all they would be immensely stupid and fight the case in court, a prospect so eminently to be desired that Mr and Mr Gibling proceeded with a delicate hesitancy that was calculated to allure.

They wrote politely to Messrs Shortstead, Publishers, of Edgware Road, apprising them of an unfortunate fact that had been brought to their notice by a client, one Mr Lockhart Flawse, that his name appeared in that extremely successful novel, *Song of the Heart*, by Miss Genevieve Goldring and published by Messrs Shortstead, and that in consequence of this unfortunate error they were forced into the regrettable course of having to request Messrs Shortstead to make good the damage done to the private, professional and marital reputation of Mr Flawse by the aspersions cast on his character in the book by a financial payment and legal costs, at the same time withdrawing all copies unsold from circulation and destroying them.

'That should set the trap,' said Mr Gibling to Mr Gibling. 'It is to be devoutly hoped that they will employ the services of some up-and-coming young man in our profession who will advise them to contest.'

Messrs Shortstead did. The reply from the least senior member of the firm of solicitors, Coole, Poole, Stoole and Folsom and Partners, one Mr Arbutus, stated that while Messrs Shortstead and the author of *Song of the Heart*, hereafter termed the novel, were prepared to offer Mr Flawse their apologies and his legal costs and if necessary some small sum for his pain and injury, they were in no way obliged nor would consider much less agree to the withdrawal of all unsold copies, etc. The letter ended on the cordial note that Coole, Poole, Stoole and Folsom and Partners looked forward to hearing from Mr Gibling. Mr Gibling and Mr Gibling rather doubted it. They held the matter in abeyance for a fortnight and then struck.

'Four hundred thousand pounds damages? Do my ears deceive me?' said Mr Folsom when Mr Arbutus showed him their reply. 'I have never in all my career read anything so monstrous. Giblings have gone mad. Of course we will contest.'

'Contest?' said Mr Arbutus, 'They must have something . . .?'

'Bluff, boy, bluff,' said Mr Folsom, 'I haven't read the book of course but such a sum is unheard-of in innocent libel. Come to that, it's unheard-of in deliberate libel. Probably a typist's error.'

But for once Mr Folsom erred. Mr Shortstead, taking his advice, instead of his own intuition which told him that *Song of the Heart* was somehow a little different in tone from Miss Goldring's other numerous novels, instructed Mr Arbutus to answer in kind and reversing the natural order of things to tell Mr Gibling and Mr Gibling to sue and be damned. And next day on the third floor of Blackstones House, Lincoln's Inn, London, when the mail was brought before him and opened by the senior clerk, that aged and austere gentleman discovered for the very first time in his life that Mr Gibling the Elder could do the hornpipe very creditably on his desktop; having done so he demanded the immediate production of two, no, three bottles of the best champagne to be sent for at no matter what cost.

'We have them by the nose,' he sang gleefully when Mr Gibling the younger arrived. 'O Lord that I should live to see this day. The nose, brother o' mine, the nose. Read it again. I must hear it.'

And Mr Gibling trembled in litigious ecstasy as the words 'Sue and be damned' quivered in the air.

'Sue and be damned,' he gibbered. 'Sue and be damned. I can hardly wait to hear that threat pronounced by counsel in court. Ah, the judge's face. The beauty, brother, the beauty of it all. The legal life is not without its precious moments. Let us savour the pleasure of this splendid day.'

Mr Partington, the senior clerk, brought in the champagne and Mr Gibling and Mr Gibling sent him to fetch a third glass. Only then did they solemnly toast Mr Lockhart Flawse of 12 Sandicott Crescent for stepping so simultaneously into their lives and out of the pages of Miss Genevieve Goldring's novel with its oh-so-appropriate title. That day there was little work done in Blackstones House, Lincoln's Inn. The drawing-up of writs is not an arduous job and the one issued by Gibling and Gibling between Lockhart Flawse, Plaintiff, and Genevieve Goldring and Messrs Shortstead, Defendants, was no different from other writs and merely stated that Elizabeth the Second, by the Grace of God, of the United Kingdom of Great Britain and Northern Ireland and of Our other Realms and Territories Queen, Head of the Commonwealth, Defender of the Faith; To Genevieve Goldring properly named Miss Magster c/o Messrs Shortstead ... 'WE COMMAND YOU that within fourteen days after the service of this Writ on you, inclusive of the day of service, you do cause an appearance to be entered for you in an action at the suit of Lockhart Flawse and take notice that in default of you doing so the Plaintiff may proceed therein, and judgement may be given in your absence.'

It was served the following day and caused little consternation in the offices of Messrs Shortstead and a great deal in those of Coole, Poole, Stoole and Folsom and Partners where Mr Arbutus, having read *Song of the Heart*, had discovered the horrid nature of the libel published on the aforesaid Lockhart Flawse; namely that he made a habit of being tied by his wife to the bed and being whipped by his wife, Jessica, and vice versa, and when not whipping or being whipped, stole money from banks in the process of which he shot dead several bank cashiers.

'We can't even plead innocent libel,' he told Mr Folsom but that worthy man had reason to think otherwise.

'No authoress in her right mind would deliberately set out to write a book in which she named a person she knew and ascribed all these perversions and crimes to him. The thing's a nonsense.' It was a view shared by Genevieve Goldring. 'Never heard of the creature,' she told Mr Shortstead and Mr Arbutus, 'and besides it's an improbable name. Frankly I can't remember having written about anyone called Lockhart Flawse with a wife named Jessica.'

'But it's down there in *Song of the Heart*,' said Mr Arbutus, 'you must have read it. After all, you wrote it.'

Genevieve Goldring snorted. 'I write five novels a year. You can't expect me to read the wretched things as well. I leave the matter in the competent hands of Mr Shortstead here.'

'But don't you check your own proofs?'

'Young man,' said Miss Goldring, 'my proofs don't need checking. Correct me if I'm wrong, Mr Shortstead.'

But Mr Shortstead, while he was beginning to hold a different point of view, held his tongue.

'Then we are to plead innocent libel?' asked Mr Arbutus.

'I see no reason to plead libel at all,' protested Miss Goldring. 'For all we know this man Flawse does tie his wife to the bed and whip her and with a name like Jessica she thoroughly deserves it. After all it's up to him to prove he doesn't.'

Mr Arbutus pointed out that truth was no defence unless in the public interest.

'I should think a bank robber and pervert was of very considerable public interest. It will probably increase the sales of my novels.'

Counsel thought otherwise. 'We haven't a leg to stand on,' said Mr Widdershins, QC. 'I advise settlement. We can't hope to win in court.'

'But won't the publicity do us good even if we pay?' asked Mr Shortstead, pushed into adopting this line by Miss Goldring who was always complaining that her novels were never sufficiently advertised. Mr Widdershins doubted it but, since he was being paid to conduct the defence, he saw no good reason to deprive himself of the financial remuneration a prolonged case was bound to bring him. 'I leave the decision to you,' he said, 'I have given my opinion and that opinion is that we will lose.'

'But they are demanding four hundred thousand pounds in settlement out of court,' said Mr Shortstead, 'and surely no court is going to award damages to that amount. It's outrageous.' It was.

The trial was held in The High Court of Justice, Queen's Bench Division, before Mr Justice Plummery. Mr Widdershins acted for the defendants and Mr Fescue had been instructed by Mr Gibling and Mr Gibling. The latter were in raptures. Mr Justice Plummery had a reputation for barbarous impartiality and a loathing for quibbling barristers. There was no recourse open to Mr Widdershins but to quibble, and to add to the difficulties of the defence there was Miss Goldring who, if she couldn't win the case, was determined to lose it as flamboyantly as possible.

Mr Shortstead sat beside her shivering in the shade of her crimson hat. One look at the plaintiff, Lockhart Flawse, had been enough to tell him that here was a clean upstanding young man of a type he had forgotten existed; who more probably owned banks than robbed them and who, if he was married, treated his wife with a tenderness that was positively chivalrous. Mr Shortstead was a good judge of character.

Mr Fescue rose to present the plaintiff's case. It was an impeccable one. Mr Lockhart Flawse of 12 Sandicott Crescent, East Pursley – and here Mr Widdershins was seen to cover his eyes with his hands and Miss Goldring's hat to quiver – was a close neighbour of the defendant, so close that he was known to her and had on one occasion been invited to tea by her. A note passed to Mr Widdershins from Miss Goldring simply said, 'Liar, bloody liar. I've never seen the little shit in my life,' at which Mr Widdershins' hopes rose a little. They were lowered by Mr Fescue's continued description of Lockhart Flawse's virtue and tribulations subsequent to the publication of *Song of the Heart*. Among these tribulations the most important had been his sacking from the firm of Sandicott & Partner, Chartered Accountants, where he had been previously employed. Evidence would be produced that his forced retirement from the lucrative profession had been the direct result of Miss Goldring's infamous attack on his private life and his wholly fictitious propensity for robbing banks and murdering cashiers. Mr Fescue, lacking the knowledge, did not mention that Mr Treyer's readiness to provide such evidence had been obtained in a private interview in which Lockhart had explained that unless Mr Treyer was evidentially co-operative he, Lockhart, would be forced by his conscience into revealing the true facts about Mr Gypsum's tax evasion and VAT avoidance to the appropriate authorities, a threat which had been made the stronger by his production of copies of all Mr Gypsum's files, both dummy and real.

Furthermore, said Mr Fescue, the plaintiff had been shunned by his neighbours to the extent that eleven houses adjacent to his address or in the same street had been left by their occupants to avoid any connection between them and a supposed murderer. And finally there was Mrs Flawse, correctly named in the novel as Jessica, who would testify that she had never once tied her husband or been tied by him to their marital bed and that there wasn't a whip in the house. Mrs Flawse's distress was of so great an order of magnitude that she had recently taken to wearing a veil to avoid being accosted (in the street) by men with a taste for bondage and flagellation, or alternately insulted by women she had formerly been able to invite to her house but who now refused her entry to their own. By the time Mr Fescue had finished he had portrayed an accurate picture of the young couple's social isolation for quite the wrong reasons, and an inaccurate one of their future financial prospects as a result of the publication of *Song of the Heart* for the right reasons, namely that the damages to be paid would be enormous.

When Mr Fescue sat down Mr Justice Plummery and the jury were clearly impressed and Mr Widdershins rose for the defence extremely handicapped. It was all very well for Miss Goldring to claim that Lockhart Flawse was a liar. It was going to be another matter to prove it. Mr Flawse did not look a liar. If anything he looked the opposite while, even behind her veil, Mrs Jessica Flawse radiated an innocence that was in marked contrast to the raddled flamboyance of his client. Booze, books and bed had all left their marks on Miss Goldring. Mr Widdershins did his best. The libel, he claimed, was entirely innocent. The defendant had no knowledge of the plaintiff's existence and had never so much as set eyes on him. The imputation that she had once invited him to tea was utterly without foundation and the fact that Miss Goldring lived in West Pursley while the plaintiff occupied a house in East was purely coincidental. However in the light of the statements made by his learned friend, Mr Fescue, the defence were prepared to apologize and make financial reparation for the damage done to the plaintiff and his wife and for the scorn, ridicule and consequential loss of his profession ... Here Miss Goldring broke away from the restraining hand of Mr Shortstead and rose to say that never, never, never would she pay one penny, one single penny to a man she had never written about in her life and that if anyone thought she would they were mistaken. Mr Justice Plummery regarded her with an immense distaste that would have withered the Sphinx at fifty yards and rendered it articulate at a hundred.

'Kindly sit down, madam,' he snarled with blood and iron in

his voice. 'What you will or will not do it is up to the Court to decide. But one thing I do assure you, a second interruption and I shall have you held for contempt. Proceed with what there is of your case, Mr Witherspin.'

Mr Widdershins' Adam's apple bobbed like a ping-pong ball on a waterspout in a fairground shooting-gallery as he tried to find words. He had no case.

'My clients plead innocent libel, m'lud,' he squeaked in direct contradiction to his instructions. Mr Justice Plummery looked at him dubiously.

'That is not what I understood,' he said.

Mr Widdershins asked for an adjournment to consult with his clients. It was granted and was spent in exultation by Mr Fescue and Mr Gibling and Lockhart, and in acrimonious arguments by Mr Widdershins and Miss Goldring. Mr Shortstead was ready in the face of the plaintiff's case to settle out of court. Miss Goldring in the face of his pusillanimity and the judge's distaste was not.

'It's all a damned lie,' she shouted, 'I never had that little shit to tea and I never used the name Lockhart fucking Flawse in any of my books.'

'But it's there in *Song of . . .*' Mr Shortstead began.

'Shut up,' said Miss Goldring. 'If it's there you must have put it there because it wasn't in the manuscript I sent you.'

'You're quite sure about that?' said Mr Widdershins, looking for some ray of hope in an otherwise hopeless case.

'I swear by Almighty God,' said Miss Goldring with a vehemence that was convincing, 'that I have never ever heard the name Flawse in my life, let alone used it in a book.'

'May we see a copy of the manuscript?' said Mr Widdershins, and Mr Shortstead sent for it. The name Flawse was there in bold pica type.

'What do you say to that?' said Mr Widdershins.

Miss Goldring said a great deal and most of it true. Mr Shortstead said little and all of it true.

'Then we shall contest the authenticity of this document,' said Mr Widdershins. 'Are we all agreed on that?'

Miss Goldring was. Mr Shortstead wasn't. 'That is the manuscript we received,' he maintained.

'That was not, is not, nor ever will be the manuscript I dictated. It's a fucking forgery.'

'You're absolutely sure about that?' said Mr Widdershins.

'I swear by Almighty God . . .'

'Very well. We will contest the case on those grounds, that this document which came into the possession of Mr Shortstead was not the original manuscript you wrote.'

'Precisely,' said Miss Goldring, 'I swear by Almighty God . . .'

She was still swearing by Almighty God and by lesser deities when she entered the witness box the following day to be cross-examined by an ebullient Mr Fescue. Mr Gibling and Mr Gibling could hardly contain themselves. In fact Mr Gibling the Elder couldn't at all and had to leave the court hurriedly while she was still in the witness box.

'Now Miss Magster,' Mr Fescue began before being stopped by the judge.

'I understood the witness's name to be Miss Genevieve Goldring,' he said, 'now you address her as Miss Magster. Which is it?'

'Miss Genevieve Goldring is an alias,' said Mr Fescue, 'her real . . .' He was interrupted by a squawk from the witness box.

'Genevieve Goldring is my pen name, my *nom de plume*,' she said.

Mr Justice Plummery studied the feather in her hat with disgust. 'No doubt,' he said, 'no doubt your profession requires an assortment of names. The court requires your real one.'

'Miss Magster,' said Miss Goldring, sullenly aware that this revelation would disillusion a large section of her public. 'But I am best known to my admirers as Miss Genevieve Goldring.'

'Again no doubt,' said the judge, 'but then from what I have gathered your admirers have peculiar tastes.'

Mr Fescue took his cue from the judge. 'I am prepared to call you Genevieve Goldring if you so prefer,' he said, 'it is not my intention to harm your professional reputation. Now is it or is it not true that in *Song of the Heart* you describe the character named Flawse as being addicted to what is known among prostitutes and their clients as bondage and flage?'

'I did not write *Song of the Heart*,' said Miss Goldring.

'But I thought you had already admitted writing it,' said the judge. 'Now I hear ...'

What he heard was a tirade from the witness box on the iniquities of publishers and editors. When she had finished, Mr Fescue turned to Mr Justice Plummery. 'Would it not be as well to examine the original manuscript and compare it with others submitted by the defendant to her publishers, m'lud?' he asked.

'The defendants have no objections,' said Mr Widdershins, and the Court adjourned once again.

Later that afternoon two experts on graphology and typography testified that the manuscript of *Song of the Heart* had been written, typed and produced by precisely the same machine as *King's Closet* and *Maid of the Moors*, both books written by Miss Goldring. Mr Fescue continued his cross-examination of the defendant.

'Having established beyond all possible doubt that you wrote *Song of the Heart*,' he said, 'is it not also true that you were and are acquainted with the plaintiff, Mr Lockhart Flawse?'

Miss Goldring began a violent denial but Mr Fescue stopped her. 'Before you commit perjury,' he said. 'I would ask you to consider the evidence given under oath by Mr Flawse that you invited him into your house and plied him with crème de menthe?'

In the witness box Miss Goldring stared at him with starting eyes. 'How did you know that?' she asked.

Mr Fescue smiled and looked to the judge and jury. 'Because Mr Flawse told me under oath yesterday,' he said gaily.

But Miss Goldring shook her head. 'About the crème de menthe,' she said weakly.

'Because the plaintiff also told me, though in private,' said Mr Fescue. 'You do, I take it, drink crème de menthe?'

Miss Goldring nodded miserably.

'Yes or no,' said Mr Fescue fiercely.

'Yes,' said Miss Goldring. Below her Mr Widdershins and Mr Shortstead both covered their eyes with their hands. Mr Fescue resumed his rout. 'Is it not also true that the carpet in your bedroom is blue flecked with gold, that your bed is heart shaped, that beside it stands a mauve pleated lampshade, that your cat's name is Pinky? Are these facts not all true?'

There was no doubting their veracity. The look on Miss

Goldring's face spoke for her. But Mr Fescue had the *coup de grâce* ready.

'And finally is it not a fact that you possess a chow named Bloggs for the sole purpose of preventing anyone you wish to keep out from entering your house without your permission and presence?' Again there was no need for an answer. Mr Fescue had his facts right: he had heard them from Lockhart who in turn had them from Jessica.

'So that,' continued Mr Fescue, 'without your permission Mr Flawse could not have been able to testify in a signed affidavit that when you invited him into the house you did so of your own free will and with the intention of seducing him and having failed of that purpose you set out deliberately and with malice aforethought to destroy his marriage, reputation and means of livelihood by portraying him in a novel as a thief, a pervert and a murderer. Is that not also true?'

'No,' shrieked Miss Goldring, 'no it isn't. I never invited him in. I never . . .' She hesitated catastrophically. She had invited a number of young men to share her bed but . . .

'I have no more questions of this witness,' said Mr Fescue and sat down.

In his summing up Mr Justice Plummery maintained that ferocious impartiality for which he was famous. Miss Goldring's evidence and behaviour in and out of the witness box had left no doubt in his mind that she was a liar, a prostitute in both the literary and sexual meanings of the word, and that she had maliciously set out to do what Mr Fescue had maintained. The jury retired for two minutes and found the libel proved. It was left to the judge to estimate the damages both personal and financial to the plaintiff as being of the order, due consideration being given to the level of inflation which presently and for the foreseeable future stood and would continue to stand at eighteen per cent, of one million pounds sterling, and that furthermore he was sending papers of the case to the Director of Public Prosecutions with the hope that the defendant would be charged with perjury. Miss Genevieve Goldring fainted and was not helped to her feet by Mr Shortstead.

That afternoon there was jubilation in the offices of Mr Gibling and Mr Gibling.

'A million with costs. A million. The highest damages ever awarded in a libel case. And with costs. Dear God, let them appeal, please let them appeal,' said Mr Gibling the Elder.

But Miss Goldring was past appealing. Mr Shortstead's insurers had communicated with him immediately following the award and had made it clear that they intended to sue both him and Miss Goldring for every penny they were being asked to pay.

And at Number 12 Sandicott Crescent Lockhart and Jessica had no qualms.

"Beastly woman,' said Jessica, 'and to think I used to love her books. And they were all lies.'

Lockhart nodded. 'And now we can start to sell the houses too,' he said. 'After so much unfortunate publicity we can't possibly stay in this neighbourhood.'

Next day the sign boards For Sale began to go up in Sandicott Crescent and Lockhart, feeling himself financially secure, decided to open the letters Miss Deyntry had given him.

Chapter sixteen

He did so with due ceremony and in the dim consciousness that he was tempting fate. 'Paper and ink will do you no good,' the old gipsy had told him and while her prediction had not been borne out by the paper and ink of Miss Goldring's novel, Lockhart harking back to her words felt that they applied more to these letters to his dead mother than to anything else. He had received them from Miss Deyntry in the hour of the gipsy's forecast and he felt that this was no coincidence. He would have been hard put to explain why but there lurked in his mind the vestigial superstitions of his ancestors and a time when a Romany's warning was taken seriously. And in other respects she had been right. Three deaths there had been and if she had rather underestimated there was still the fact that she had been precise about the unfilled grave. The remains of the late Mrs

Simplon had needed no grave. And what about the hanged man on a tree? Certainly the Police Superintendent had hung from a tree but not in the manner of the old woman's sinister prediction. Finally there was the matter of his gift. 'Till ye come to your gift again.' Possibly that referred to the million pounds' damages from the libel suit. But again Lockhart doubted it. She had meant another kind of gift than money.

Nevertheless Lockhart took courage and opened the letters one by one, starting from the first which was dated the year of his birth and came from South Africa and ended with the last dated 1964 and addressed from Arizona. His father, if father the writer was, had been a travelling man and Lockhart soon realized why. Miss Deyntry had been right. Grosvenor K. Boscombe had been a mining engineer and his work had taken him across the globe in search of precious metals, oil, gas and coal, anything in fact that the millenniums had covered and modern mining methods could discover. Possibly he was a mining engineer and a highly successful one at that. His last letter from Dry Bones, Arizona, in which he announced his marriage to a Miss Phoebe Tarrent also indicated that he had struck it rich in natural gas. But whatever his success as a mining engineer, Grosvenor K. Boscombe had little talent for writing letters. There was no glimmer of that passion or sentiment Lockhart had expected, and certainly no suggestion that Mr Boscombe had done anything to qualify as Lockhart's long-lost father. Mr Boscombe stuck to the occupational hazards of his profession and spoke of his boredom. He described sunsets over the Namibian, Saudi Arabian, Libyan and the Sahara deserts in almost identical terms in letters years apart. By the time he had ploughed his way through all the letters Lockhart had crossed correspondentially most of the major deserts of the world, a laborious process made more so by virtue of Mr Boscombe's inability to spell any word with more than four syllables correctly or even consistently. Thus Saudi Arabia went through half a dozen permutations from Sordy Rabier to Sourday Ayrabbia. The only word the man could spell was 'Bore' and it was appropriate. Grosvenor K. Boscombe was boring wherever he went and apart from regarding the world as a gigantic pin cushion into which it was his profession to push immensely long hollow pins, his only moment of even approximate passion came when he and the boys, whoever they were, punctured some underground pressure point and 'then she fare blue'. The phrase recurred less frequently than the sunsets, and dry holes predominated over gushers but she blue farely often all the same and his strike at Dry Bones, Arizona, put Mr Boscombe in his own words 'up amung the lucky ones with mor greenbacks than a man wuld nede to carpit the moon.' Lockhart interpreted that as meaning his possible father was rich and unimaginative. Lockhart knew exactly what he intended to do with his money and carpeting the moon didn't enter his list of priorities. He meant to find his father and do old Mrs Flawse out of any part of the estate and if Boscombe was his father, he was going to thrash him within an inch of his life in accordance with his grandfather's will.

Having read all the letters he allowed Jessica to read them too.

'He doesn't seem to have had a very interesting life,' she said. 'The only things he talks about are deserts and sunsets and dogs.'

'Dogs?' said Lockhart. 'I missed that bit.'

'It's at the end of each letter. "Please rember me to yure father and the dawgs it sure was a priv ledge nowing youall. Ever thyne, Gros." and there's another bit here about just luving dawgs.'

'That's reassuring,' said Lockhart, 'his loving dogs. I mean if he is my father it shows we've got something in common. I've never had much time for sunsets. Dogs are another kettle of fish.'

On the carpet in front of the fire Colonel Finch-Potter's ex-bull-terrier snoozed contentedly. Adopted by Lockhart he had, unlike his master, recovered from the effects of his night of passion and while the Colonel fought legal battles and wrote to his MP to get himself released from the mental hospital to which he had been committed, his pet settled cheerfully into his new home. Lockhart looked at him with gratitude. The bull-terrier had played a very considerable part in clearing Sandicott Crescent of unwanted tenants and Lockhart had appropriately renamed him Bouncer.

'I suppose we could always tempt this Boscombe man over here by offering him some extra-special sort of pedigree dog,' he pondered aloud.

'Why do you have to tempt him over?' said Jessica. 'We can

afford to fly to America to see him ourselves with all the money we've got.'

'All the money isn't going to buy me a birth certificate and without one I can't get a passport,' said Lockhart who had never forgotten his experience of non-entity at the National Insurance office and besides, he meant to put this disadvantage to good use in other matters. If the State was not prepared to contribute to his well-being when in need, he saw no need to contribute one penny by way of taxes to the State. There were virtues to non-existence after all.

And as the winter months rolled by the money rolled in. Messrs Shortstead's insurance company paid one million pounds into Lockhart's bank account in the City and money rolled into Jessica's account at East Pursley and the For Sale notices came down and new occupiers moved in. Lockhart had timed his campaign of eviction with financial precision. Property values were up and not one of the houses went for less than fifty thousand pounds. By Christmas Jessica's account stood at £478,000 and her standing with the bank manager even higher. He offered her financial advice and suggested she should invest the money. Lockhart told her not to do anything so foolish. He had plans for that money and they had nothing to do with stocks and shares and even less to do with Capital Gains Tax which the bank manager was at pains to point out she would inevitably have to pay. Lockhart smiled confidently and went on footling about in the workshop in the garden. It helped to pass the time while the houses were sold and besides, ever since his success as a radio mechanic in the Wilsons' attic, he had become quite an expert and had bought all the necessary ingredients for a hi-fi system which he then constructed. In fact he went in for gadgetry with all his grandfather's enthusiasm for breeding hounds and in no time at all Number 12 was wired for sound so that Lockhart, moving from room to room could, by the mere manipulation of a pocket tuner, switch one loudspeaker off and another one on and generally accompany himself musically wherever he went. On tape recorders he went hog wild and indulged his fancy from minute ones with batteries to vast ones with specially constructed drums a yard wide that held a tape that would play continuously for twenty-four hours and then reverse themselves and start all over again *ad infinitum*.

And in just the same way he could play his tapes all day he could record as long and in whatever room he happened to be. Every so often he would find himself breaking out into song, strange songs of blood and battle and feuds over cattle which were as surprising to him as they were out of place in Sandicott Crescent and seemed to spring spontaneously from some inner source beyond his comprehension. Words reverberated in his head and increasingly he found himself speaking aloud a barely intelligible dialect that bore but little resemblance even to the broadest brogue of the North Tyne. And rhyme came with the words and behind it all a wild music swirled like the wind haunting the chimney on a stormy night. There was no compassion in that music, no pity or mercy, any more than there was in the wind or other natural phenomena, only harsh and naked beauty which took him by force out of the real world in which he moved into another world in which he had his being. His being? It was a strange notion, that one had one's being in much the same way as his grand-uncle, an apostate from the ethical religion of self-help and hero-worship which his grandfather espoused, had the living of St Bede's Church at Angoe.

But Lockhart's mind dwelt less on these subtleties than on the practical problems facing him and the words and the wild music came out only occasionally when he was not feeling himself. And here it had to be admitted he was increasingly feeling himself in ways which his grandfather, a devotee of that Fouler whose great work, *Usage and Self-Abusage*, was the old man's guide in matters of masturbation, would have deplored. The strain of not imposing himself upon his angelic Jessica had begun to tell and sexual fantasies began to fester in his mind as he tinkered in his workshop with a soldering iron. They had the same ancestral and almost archetypal quality as the primeval forests that had flickered in Bouncer's mind under the influence of LSD and with them came guilt. There were even moments when he considered assuaging his desire in Jessica but Lockhart thrust the idea from him and used the sheepskin buffer on the electric drill instead. It was not a satisfactory remedy but it sufficed for the present. One day when he was master of Flawse Hall, and owner of five thousand acres, he would raise a family, but not till then. In the meantime he and Jessica would live chaste lives and resort to the electric drill and manual methods. Lockhart's reasoning was primitive but it stemmed from the feeling that he had yet to master his fate and until that moment came he was impure.

It came sooner than he expected. In late December the phone rang. It was Mr Bullstrode calling from Hexham.

'My boy,' he said in sombre tones. 'I have bad news. Your father, I mean your grandfather, is dangerously ill. Dr Magrew sees little hope of his recovering. I think you should come at once.'

Lockhart with death in his heart for old Mrs Flawse drove north in his new car, a three-litre Rover, leaving Jessica in tears.

'Is there nothing I can do to help?' she asked but Lockhart shook his head. If his grandfather was dying thanks to anything old Mrs Flawse had done, he did not want the presence of her daughter to hinder his plans for the old witch. But when he drove over the track to the gated bridge below the Hall it was to learn from Mr Dodd that the man had fallen, if not of his own volition at least unassisted by his wife who had been in the kitchen garden at the time. Mr Dodd could vouch for that.

'No banana skins?' said Lockhart.

'None,' said Mr Dodd. 'He slipped in his study and hit his head on the coal scuttle. I heard him fall and carried him up-stairs.'

Lockhart went up the stairs and brushing Mrs Flawse's lamentations aside with a 'Hush, woman' went into his grand-father's bedroom. The old man was lying in bed and beside him sat Dr Magrew feeling Mr Flawse's pulse.

'His heart's strong enough. It's his head I'm worried about. He should be X-rayed for a fracture but I dare not move him over the broken road,' he said. 'We must trust to the good Lord and the strength of his constitution.'

As if to give a demonstration of that strength old Mr Flawse opened an evil eye and damned Dr Magrew for a scoundrel and a horse thief before shutting it and sinking back into a coma. Lockhart and Dr Magrew and Mr Dodd went downstairs.

'He could go at any moment,' said the doctor, 'and then again he may linger for months.'

'It is a hope much to be desired,' said Mr Dodd looking significantly at Lockhart, 'he canna die before the father's found.' Lockhart nodded. The same thought was in his mind. And that night after Dr Magrew had left with the promise to return in the morning, Lockhart and Mr Dodd sat in the kitchen without Mrs Flawse and conferred.

'The first thing to see to is that woman doesna go near him,' said Mr Dodd. 'She'd stifle the man with a pillow had she but half the chance.'

'Gan lock her door,' said Lockhart, 'we'll feed her through the keyhole.'

Mr Dodd disappeared and returned a few minutes later to say that the bitch was chained in her kennel.

'Now then,' said Lockhart, 'he mustn't die.'

' 'Tis in the lap of the Gods,' said Mr Dodd, 'you heard the doctor.'

'I heard him and I still say he mustn't die.'

A bellow of oaths from upstairs indicated that Mr Flawse was living up to their hopes.

'He does that every now and then. Shouts and abominates the likes of all around.'

'Does he indeed?' said Lockhart. 'You put me in mind of an idea.'

And the next morning before Dr Magrew arrived he was up and away over the broken road and down through Hexham to Newcastle. He spent the day in radio and hi-fi shops and returned with a carload of equipment.

'How is he?' he asked as he and Mr Dodd carried the boxes into the house.

'Ever the same. He shouts and sleeps and sleeps and shouts but the doctor doesna hold out too much hope. And the old bitch has been adding her voice to the din. I told her to still herself or she'd have no food.'

Lockhart unpacked a tape recorder and presently he was sitting by the old man's bed while his grandfather shouted abominations into the microphone.

'Ye damned skulking swine of a blackhearted Scot,' he yelled as Lockhart fixed the throat mike round his neck, 'I'll have no more of your probing and pestering. And take that satanic stethoscope from me chest, ye bluidy leech. 'Tis not my heart that's gan awry but my head.'

And all night he blathered on against the infernal world and its iniquities while Lockhart and Mr Dodd took turns to switch the tape recorder on and off.

That night the snow set in and the road across Flawse Fell became impassable. Mr Dodd heaped coals on the fire in the bedroom and Mr Flawse mistook them for the flames of hell. His language became accordingly more violent. Whatever else, he was not going gently into that dark underworld in which he had professed such unbelief.

'I see you, you devil,' he shouted, 'by Lucifer I'll have ye by the tail. Get ye gone.'

And ever and anon he rambled. ' 'Tis hunting weather, ma'am, good day to ye,' he said quite cheerfully, 'the hounds'll have the scent na doubt. Would that I were young again and could ride to the pack.'

But as each day passed he grew weaker and his thoughts turned to religion.

'I dinna believe in God,' he murmured, 'but if God there be the old fool made an afful mess in the making of this world. Old Dobson the stonemason of Belsay could have made better and he was a craftsman of small talent for all the Grecians taught him in the building of the Hall.'

Lockhart sitting by the tape recorder switched it off and asked who Dobson was but Mr Flawse's mind had gone back to the Creation. Lockhart switched the tape recorder on again.

'God, God, God,' muttered Mr Flawse, 'if the swine doesna exist he should be ashamed of the fact and that's the only creed a man must hold to. To act in such a way that God be put to shame for not existing. Aye, and there's more honour among thieves than in a rabble of godly hypocrites with hymnbooks in their hands and advantage in their hearts. I havena been to church in fifty years save for a burial or two. I willna go now. I'd as soon be bottled like that heretical utilitarian Bentham than be buried with my bloody ancestors.'

Lockhart took note of his words and none of Mrs Flawse's complaints that they had no right to lock her in her room and that it was insanitary to boot. Lockhart had Mr Dodd hand her a roll of toilet paper with instructions to empty the contents of her pot out the window. Mrs Flawse did, to the detriment of Mr Dodd who was passing underneath at the time. After that Mr Dodd gave the window a wide berth and Mrs Flawse no dinner for two days.

And still it snowed and Mr Flawse lingered on blaspheming and blaming the absent Dr Magrew for meddling with him when all the time it was Lockhart or Mr Dodd with the tape recorder. He heaped coals of fire on Mr Bullstrode's head too and called out that he never wanted to see that litigious bloodsucker again which, considering that Mr Bullstrode was unable to make his way to the Hall thanks to the snow, seemed highly probable.

Between these outbursts he slept and slowly slipped away. Lockhart and Mr Dodd sat in front of the kitchen fire and laid their plans for his imminent end. Lockhart had been particularly impressed by the old man's repeated wish not to be buried. Mr Dodd on the other hand pointed out that he didn't want to be cremated either if his attitude to the fire in the bedroom was anything to go by.

'It's either one or t'other,' he said one night. 'He'd keep while the cold lasts but I doubt he'd be pleasant company come the summer.'

It was Lockhart who found the solution one evening as he stood in the peel tower and stared at the dusty flags and the ancient weapons and heads that hung on the wall, and when in the cold hour before dawn old Mr Flawse, muttering a last imprecation on the world, passed from it, Lockhart was ready.

'Keep the tape recorders going today,' he told Mr Dodd, 'and let no one see him.'

'But he's nothing left to say,' said Mr Dodd. But Lockhart switched the tape from record to play and from beyond the shadow of death old Mr Flawse's voice echoed through the house. And having shown Mr Dodd how to change the cassettes to avoid too much repetition, he left the house and struck across the fells towards Tombstone Law and Miss Deyntry's house in Farspring. It took him longer than he expected. The snow was deep and the drifts against the stone walls deeper still and it was already afternoon when he finally slid down the slope to her house. Miss Deyntry greeted him with her usual gruffness.

'I thought I'd seen the last of you,' she said as Lockhart warmed himself in front of the stove in her kitchen.

'And so you have,' said Lockhart, 'I am not here now and I am not going to borrow your car for a few days.'

Miss Deyntry regarded him dubiously. 'The two statements do not fit together,' she said, 'you are here and you are not going to borrow my car.'

'Rent it then. Twenty pounds a day and it never left your garage and I was never here.'

'Done,' said Miss Deyntry, 'and is there anything else you'd be needing?'

'A stuffer,' said Lockhart.

Miss Deyntry stiffened. 'That I can't provide,' she said. 'Besides, I understood you to be married.'

'Of animals. Someone who stuffs animals and lives a fair way off.'

Miss Deyntry sighed with relief. 'Oh, a taxidermist,' she said. 'There's an excellent one in Manchester. I know him only by repute of course.'

'And you'll not know even that from now on,' said Lockhart and wrote down the address, 'your word on it.' He placed a hundred pounds on the table and Miss Deyntry nodded.

That night Mr Taglioni, Taxidermist & Specialist in Permanent Preservation, of 5 Brunston Road was interrupted in his work on a Mrs Pritchard's pet and late poodle, Oliver, and called to the front door. In the darkness outside stood a tall figure whose face was largely obscured by a scarf and a peaked hat.

'Yes,' said Mr Taglioni, 'can I help you?'

'Perhaps,' said the figure. 'Do you live alone?'

Mr Taglioni nodded a trifle nervously. It was one of the disadvantages of his occupation that few women seemed disposed to share a house with a man whose livelihood consisted of stuffing other things and those dead.

'I am told you are an excellent taxidermist,' said the figure pushing past Mr Taglioni into the passage.

'I am,' said Mr Taglioni proudly.

'You can stuff anything?' There was scepticism in the voice.

'Anything you care to mention,' said Mr Taglioni, 'fish, fox, fowl or pheasant, you name it I'll stuff it.'

Lockhart named it. 'Benvenuto Cellini!' said Mr Taglioni lapsing into his native tongue, 'Mamma mia, you can't be serious?'

But Lockhart was. Producing an enormous revolver from his raincoat pocket he pointed it at Mr Taglioni.

'But it's not legal. It's unheard of. It's ...'

The revolver poked into his belly. 'I named it, you stuff it,' said the masked figure. 'I'll give you ten minutes to collect your tools and anything else you need and then we'll go.'

'What I need is brandy,' said Mr Taglioni and was forced to drink half the bottle. Ten minutes later a blindfolded, drunk and partially demented taxidermist was bundled into the back seat of Miss Deyntry's car and driven north and by three o'clock in the morning the car was hidden in an abandoned lime kiln near Black Pockrington. Across the fell there stalked a tall black figure and over his shoulder he carried the insensible Mr Taglioni. At four they entered the Hall and Lockhart unlocked the door to the wine cellar and laid the taxidermist on the floor. Upstairs Mr Dodd was awake.

'Make some strong coffee,' Lockhart told him, 'and then come with me.'

When half an hour later Mr Taglioni was coaxed back to consciousness by having scalding hot coffee poured down his throat, the body of the late Mr Flawse lying on the table was the first thing to meet his horrified gaze. Lockhart's revolver was the second, a masked Mr Dodd the third.

'And now to work,' said Lockhart. Mr Taglioni gulped.

'Liebe Gott, that I should have to do this thing ...'

'That is not a thing,' said Lockhart grimly and Mr Taglioni shuddered.

'Never in my life have I been called upon to stuff a person,' he muttered, rummaging in his bag. 'Why not ask an embalmer?'

'Because I want the joints to move.'

'Joints to move?'

'Arms and legs and head,' said Lockhart. 'He must be able to sit up.'

'Legs and arms and neck maybe but hips is impossible. Either sitting or standing. It must be one or the other.'

'Sitting,' said Lockhart. 'Now work.'

And so while his widow lay sleeping upstairs unaware of her recent but long-awaited bereavement, the grisly task of stuffing Mr Flawse began in the cellar. When she did wake, the old man could be heard shouting from his bedroom. And in the cellar Mr Taglioni listened and felt terrible. Mr Dodd didn't feel much better. The business of carrying buckets upstairs and disposing of their ghastly contents in the cucumber frames where they wouldn't be seen because of the snow on the glass above was not one he relished.

'They may do the cucumbers a world of good,' he muttered on his fifth trip, 'but I'm damned if they do me. I won't be able to touch cucumbers again without thinking of the poor old devil.'

He went down to the cellar and complained to Lockhart. 'Why can't we use the earth closet instead?'

'Because he didn't want to be buried and I'll see his wishes carried out,' said Lockhart.

'I wish you'd carry out a few of his innards as well,' said Mr Dodd bitterly.

What Mr Taglioni said was largely unintelligible. What he had to say he muttered in his native Italian and when Lockhart inadvisedly left the cellar for a moment he returned to find that the taxidermist had, to relieve the strain of emptying Mr Flawse, filled himself with two bottles of that late gentleman's crusted port. The combination of a drunk taxidermist elbow-deep in his lamented employer was too much for Mr Dodd. He staggered up the stairs and was greeted by the unearthly voice of the late Mr Flawse bellowing imprecations from the bedroom.

'The devil take the lot of you, ye bloodsucking swine of Satan. You couldn't be trusted not to steal the last morsel of meat from a starving beggar,' the late man bawled very appositely, and when an hour later Lockhart came up and suggested that something substantial for lunch like liver and bacon might help the taxidermist sober up, Mr Dodd would have none of it.

'Ye'll cook whatever you damned well please,' he said, 'but I'll not be eating meat this side of Candlemas.'

'Then you'll go back down and see he doesn't help himself to more wine,' said Lockhart. Mr Dodd went gingerly down to the cellar to find that Mr Taglioni had helped himself to just about everything else. What remained of Mr Flawse was not a pleasant sight. A fine figure of a man in his day, in death he was not at his best. But Mr Dodd steeled himself to his vigil while Mr Taglioni babbled on unintelligibly and delving deeper into the recesses finally demanded more lights. The expression was too close to the bone for Mr Dodd.

'You've had his bloody liver,' he shouted, 'what more bleeding lights do you need? They're in the fucking cucumber frame and if you think I'm going to get them, you can think again.'

By the time Mr Taglioni had managed to explain that by lights he meant more illumination, Mr Dodd had been sick twice and the taxidermist had a bloody nose. Lockhart came down to separate them.

'I'm not staying down here with this foreign ghoul,' said Mr Dodd vehemently. 'The way he goes on you'd not think he knew his arse from his elbow.'

'All I ask for is lights,' said the Italian, 'and he goes berserk like I asked for something terrible.'

'You'll get something terrible,' said Mr Dodd, 'if I have to stay down here with you.'

Mr Taglioni shrugged. 'You bring me here to stuff this man. I didn't ask to come. I asked not to come. Now when I stuff him you say I get something terrible. Do I need telling? No. That I don't need. What I got is something terrible enough to last me a lifetime, my memories. And what about my conscience? You think my religion permits me to go round stuffing men?'

Mr Dodd was hustled upstairs by Lockhart and told to change the tapes. The late Mr Flawse's repertoire of imprecations was getting monotonous. Even Mrs Flawse complained.

'That's the twenty-fifth time he's told Dr Magrew to get out of the house,' she shouted through her bedroom door. 'Why doesn't the wretched man go? Can't he see he's not wanted?'

Mr Dodd changed the cassette to one labelled 'Heaven and Hell, Possible Existence of.' Not that there was any possibility in his own mind of doubting the existence of the latter. What was going on in the cellar was proof positive that Hell existed. It was Heaven he wanted to be convinced about, and he was just listening to the old man's deathbed argument borrowed in part from Carlyle about the unseen mysteries of the Divine Spirit when he caught the sound of steps on the stairs. He glanced out the door and saw Dr Magrew coming up. Mr Dodd slammed the door and promptly switched the cassette back to the previous one. It was marked 'Magrew and Bullstrode, Opinions of.' Unfortunately he chose Mr Bullstrode's side and a moment later Dr Magrew was privileged to hear his dear friend, the solicitor, described by his dear friend, Mr Flawse, as litigious spawn of a syphilitic whore who should never have been born but having been should have been gelded at birth before he could milk the likes of Mr Flawse of their wealth by consistently bad advice. This opinion had at least the merit of stopping the doctor in his tracks. He had always valued Mr Flawse's judgement and was interested to hear more. Meanwhile Mr Dodd had gone to the window and looked out. The snow had thawed sufficiently to let the doctor's car through to the bridge. Now he had to think of some means of denying him access to his departed patient. He was saved by Lockhart who emerged from the cellar with the tray on which stood the remnants of Mr Taglioni's lunch.

'Ah, Dr Magrew,' he called out, shutting the cellar door firmly behind him, 'how good of you to come. Grandfather is very much better this morning.'

'So I can hear,' said the doctor as Mr Dodd tried to change the cassette and Mr Taglioni, revivified by his lunch, burst into a foul imitation of Caruso. 'Quite remarkably better by the sound of it.'

From her bedroom Mrs Flawse demanded to know if that damned doctor was back again.

'If he tells Dr Magrew to get out of the house just one more time,' she wailed, 'I think I'll go off my head.'

Dr Magrew hesitated between so many injunctions. From the bedroom Mr Flawse had switched to politics and was berating the Baldwin government of 1935 for its pusillanimity while at the same time someone in the cellar was bawling about Bella bella carissima. Lockhart shook his head.

'Come down and have a drink,' he said. 'Grandfather's in an odd frame of mind.'

Certainly Dr Magrew was. In the course of separating Mr Dodd from the taxidermist Lockhart had, to put it mildly, been bloodied and the presence in a coffee cup on the tray of what from Dr Magrew's experience he could have sworn to be a human appendix dropped there absent-mindedly by Mr Taglioni, left him badly in need of a drink. He staggered down the staircase eagerly and presently was gulping down Mr Dodd's special distilled Northumbrian whisky by the tumbler.

'You know,' he said when he felt a little better, 'I had no idea your grandfather had such a low opinion of Mr Bullstrode.'

'You don't think that could just be the result of his concussion? The fall affected his mind as you said yourself.'

Down below Mr Taglioni, left to himself, had hit the crusted port again and with it Verdi. Dr Magrew stared at the floor.

'Am I imagining things,' he asked, 'but is there someone singing in your cellar?'

Lockhart shook his head. 'I can't hear anything,' he said firmly.

'Christ,' said the doctor looking wildly round, 'you really can't?'

'Only grandfather shouting upstairs.'

'I can hear that too,' said Dr Magrew. 'But ...' He stared demoniacally at the floor. 'Well, if you say so. By the way, do you always wear a scarf over your face in the house?'

Lockhart took it off with a sanguine hand. From the cellar came a fresh burst of Neapolitan.

'I think I had better be gone,' said the doctor, staggering to his feet, 'I'm delighted your grandfather is making such good progress. I'll call again when I feel a little better myself.'

Lockhart escorted him to the door and was seeing him out when the taxidermist struck again.

'The eyes,' he shouted, 'my God I forgot to bring his eyes. Now what are we going to do?'

There was no doubting what Dr Magrew was going to do. He took one last demented look at the house and trundled off at a run down the drive to his car. Houses in which he saw human appendixes in otherwise empty coffee cups and people announced that they had forgotten to bring their eyes were not for him. He was going home to consult a fellow practitioner.

Behind him Lockhart turned blandly back into the Hall and calmed the distraught Mr Taglioni.

'I'll bring some,' he said, 'don't worry. I'll fetch a pair.'

'Where am I?' wailed the taxidermist. 'What is happening to me?'

Upstairs Mrs Flawse knew exactly where she was but had no idea what was happening to her. She peered out of the window in time to see the persistent Dr Magrew running to his car and then Lockhart appeared and walked to the peel tower. When he returned he was carrying the glass eyes of the tiger his grandfather had shot in India on his trip there in 1910. He thought they would do rather well. Old Mr Flawse had always been a ferocious man-eater.

Chapter seventeen

All that day and the next and the one following Mr Taglioni continued his gruesome task while Lockhart cooked and Mr Dodd sat in his shed and stared resentfully at the cucumber frames. In her bedroom Mrs Flawse had stood all she could of her blasted husband's voice echoing from across the landing about Heaven and Hell and guilt, sin and damnation. If the old fool would either die or stop repeating himself she wouldn't have minded but he went on and on and on, and by the third night Mrs Flawse was prepared to brave snow, sleet and storm and even heights to escape. She tied her sheets together and then tore her blankets into strips and knotted them to the sheets and the sheets to the bed and finally, donning her warmest clothes, she clambered out of the window and slid rather than climbed to the ground. The night was dark and the snow melted and against the black background of mud and moor she was invisible. She slushed off down the drive towards the bridge and had just crossed it and was trying to undo the gates when behind her she heard the sound that had welcomed her to Flawse Hall, the baying of hounds. They were still in the yard but a light shone in the window that had been her bedroom and the light had been off when she left.

She turned from the gate and ran or rather stumbled alongside The Cut in a desperate attempt to reach the hillside by the tunnel, and as she ran she heard the creak of the wooden gates to the yard and the louder baying of the hounds. The Flawse pack was on the scent again. Mrs Flawse fled on into the darkness, tripped and fell, got up, tripped again and this time fell into The Cut. It wasn't deep but the cold was intense. She tried to climb the far bank but slipped back and giving up, waded on knee-deep in the icy water towards the dark shadow of the hill and the darker hole of the great tunnel. It loomed larger and more awful with each uncertain step she took. Mrs Flawse hesitated. The black hole ahead spoke to her of Hades, the baying pack behind of Pluto, no gay cartoon of Disneyland, but rather that dread god of the infernal regions at whose altar of mere wealth she had unconsciously worshipped. Mrs Flawse was not an educated woman but she knew enough to tell that she was caught between the devil and, by way of taps, toilets, and sewers provided by the Gateshead and Newcastle Waterworks, the deep blue sea. And then as she hesitated the baying hounds were halted in their tracks and against the skyline she could see in silhouette a figure on a horse thrashing about him with a whip.

'Get back, ye scum,' shouted Lockhart, 'back to your kennels, ye scavengers of hell.'

His voice drifting with the wind reached Mrs Flawse and for once she felt grateful to her son-in-law. A moment later she knew better. Addressing Mr Dodd as he had addressed the hounds, Lockhart cursed the man for his stupidity.

'Have you forgotten the will, you damned old fool?' he demanded. 'Let the old bitch but go one mile beyond the radius of the Hall and she will forfeit the estate. So let her run and be damned.'

'I hadna thought of that,' said Mr Dodd contritely and turned his horse to follow the pack back to Flawse Hall while Lockhart rode behind. Mrs Flawse no longer hesitated. She too had forgotten the clause in the will. She would not run and be damned. With a desperate effort she scrambled from The Cut and stumbled back to the Hall. Once there she had not the strength to climb the sheets to her bedroom but tried the door. It was unlocked. She went inside and stood shivering in the darkness. A door was open to the kitchen and a light shone beneath the cellar door. Mrs Flawse needed a drink, a strong drink to warm her blood. She stepped quietly to the cellar door and opened it. A moment later her screams echoed and re-echoed through the house for there before her very eyes, naked and with an enormous scar from groin to gullet, sat old Mr Flawse on a bare wood table stained with blood and his eyes were the eyes of a tiger. Behind him stood Mr Taglioni with a piece of cotton waste which he appeared to be stuffing into her husband's skull and while he worked he hummed a tune from *The Barber of Seville*. Mrs Flawse took one look and having screamed passed out. It was Lockhart who carried her gibbering dementedly back to her room and dropped her on the bed. Then he hauled up the sheets and blankets and knotted her to the bedstead.

'Ye'll go no more a-wandering by the light of the moon,' he said cheerfully and went out locking the door. It was true. When Mr Dodd took her breakfast up he found Mrs Flawse staring dementedly at the ceiling, gibbering to herself.

Down in the cellar Mr Taglioni gibbered too. Mrs Flawse's eruption and hysteria in the cellar had completed his demoralization. It had been bad enough to stuff a dead man but to have his work interrupted in the middle of the night by a wailing widow had been too much for him.

'Take me home,' he pleaded with Lockhart, 'take me home.'

'Not before you've finished,' said Lockhart implacably. 'He's got to speak and wave his hands.'

Mr Taglioni looked up at the masked face.

'Taxidermy's one thing. Marionettes another,' he said. 'You wanted him stuffed, you got him stuffed. Now you say I got to make him speak. What you want? Miracles? You better ask God for those.'

'I'm not asking anyone. I'm telling,' said Lockhart and produced the small loudspeaker. 'You put that where his larynx is ...'

'Was,' said Mr Taglioni, 'I no leave nothing inside.'

'Was then,' continued Lockhart, 'and then I want this receiver put in his head.' He showed Mr Taglioni the miniature receiver. Mr Taglioni was adamant.

'No room. His head is stuffed with cotton wool.'

'Well take some out and put this in and leave space for the

batteries. And while you're about it I want his jaw to move. I've an electric motor here. Look, I'll show you.'

For the rest of the morning, the late Mr Flawse was wired for sound and by the time they had finished it was possible to hear his heart beat when a switch was pulled. Even his eyes, now those of the tiger, swivelled in his head at the touch of a button on the remote control. About the only thing he couldn't do was walk or lie down flat. For the rest he looked rather healthier than he had done of late and certainly sounded as articulate.

'Right,' said Lockhart when they had tested him out, 'Now you can drink your fill.'

'Who?' said Mr Taglioni, by this time thoroughly confused. 'Him or me?'

'You,' said Lockhart and left him to his own devices and the contents of the wine cellar. He went upstairs to find that Mr Dodd was also drunk. The sound of his Master's voice issuing from that fearful effigy in the cellar had been too much even for his sturdy soul and he was half-way through a bottle of his own Northumbrian brew. Lockhart took the whisky from him.

'I'll need your help to get the old man to bed,' he said, 'he's stiff in the hip joints and needs levering round corners.'

Mr Dodd demurred but eventually between them they got Mr Flawse, clad in his red flannel nightgown, into bed where he sat up bellowing and calling on the Almighty to save his soul.

'You've got to admit he's very realistic,' said Lockhart. 'It is just a pity we didn't think of taping his utterances earlier.'

'It's more a pity we ever thought of taping them at all,' said Mr Dodd drunkenly, 'and I wish his jaw wouldna go up and down like that. It puts me in mind of a goldfish with asthma.'

'But the eyes are about right,' said Lockhart. 'I got them from the tiger.'

'Ye dinna have to tell me,' said Mr Dodd and surprisingly broke into Blake. 'Tiger, tiger burning bright in the forests of the night. What demented hand and eye framed thy awful circuitry?'

'I did,' said Lockhart proudly, 'and I'm fixing him a wheelchair so that he can move about the house on his own and I'll direct it by remote control. That way no one will suspect he isn't still alive and I'll have time to see if this Mr Boscombe in Arizona is my father.'

'Boscombe? A Mr Boscombe?' said Mr Dodd. 'And for why would you be thinking he was your father?'

'He wrote a great many letters to my mother,' said Lockhart and explained how he had got them.

'Ye'll be wasting your time ganning after the man,' said Mr Dodd. 'Miss Deyntry was right. I recall the little man and he was a poor wee thing that your mither had no time for. You had best look closer home.'

'He's the only lead I've got,' said Lockhart, 'unless you can suggest a more likely candidate.'

Mr Dodd shook his head. 'I'll tell you this though. The auld bitch has got wind of what ye're up to and knows the old man is dead. If ye gan off to America she'll find a way out of the house to alert Mr Bullstrode. Ye saw what she did the other night. The woman's desperate dangerous and there's the Italian down below is a witness to the deed. Ye hadna thought of that.'

Lockhart pondered a while. 'I was going to take him back to Manchester,' he said. 'He has no idea where he has been.'

'Aye but he's a fine knowledge of the house and he's seen our faces,' said Mr Dodd, 'and with the woman hollering that the man was stuffed it will take no time for the law to put two and two together.'

Down in the cellar Mr Taglioni had put far more than two and two together and was drinking himself insensible on crusted port. He sat surrounded by empty bottles proclaiming in garbled tones that he was the finest stuffer in the world. It was not a word he liked to use but his tongue could no longer wrap itself round anything so polysyllabic as taxidermist.

'There he goes again with his blathering and boasting,' said Mr Dodd as they stood at the top of the cellar steps, 'the finest stuffer in the world indeed. The word has too many meanings for my liking.'

Mrs Flawse shared his distaste. Tied to the bed on which she herself had been stuffed by her late stuffed husband Mr Taglioni's repertoire filled her with dread. Mr Flawse did not help. Mr Dodd had inserted a tape cassette labelled 'Family History, Findings In', which thanks to Lockhart's electronic ingenuity no sooner ended than it rewound itself and repeated its findings *ad*

177

nauseam. Since the tape was forty-five minutes long and took three to rewind Mrs Flawse was subjected from below to Mr Taglioni's drunken boasts and from the bedroom across the landing to endless re-runs of the tale of Headman Flawse, Bishop Flawse going to the stake, and a recitation of Minstrel Flawse's song beneath the gibbet. It was this last which affected her.

'I gan noo wha ma organs gan
    When oft I lay abed,
So rither hang me upside doon
    Than by ma empty head.'

The first stanza was bad enough but the rest were even worse. By the time Mrs Flawse had heard the old man apparently demand fifteen times that Sir Oswald's arse be prised apart and he be given back his prick because he couldn't wait for Oswald to die before he had a pee, his widow was in much the same condition. Not that she wanted a prick, but she certainly couldn't wait much longer to have a pee. And all day Lockhart and Mr Dodd sat out of earshot in the kitchen debating what to do.

'We canna let the Latin go,' said Mr Dodd. 'It would be better to dispose of him altogether.'

But Lockhart's mind was working along more economical lines. Mr Taglioni's repeated boast that he was the world's finest stuffer and the ambiguity of that remark gave him pause for thought. And Mr Dodd's attitude was strange. His adamant denial that Mr Boscombe in Dry Bones was Miss Flawse's lover and his own father had been convincing. When Mr Dodd said something it was invariably true. Certainly he didn't lie to Lockhart – or hadn't in the past. And now he was stating categorically that the letters were no clue. It was what Miss Deyntry and the old Romany had warned him. 'Paper and ink will do you no good.' Lockhart accepted the fact and yet without Mr Boscombe he was without the possibility of finding his father before it was known that his grandfather was dead. Mr Dodd was right on that point. Mrs Flawse knew and knowing would tell as soon as she was released. Her screams rising to a crescendo that drowned even old Mr Flawse's Family History and Mr Taglioni's garbled utterances decided Lockhart to go to her relief. By the time he unlocked the bedroom door she was screaming that if she didn't have a pee soon it was less a question of anyone else dying than of her bursting. Lockhart untied her and she wobbled to the earth closet. When she returned to the kitchen Lockhart had made up his mind.

'I have found my father,' he announced. Mrs Flawse stared at him with loathing.

'You're a liar,' she said, 'a liar and a murderer. I saw what you had done to your grandfather and don't think . . .'

Lockhart didn't. Between them he and Mr Dodd dragged Mrs Flawse up to her room and tied her again to the bed. This time they gagged her.

'I told you the auld witch knew too much,' said Mr Dodd, 'and since she's lived for money she'll not die without it, threaten her how you may.'

'Then we must forestall her,' said Lockhart and went down to the cellar. Mr Taglioni, on to his fifth bottle, regarded him hazily through bloodshot eyes.

'Finest taxi . . . stuffer in the world. Me,' he burbled, 'fox, flowl, phleasant, you name it I'll stuff it. And now I've stuffed a man. Whatcha think of that?'

'Daddy,' said Lockhart and put his arm round Mr Taglioni's shoulder affectionately, 'my own dear daddy.'

'Daddy? Whose flucking daddy?' said Mr Taglioni, too drunk to appreciate the new role he was being cast in. Lockhart helped him to his feet and up the stairs. In the kitchen Mr Dodd was busy at the stove making a pot of coffee. Lockhart propped the taxidermist up against the settle where he tried to focus his eyes on these new and circling surroundings. It took an hour and a pint of black coffee together with a great deal of stew to sober him up. And all the time Lockhart insisted on calling him daddy. If anything more was needed to unnerve the Italian it was this.

'I'm not your flucking daddy,' he said, 'I don't know what you're talking about.'

Lockhart got up and went to his grandfather's study and unlocked the safe hidden behind the collected works of Surtees. When he returned he was carrying a washleather bag. He beckoned to Mr Taglioni to come to the table and then emptied the bag's contents out in front of him. A thousand gold sovereigns littered the scrubbed pine table. Mr Taglioni goggled at them.

'What's all that money doing there?' he asked. He picked a sovereign up and fingered it. 'Gold. Pure gold.'

'All for you, daddy,' said Lockhart.

For once Mr Taglioni didn't question the word. 'For me? You're paying me in gold for stuffing a man?'

But Lockhart shook his head. 'No, daddy, for something else.'

'What?' said the taxidermist suspiciously.

'For being my father,' said Lockhart. Mr Taglioni's eyes swivelled in his head almost as incredulously as the tiger's did in the old man.

'Your father?' he gasped. 'You want me to be your father? For why should I be your father? You must have one already.'

'I am a bastard,' said Lockhart but Mr Taglioni knew that already.

'So even a bastard must have a father. Your mother was a virgin?'

'You leave my mother out of this,' said Lockhart and Mr Dodd shoved a poker into the glowing fire of the range. By the time it was red-hot Mr Taglioni had made up his mind. Lockhart's alternatives left him little choice.

'Okay, I agree. I tell this Mr Bullstrode I am your father. I don't mind. You pay me this money. Is fine with me. Anything you say.'

Lockhart said a lot more. They concerned the likely prison sentence to be pronounced on a taxidermist who had stuffed an old man, having in all likelihood first murdered him for the thousand gold sovereigns in his safe.

'I no murdered anyone,' said Mr Taglioni frantically, 'you know that. He was dead when I came here.'

'You prove it,' said Lockhart. 'Where are his vital organs to be examined by a police surgeon and forensic expert to say when he died?'

'In the cucumber frames,' said Mr Dodd involuntarily. It was a circumstance that haunted his mind.

'Never mind that,' said Lockhart, 'the point I'm making is that you'll never be able to prove you didn't kill my grandfather and this money is the motive. Besides, we don't like foreigners in these parts. The jury would be biased against you.'

Mr Taglioni acknowledged that likelihood. Certainly everything else in whatever parts he was seemed to have a bias against him.

'Okay, okay. I say what you want me to say,' he said, 'and then I go with all this money? Right?'

'Right,' said Lockhart, 'you have my word as a gentleman.'

That night Mr Dodd went to Black Pockrington and, having first collected Miss Deyntry's car from the old lime kiln, drove to Hexham to inform Mr Bullstrode that he and Dr Magrew were required next day at the Hall to certify the sworn statement of Lockhart's father that he was indeed responsible for Miss Flawse's pregnancy. He then returned the car to Divit Hall.

Lockhart and Mr Taglioni sat on in the kitchen while the Italian learnt his lines. Upstairs Mrs Flawse struggled with her own. She had made up her mind that nothing, not even the prospect of a fortune, was going to keep her lying there in wait for a similar end to that of her husband. Come hell or high water she was going to get loose from the bed and absent from the Hall, and not even the thought of being pursued by the Flawse pack would deter her from making her escape. Unable to express herself vocally because of the gag, she concentrated on the ropes that tied her to the iron bedstead. She pushed her hands down and pulled them back over and over again with a tenacity that was a measure of her fear.

And in Hexham Mr Bullstrode pertinaciously tried to persuade Dr Magrew to return with him to Flawse Hall the next morning. Dr Magrew was not easily induced. His last visit had had a quite remarkable adverse effect on him.

'Bullstrode,' he said, 'it does not come easily to me in my professional capacity to reveal the confidences of a man I have known so many years and who may and indeed probably is at this moment on his deathbed, but I have to tell you that old Edwin had harsh things to say about you when last I heard him.'

'Indeed,' said Mr Bullstrode, 'he was doubtless rambling in delirium. You cannot rely on the sayings of a senile old man.'

'True,' said Dr Magrew, 'but there was a certain precision about some of his comments that didn't suggest senility to me.'

'Such as?' said Mr Bullstrode. But Dr Magrew was not prepared to say. 'I will not repeat slander,' he said, 'but I am not of a mind to go back to the Hall until Edwin is either dead or ready to apologize to you.'

Mr Bullstrode took a more philosophical and financially advantageous view of the matter. 'As his personal physician you know best,' he said, 'but for myself I do not intend to forgo my professional fee as his solicitor, and the estate is a large one and will take a good deal of winding up. Besides, the will is sufficiently ambiguous to provide fertile ground for litigation. Now if Lockhart has found his father I doubt very much if Mrs Flawse will not contest the issue and the pickings of such a lengthy court action would be considerable. It would be foolish after so many years amicable acquaintance with Edwin to fail him in his hour of need.'

'Be it on your own head,' said Dr Magrew. 'I will come with you but I warn you there are strange occurrences going on at the Hall and I care not for them.'

Chapter eighteen

He liked them even less when the following morning Mr Bullstrode stopped his car at the gated bridge and waited for Mr Dodd to come and unlock it. Even at this distance Mr Flawse's voice could be heard cursing the Almighty and blaming him for the state of the universe. As usual Mr Bullstrode's point of view was more pragmatic.

'I cannot say I agree with his sentiments,' he said, 'but if as you assert he has said some unkind words about me it would appear that I am at least in good company.'

He wasn't ten minutes later. Mr Taglioni's appearance did not inspire confidence. The taxidermist had been through too many inexplicable horrors to be at his best and while Lockhart had spent half the night seeing to it that his 'father' was word perfect in his new role, drink, fear and sleeplessness had done nothing to improve his looks. Mr Taglioni's clothes too had suffered. Provided by Lockhart from his grandfather's wardrobe to replace the bloodstained garments the taxidermist had been wearing before, nothing fitted at all precisely. Mr Bullstrode looked at him with dismay and Dr Magrew with medical concern.

'He doesn't look a very fit man to me,' he whispered to the solicitor as they followed Lockhart into the study.

'I cannot express an opinion on his health,' said Mr Bullstrode, 'but the word fit does not apply to his apparel.'

'It doesn't apply to a man who is shortly to be flogged within an inch of his life,' said Dr Magrew. Mr Bullstrode stopped in his tracks.

'Good Lord,' he muttered, 'that stipulation had quite passed out of my mind.'

It had never entered Mr Taglioni's. All he wanted to do was to get out of this dreadful house with his life, reputation and money still intact.

'What are we waiting for?' he asked as Mr Bullstrode hesitated.

'Quite,' said Lockhart, 'let us get on with the business.'

Mr Bullstrode swallowed. 'Would it not be more proper to have present your grandfather and his wife?' he inquired. 'After all the one drew the will and last testament up and the other would appear to be about to be deprived of those benefits she would otherwise have received under it.'

'My grandfather has stated that he does not feel up to leaving his bed,' said Lockhart and waited while Mr Flawse's voice made fresh inroads into, this time, Dr Magrew's professional reputation. 'I think I can safely say the same for my step-grandmother. She is at present indisposed and naturally my father's appearance here today, with all its consequences for her financially, might be said to chafe her more than a little.'

It was no more than the truth. A night spent rubbing the ropes that bound her hands up and down against the iron bedstead had indeed chafed her but she still persisted while down in the study Mr Taglioni repeated word for word what he had been taught. Mr Bullstrode wrote down his words and was in spite of himself impressed. Mr Taglioni stated that he had been employed as a casual labourer by the Waterworks at the time and being an Italian had naturally attracted the attention of Miss Flawse.

'I couldn't help it,' he protested, 'I am Italian and English ladies, you know how English ladies like . . .'

'Quite,' said Mr Bullstrode who knew what was coming and wasn't prepared to listen to it. 'And so you fell in love?' he continued to improve upon the singularly distressing tastes in the matter of foreigners displayed by the late Miss Clarissa Flawse.

'Yes. We fall in love. You could put it like that.'

Muttering to himself that he wished to hell he couldn't Mr Bullstrode wrote this down. 'And then what?'

'What do you think? I stuff her.'

Mr Bullstrode wiped his bald head with a handkerchief while Dr Magrew's eyes blazed lividly at the Italian.

'You had sexual intercourse with Miss Flawse?' said Mr Bullstrode when he could bring himself to speak.

'Sexual intercourse? I don't know. We fuck. Right? First I fuck her. Then she fuck me. Then—'

'So help me God someone else is going to fuck you if you don't shut up,' shouted Dr Magrew.

'Now what I say wrong?' asked Mr Taglioni. 'You . . .'

Lockhart intervened. 'I don't think we need go into any further details,' he said pacifically. Mr Bullstrode expressed his fervent agreement. 'And you are prepared to swear on oath that to the best of your knowledge you are the father of this man?' he asked.

Mr Taglioni said he was. 'Then if you'll just sign here,' Mr Bullstrode went on and handed him the pen. Mr Taglioni signed.

His signature was witnessed by Dr Magrew.

'And may one ask what your present occupation is?' Mr Bullstrode asked inadvisedly.

'You mean what I do?' said Mr Taglioni. Mr Bullstrode nodded. Mr Taglioni hesitated and then, after so many lies, decided to tell the truth. Before Dr Magrew could get at him Lockhart had hustled the Italian out of the room. Behind him Mr Bullstrode and Dr Magrew were left speechless.

'Did you ever hear the like?' said Dr Magew when at last his palpitations had abated somewhat. 'The bloody swine has the gall to stand there and . . .'

'My dear Magrew,' said Mr Bullstrode, 'I can only say that I now understand why the old man stipulated in his will that the bastard's father should be flogged to within an inch of his life. He must have had some inkling, you know.'

Dr Magrew agreed. 'Personally I would have preferred him to have stipulated something stronger,' he said, 'like half a mile beyond it.'

'Beyond what?' asked the solicitor.

'Beyond his life,' said Dr Magrew and helped himself to some of Mr Flawse's whisky which stood on a tray in the corner. Mr Bullstrode joined him.

'That raises a very interesting point,' he said when they had drunk one another's health and the ill-health of Mr Taglioni. 'Which is quite simply what constitutes "within an inch of his life". The question of measurement would seem to me to be crucial.'

'I hadn't thought of that,' said Dr Magrew, 'and now that you mention it I can see great objections. A more exact statement would, I suppose, have been within an inch of his death.'

'That still doesn't answer the question. Life is time. We speak of a man's lifetime, not his life-space. And an inch is not a function of time.'

'But we also speak of a long life,' said Dr Magrew, 'and that surely implies spatial extension. Now if we assume that by a long life we mean eighty years, and I think that a fair estimate, I suppose we can take as our standard three-score years and ten. Personally I am glad to suspect from the colour of that wretched Italian's complexion and his general physique that the swine has a far shorter life expectancy than that laid down in the Bible. Let us say to be on the safe side, sixty years. Now we have to transfer an inch to a scale of time relative to sixty years ...'

They were interrupted by the entrance of Lockhart who announced that to avoid disturbing his grandfather and distressing Mrs Flawse he had decided to conduct the second part of the ceremony in the peel tower.

'Dodd's getting him ready for the flogging,' he said. 'The two old men followed him out still deep in disputation as to what constituted to within an inch of life.

'An inch of life,' said Dr Magrew, 'leaves us in fact two inches to play with, one before death and one after. Now death itself is an indeterminate state and before acting it would be as well to decide what we mean by it. Some authorities define it as the moment the heart stops beating; others would have it that the brain being the organ of consciousness is capable of subsisting beyond the moment of time in which the heart stops functioning. Now, sir, let us define . . .'

'Dr Magrew,' said Mr Bullstrode as they crossed the dwarf garden, 'as a lawyer I am not qualified to judge the issue. The term "to within an inch of his life" does not allow of the man dying. I would not have been party to a last will and testament which stipulated the murder of Lockhart's father no matter how strongly I may feel about the matter personally. Murder is against the law . . .'

'So is flogging,' said Dr Magrew. 'To lay down in a will that a man must be flogged to within an inch of his life is to make us both parties to a crime.'

They had entered the peel tower and his voice echoed among the dusty battle-flags and ancient armour. An eyeless tiger bared its teeth above the great open hearth. Manacled to the opposite wall, Mr Taglioni gave voice to his objections.

'What do you mean flogged?' he screamed but Mr Dodd put a bullet in his mouth.

'To give him something to bite on,' he explained. 'It was an old custom in the army.'

Mr Taglioni spat the bullet out. 'You crazy?' he yelled. 'What more do you want from me? First I got to . . .'

'Keep the bullet between your teeth,' interrupted Mr Dodd and replaced it. Mr Taglioni struggled with the bullet and finally got it into a corner of his cheek where it bulged like a quid of tobacco.

'I tell you I don't awant to be flogged. I came here to stuff someone. I stuff him. Now . . .'

'Thank you, Mr Dodd,' said Mr Bullstrode as that servant silenced the Italian with his grimy handkerchief. 'If anything persuades me that the will ought to be carried out according to the spirit of the law rather than the letter it is his constant reference to stuffing. I find the term singularly objectionable, I must say.'

'And was I not mistaken in thinking that the gender was wrong too?' said Dr Magrew. 'I could have sworn he said "Him".'

Mr Taglioni would have sworn too if he could but Mr Dodd's handkerchief in combination with the bullet was doing things to his taste buds and his breathing that took what was left of his mind off external circumstances. He turned from white to damson. In a far corner of the hall Lockhart was practising with his horsewhip on a figure in armour and the room rang to the clang of the whip. The sound recalled Mr Bullstrode to his professional rectitude.

'I am still unpersuaded that we should proceed before determining the exact measurement of an inch of life,' he said. 'Perhaps we should consult Mr Flawse himself to find out what precisely he meant.'

'I doubt you'll get a rational answer out of the man,' said Mr Dodd, all the while wondering which cassette would give an even approximate answer to the question. He was saved the trouble by Dr Magrew. Mr Taglioni's complexion had progressed from damson to off-black.

'I think it would be as well to allow your father some air,' he told Lockhart, 'my Hippocratic oath will not allow me to attend death by suffocation. Of course if this were a hanging . . .'

As Mr Dodd removed the handkerchief and bullet Mr Taglioni regained a better complexion and a volubility that was wasted on his audience. He stood shouting in Italian. Finally, unable to hear themselves dispute, Dr Magrew and Mr Bullstrode went out into the garden in disgust.

'I find his cowardice contemptible,' said Mr Bullstrode, 'but the Italians fought very badly in the war.'

'Which hardly helps us solve our present problem,' said Dr Magrew, 'and as a man of some compassion even for such swine I would suggest that we act in strict accordance to the will and flog the brute to within an inch of his life.'

'But . . .' began Mr Bullstrode. Dr Magrew went back into the hall and spoke to Mr Dodd above the din. Presently Mr Dodd left the hall and returned five minutes later with a ruler and a pencil. Dr Magrew took them and approached Mr Taglioni. Placing the ruler an inch from his shoulder and marking the point with the pencil he proceeded down the Italian's right side making pencil marks on the stucco wall and joining them together so that they formed an outline one inch from the man.

'I think that is precise,' he announced proudly. 'Lockhart, my boy, you may go ahead and flog the wall up to the pencil line and you will have flogged the man to within an inch of his life. I think that satisfies to the letter the conditions of your grandfather's will.'

But as Lockhart advanced with the whip, Mr Taglioni fulfilled the old man's last testament to the spirit. He slumped down the wall and was silent. Lockhart looked at him in annoyance.

'Why's he gone that funny colour?' he asked. Dr Magrew opened his bag and took out his stethoscope. A minute later he shook his head and pronounced Mr Taglioni dead.

'That's torn it,' said Mr Bullstrode, 'now what the hell do we do?'

But the question was to remain unanswered for the time being. From within the house there came a series of terrible shrieks. Mrs Flawse had freed herself and had evidently discovered the full extent of her late husband's dismemberment. As the little group in the peel hall stood and, with the exception of Mr Taglioni, listened, the shrieks turned to insane laughter.

'Curse the woman,' said Mr Dodd and charged towards the door, 'I should have known better than to have left the bitch alone so long.' He dashed across the yard and into the house. Lockhart and his grandfather's two old friends followed. As they entered the Hall they saw Mrs Flawse standing at the top of the stairs while Mr Dodd writhed at the bottom and clutched his groin.

'Get her from behind,' he advised Lockhart, 'she's got me in the front.'

'The woman's insane,' said Dr Magrew unnecessarily as Lockhart headed for the back stairs. Mrs Flawse was bawling about the old man being dead and not lying down.

'Go see for yourselves,' she cried and scuttled into her room. Dr Magrew and Mr Bullstrode went cautiously up the stairs.

'If as you say the woman is *non compos mentis*,' said Mr Bullstrode, 'that only makes what has just occurred all the more regrettable. Having parted with her mind she has also relinquished any right to the estate under the will thus negating the necessity for that disgusting foreigner's statement.'

'Not to mention the swine's death,' said Dr Magrew. 'I suppose we had better pay our compliments to Edwin.'

They turned towards old Mr Flawse's bedroom while at the foot of the stairs Mr Dodd tried to dissuade them.

'He's not seeing anyone,' he shouted but the truth of this remark escaped them. By the time Lockhart, coming stealthily up the back stairs to avoid being kicked in the groin by his demented mother-in-law, arrived, the landing was empty and Dr Magrew had taken his stethoscope out and was applying it to Mr Flawse's chest. It was not the wisest of moves and Mr Flawse's subsequent ones were appalling to behold. Either the doctor's bedside manner or Mr Bullstrode's accidental treading on the remote control activated the mechanism for the old man's partial animation. His arms waved wildly, the tiger's eyes rolled in his head, his mouth opened and shut and his legs convulsed. Only the sound was off, the sound and the bedclothes which his legs kicked off the bed so that the full extent of his rewiring was revealed. Mr Taglioni had not chosen the kindest spot for the wires to extrude and they hung like some terrible electronic urethra. As Mr Taglioni had said at the time, it was the last place anyone examining him would think of looking. It was certainly the last place Dr Magrew and Mr Bullstrode wanted to look but by the very complexity of the wires they couldn't take their eyes off the thing.

'The junction box and earth,' Lockhart explained adding a cricketing term to their confusion, 'and the aerial. The amplifier is under the bed and I've only got to turn the volume up ...'

'Don't, for God's sake, don't do anything of the sort,' pleaded Mr Bullstrode, unable to distinguish between spatial volume and output and convinced that he was about to be privy to an erection. Mr Flawse's reactions were awful enough without that dreadful addition.

'I've got him on ten watts per channel,' Lockhart went on but Dr Magrew interrupted. 'As a medical man I have never been in favour of euthanasia,' he gasped, 'but there's such a thing as sustaining life beyond the bounds of human reason and to wire a man's ... Dear God!'

Ignoring Mr Bullstrode's plea Lockhart had turned the volume up and besides twitching and jerking the old man now gave voice.

'Twas ever thus with us,' he bellowed, a statement Dr Magrew felt certain must be untrue, 'Flawse blood runs in our veins and carries with it the bacteria of our ancestral sins. Aye, sins and sanctity so intertwined there's many a Flawse gone to the block a martyr to his forebears' loves and lusts. Would that it were not so, this determinism of inheritance, but I have known myself too well to doubt the urgency of my inveterate desires . . .'

There was equally no doubting the urgency of Dr Magrew's and Mr Bullstrode's desires. They wanted to get the hell out of the room and away as fast as their legs would carry them but the magnetism of the old man's voice (the cassette was labelled 'Flawse, Edwin Tyndale, Self-Opinions of') held them – that and Lockhart and Mr Dodd standing implacably between them and the door.

'And I must say, congenitally speaking, that I am as much a moss trooper at heart as I am an Englishman and a man of so-called civilization, albeit that civilization to which I was born and bred has gone and taken with it that pride in being an Englishman which so sustained us in the past. Where is the proud craftsman now, and where the self-reliance of the working man? Where too the managers of men and great machines that were the envy of the world? All gone and in their place the Englishman a beggar has become, the world's beggar, whining cap in hand for alms to help support him though he does no work nor now produces goods the world will buy. All cloth is shoddy and all standards dropped. And this because no politician dared to tell the truth but bowed and cringed and bought their votes to empty power by promises as empty as themselves. Such scum as Wilson, aye and Tories too, would make Keir Hardy and Disraeli both agree, this was not their meaning of democracy, this bread and circuses that makes of men a mass and then despises them. So has old England gone to pot since I was born and laws being broken by the men who passed them from Bills to Acts of Parliament, being broken by the Ministers themselves, what law is left a man should now obey when all are outlawed by bureaucracy. Aye, bureaucrats who pay themselves with money begged and borrowed, or stolen from the pockets of the working man. These civil-service maggots on the body politic who feed upon the rotting corpse of England that they killed . . .'

Lockhart switched the old man off and Dr Magrew and Mr Bullstrode breathed a sigh of terrible relief. It was short-lived. Lockhart had more in store for them.

'I had him stuffed,' he said proudly, 'and you, doctor, proclaimed him healthy when he was already dead. As Dodd's my witness so you did.'

Mr Dodd nodded. 'I heard the doctor so proclaim,' he said.

Lockhart turned to Mr Bullstrode. 'And you were instrumental in the killing of my father,' he said. 'The sin of patricide . . .'

'I did nothing of the sort,' said the solicitor. 'I refuse . . .'

'Did you or did you not draw up my grandfather's will?' he asked. Mr Bullstrode said nothing. 'Aye, you did and thus we three all stand convicted of complicity in murder. I would have you consider the consequences carefully.'

Already it seemed to Dr Magrew and Mr Bullstrode that in Lockhart's voice they heard the unmistakable tone of the old man sitting stuffed beside them, the same unshakable arrogance and that dread logic that neither port nor learned disputation nor, now it seemed, even death could totally dispel. They followed his instructions to the letter and considered the consequences very well indeed.

'I must confess to finding myself perplexed,' said Mr Bullstrode finally. 'As your grandfather's oldest friend I feel bound to act to his best advantage and in a way he would have liked.'

'I doubt very much he would have liked being stuffed,' said Dr Magrew. 'I know I wouldn't.'

'But on the other hand, as an officer of the law and a Commissioner of Oaths I have my duty to perform. My friendship contradicts my duty. Now if it were possible to say that Mr Taglioni died a natural death . . .'

He looked expectantly at Dr Magrew.

'I can't believe a coroner would find the circumstances propitious to such a verdict. A man chained by his wrists to a wall may die a natural death but he chose an unnatural position to do it in.'

There was a gloomy silence and finally Mr Dodd spoke. 'We

could add him to the contents of the cucumber frames,' he said.

'The contents of the cucumber frames?' said Dr Magrew and Mr Bullstrode simultaneously, but Lockhart ignored their curiosity.

'My grandfather expressed a wish not to be buried,' he said, 'and I intend to see his wishes carried out.'

The two old men looked unwillingly at their dead friend. 'I cannot see him sitting to anyone's advantage in a glass case,' said Dr Magrew, 'and it would be a mistake to suppose we can maintain the fiction of his life perpetually. I gather that his widow knows.'

Mr Dodd agreed with him.

'On the other hand,' said Lockhart, 'we can always bury Mr Taglioni in his place. Grandfather is so jointed it would take a conspicuously right-angled coffin to fit him in and I don't suppose the publicity attached to such a contraption would do us any good.'

Mr Bullstrode and Dr Magrew were of the same opinion.

'Then Mr Dodd will find him a suitable sitting place,' said Lockhart, 'and Mr Taglioni will have the honour of joining the Flawse ancestors at Black Pockrington. Dr Magrew, I trust you have no objections to making out a certificate of death, of natural death, for my grandfather?'

Dr Magrew looked doubtfully at his stuffed patient.

'Let us just say that I won't let appearances to the contrary influence my judgement,' he said. 'I suppose I could always put it that he shuffled off this mortal coil.'

'A thousand natural shocks that flesh is heir to, would certainly seem to fit the case,' said Mr Bullstrode.

And so it was agreed.

Two days later a solemn cortège left Flawse Hall led by the brougham in which lay the coffin containing Mr Taglioni. It made its melancholy way along the gated road to the church at Black Pockrington where, after a short service in which the Vicar spoke movingly and with unconscious percipience about the dead man's love of wild life and its preservation, the taxidermist was laid to rest beneath a tombstone which proclaimed him Edwin Tyndale Flawse of Flawse Hall. Born 1887 and

Gone to His Maker 1977. Below Lockhart had had inscribed a suitably enigmatic verse for them both.

'Ask not who look upon this stone
If he who lies here, lies alone.
Two fathers share this plot of land;
The one acquired, the other grand.'

Mr Bullstrode and Dr Magrew looking upon it found it appropriate if not in the best of taste.

'I dislike the emphasis on lies,' said Dr Magrew.

'I still have grave reservations about Mr Taglioni's claim to be the bastard's father,' said Mr Bullstrode. 'That "acquired" has a nasty ring to it but I don't suppose we shall ever know the whole truth.'

'I sincerely hope no one else does,' said Dr Magrew. 'Do we know if he left a widow?'

Mr Bullstrode said he thought it best not to inquire. Certainly Mr Flawse's widow did not attend the funeral. She wandered the house dementedly and occasionally wailed, but her cries were drowned by the whines of the Flawse hounds baying the passing of their creator. And occasionally as if in royal salute there came the boom of a gun firing on the artillery range to the west.

'I wish the old bitch would go the same way herself,' said Lockhart after the funeral breakfast. 'It would save a lot of trouble.'

'Aye, it would that,' Mr Dodd agreed. 'It never does to have your mither-in-law living in the same house with a young couple. And you'll be moving in with your wife shortly na doubt.'

'As soon as I have made financial arrangements, Mr Dodd,' said Lockhart. 'I have one or two matters still to attend to in the south.'

Next day he caught the train from Newcastle and by evening was back in Sandicott Crescent.

Chapter nineteen

There everything had changed. The houses had all been sold, even Mr O'Brain's, and the Crescent was once more its quiet undisturbed suburban self. In Jessica's bank account £659,000 nestled to her credit, the manager's effusiveness and the great expectations of the Chief Collector of Taxes who could hardly wait to apply the regulations governing Capital Gains. Lockhart's million pounds in damages from Miss Goldring and her erstwhile publishers were lodged in a bank in the City acquiring interest but otherwise untouchable by the tax authorities whose mandate did not allow them to lay hands on wealth obtained by such socially productive methods as gambling, filling in football pool coupons correctly, playing the horses or winning £50,000 by investing one pound in Premium Bonds. Even bingo prizes remained inviolate. So for the time being did Jessica's fortune and Lockhart intended it to remain that way.

'All you have to do,' he told her next morning, 'is to see the manager and tell him you are withdrawing the entire sum in used one-pound notes. You understand?'

Jessica said she did and went down to the bank with a large empty suitcase. It was still large and empty when she returned.

'The manager wouldn't let me,' she said tearfully, 'he said it was inadvisable and anyway I have to give a week's notice before I can withdraw money in my deposit account.'

'Oh did he?' said Lockhart. 'In that case we will go down again this afternoon and give him a week's notice.'

The meeting in the bank manager's office did not go smoothly. The knowledge that so valued a customer intended to ignore his advice and withdraw such an enormous sum in such small denominations had rubbed away a great deal of his effusiveness.

'In used one-pound notes?' he said incredulously. 'You surely can't mean that. The work involved . . .'

'Will go some way to making good the profit you have received from my wife's deposit,' said Lockhart. 'You charge higher rates for overdrafts than you pay for deposits.'

'Yes, well we have to,' said the manager. 'After all . . .'

'And you also have to return the money to customers when they require it and in the legal tender they choose,' continued Lockhart, 'and if my wife wants used one-pound notes.'

'I can't imagine what for,' said the manager, 'I would have thought it the height of folly for you to leave this building with a suitcase of untraceable notes. You might be robbed in the street.'

'We might equally well be robbed in here,' said Lockhart, 'and to my way of thinking we have been by the discrepancy between your rates of interest. The value of that money has been depreciating thanks to inflation ever since you've had it. You won't deny that.'

The manager couldn't. 'It's hardly our fault that inflation is a national problem,' he said. 'Now if you want some advice as to the best investment . . .'

'We have one in mind,' said Lockhart. 'Now, we will abide by our undertaking not to withdraw the money without giving you a week's notice provided you let us have the money in used pound notes. I hope that is clear.'

'Yes,' said the manager for whom it wasn't but who didn't like the look on Mr Flawse's face. 'If you will come in on Thursday it will be ready for you.'

Jessica and Lockhart went back to Number 12 and spent the week packing.

'I think it would be best to send the furniture up by British Rail,' said Lockhart.

'But don't they lose things? I mean look what happened to mummy's car.'

'They have the advantage, my dear, that while things frequently don't arrive at their proper destination they invariably fail to be returned to their point of departure. I rely on this inefficiency to prevent anyone knowing where we have gone to.'

'Oh, Lockhart, you are clever,' said Jessica. 'I hadn't thought of that. But why are you addressing that packing-case to Mr Jones in Edinburgh? We don't know any Mr Jones in Edinburgh.'

'My love,' said Lockhart, 'no more we do and no more does British Rail but I will be there at the station with a rented van to collect it and I very much doubt if anyone will be able to trace us.'

'You mean we're going to hide?' said Jessica.

'Not hide,' said Lockhart, 'but since I have been classified as statistically and bureaucratically non-existent and thereby ineligible to those benefits the Welfare State is said to provide, I have not the slightest intention of providing the State with any of those benefits we have been able to accrue. In short not one penny in income tax, not one penny in Capital Gains Tax, and not one penny in anything. I don't exist and being non-existent intend to reap my reward.'

'I hadn't thought of it like that,' said Jessica, 'but you're quite right. After all fair's fair.'

'Wrong,' said Lockhart. 'Nothing is fair.'

'Well, they do say "All's fair in love and war", darling,' said Jessica.

'Which is to invert the meaning of the word,' said Lockhart, 'or to reduce it to mean that there are no rules governing one's conduct. In which case all is fair in love, war and tax evasion. Isn't that true, Bouncer?'

The bull-terrier looked up and wagged his stump. He had taken to the Flawse family. They seemed to look with favour on those ferocious attributes for which he and his fellow bull-terriers had been bred, namely the biting of things and hanging on like grim death.

And so by the following Thursday the contents of the house had been packed and dispatched to Edinburgh by British Rail to be collected there by Mr Jones and it only remained to go to the bank and fill the suitcase with the used one-pound notes. Lockhart had already withdrawn his million in the same form from his bank in the City. The manager there had been more cooperative, largely thanks to Lockhart's explanation that he needed the money immediately as he was conducting a little transaction concerning oil wells with the Sheik of Araby who wanted his money in coinage, and preferably in five penny pieces. The thought of counting one million pounds out in fivepenny pieces had so daunted the manager that he had done his utmost to persuade Lockhart to accept one-pound notes. And Lockhart had reluctantly agreed provided they were used.

'Why used?' asked the manager. 'Surely new notes would be preferable?'

'The Sheik has a suspicious mind,' said Lockhart. 'He asked

for coins to ensure that they were real money and not forged. If I take him new notes he will immediately suppose he is being swindled.'

'But he could easily check with us or the Bank of England,' said the manager, who had not kept up with Britain's declining reputation in currency matters.

'Good God,' he muttered when Lockhart explained the Sheik genuinely believed the old saying that an Englishman's word was his bond and consequently thought all Englishmen liars by virtue in the fall in the value of British bonds, 'that it should have come to this.'

But he had handed over one million pounds in used notes and had been thankful to see the back of such a disillusioning customer.

The bank manager in East Pursley was less easily persuaded.

'I still think you are acting most unwisely,' he told Jessica when she entered with the suitcase. 'Your mother, I feel sure, would never have followed such a very rash procedure. She was always extremely careful where money was concerned and she had a shrewd mind financially speaking. I can recall her advice in 1972 to buy gold. I wish now that I had followed it.'

And Mrs Flawse's interest in gold continued. As he spoke she was following its trail from the Hall and every few yards along the path she stopped to pick up another gold sovereign. Ahead of her Mr Dodd walked steadily and every so often dropped another from the late Mr Taglioni's reimbursement. By the time he had covered a thousand yards he had dropped two hundred sovereigns on the path, one every five yards. After that he lengthened the space to twenty yards but still Mrs Flawse, oblivious to all else, followed, muttering greedily to herself. By the two-thousand-yard mark Mr Dodd had dropped two hundred and fifty and Mrs Flawse had picked as many up. And all the time the trail of glittering gold led west past the pine trees by the reservoir out on to the open fell. At three thousand yards Mr Dodd had still seven hundred sovereigns left in the wash-leather bag. He paused beneath a sign which said 'DANGER. MINISTRY OF DEFENCE FIRING-RANGE. ENTRY STRICTLY FORBIDDEN', and considered its message and the morality of his action. Then observing the mist that drifted across the artillery range and being a man of honour decided that he must proceed. 'What's good for the goose is good for the gander,' he muttered and then changed it to what was bad for the goose necessitated some risk to the gander. He dropped more coins, this time closer together to quicken the pace. At four thousand yards he was down to five hundred sovereigns and at five thousand the washleather bag still held four hundred. And as the money thickened on the ground so did the mist above it. At eight thousand yards Mr Dodd emptied the remnants on the ground, scattering them in the heather to be searched for. Then he turned and ran. Mrs Flawse was nowhere to be seen but her demented muttering came though the mist. So did the first shell. It burst on the hillside and sent shrapnel scudding past Mr Dodd's head and he redoubled his pace. Mrs Flawse didn't. Deaf to the sound of the artillery she walked on, stopping and stooping and gathering the golden hoard which like some legend come to life held her attention to the exclusion of all else. If this trail of bullion continued she would be a rich woman. The market value of each old sovereign was twenty-six pounds and gold had been rising. And already she had collected seven hundred of the glittering coins. Mrs Flawse foresaw a splendid future. She would leave the Hall. She would live in luxury with yet another husband, a young one this time to be bullied and put to work and made to serve her sexual requirements. With each stop and stoop she was more inflamed with greed and lust and made an audit of her good fortune. Finally at eight thousand yards the trail dwindled and stopped. But the gold gleamed in the heather all round and she scrabbled with her fingers for each remaining one. 'I mustn't miss any,' she muttered.

At four thousand yards to the south the men of the Royal Artillery were equally determined not to miss their target. They couldn't see it but the range was right and having bracketed it they prepared to fire a salvo. Ahead of them Mrs Flawse found the last coin and sat on the ground with the gold gathered in her skirt and began to count. 'One, two, three, four, five . . .' She got no further. The Royal Artillery had lived up to their reputation and the six-gun salvo had scored a direct hit. Where Mrs Flawse had been sitting there was a large crater around whose perimeter lay scattered, like golden confetti from some extravagant wedding, one thousand sovereigns. But then Mrs Flawse had always married money. Or, as she had been told as a child by her avaricious mother, 'Don't marry money, my dear, go where money is.' And Mrs Flawse had gone.

Mr Dodd had too but in a much more lively manner. He went with a clear conscience. He had put his own life at risk to be rid of the auld bitch and as the poet had it 'Liberty's in every blow! Let us do or die!' and Mr Dodd had done for liberty what he could and was still alive. As he strode back to Flawse Hall he was whistling 'Gin a body meet a body, Coming through the rye. Gin a body kill a body, Need a body cry?' Aye, old Robbie Burns knew what he was talking about, he thought, even with a little amendment to his meaning. And when he reached the Hall he lit a fire in the old man's study and fetching his pipes sat on the settle in the kitchen and played 'Twa Corbies' in elegiac recognition that o'er Mrs Flawse's white bones already bare the wind shall blaw for evermair. He was still playing when the sound of a horn blown from the locked gate on the bridge sent him running down the drive to welcome Lockhart and his wife.

'The Flawses are back at the Hall,' he said as he opened the gate. 'It's a grand day.'

'Aye, it's good to be back for good,' said Lockhart.

That evening Lockhart dined in his grandfather's place at the oval mahogany table with Jessica sitting opposite him. By candlelight she looked more innocent and lovely than ever and Lockhart lifted his glass to her. He had come into his gift again as the gipsy had foretold and the knowledge that he was now truly head of the Flawse family freed him from the imposed chasteness of the past. Later while Bouncer and the collie eyed one another warily in the kitchen and Mr Dodd played a gay tune of his own composing to celebrate the occasion, Lockhart and Jessica lay not only in one another's arms but something more.

Such was their happiness that it was not until after a late breakfast that any mention was made of Mrs Flawse's absence.

'I havena seen her since yesterday,' said Mr Dodd. 'She was away across the fell in rather better spirits than of late.'

199

Lockhart investigated her bedroom and found the bed had not been slept in.

'Aye, there's a discrepancy there,' Mr Dodd agreed, 'but I have a notion she's taking her rest all the same.'

But Jessica was too enchanted by the house to miss her mother. She went from room to room looking at the portraits and the fine old furniture and making plans for the future.

'I think we'll have the nursery in grandfather's old dressing-room,' she told Lockhart, 'don't you think that would be a good idea? Then we'll have baby near us.'

Lockhart agreed with everything she suggested. His mind was on other things than babies. He and Mr Dodd conferred in the study.

'You've put the money in the whisky wall with the man?' he asked.

'Aye, the trunk and the suitcases are well hidden,' said Mr Dodd, 'but you said that no one will come looking.'

'But I cannot be certain,' said Lockhart, 'and it's necessary to prepare for contingencies and I dinna intend to be dispossessed of my gains. If they cannot find the money they can seize the house and everything in it. I have mind to prepare for that eventuality in advance.'

'It would be a hard place to take by force,' said Mr Dodd, 'but perhaps you have other intentions.'

Lockhart said nothing. His pen doodled on the pad in front of him and drew a moss trooper pendant.

'I would rather avoid that necessity,' he said after a long silence. 'I'll have a word with Mr Bullstrode first. He always dealt with my grandfather's tax problems. You'll go to the telephone in Pockrington and send for him.'

Next day Mr Bullstrode arrived to find Lockhart sitting at the desk in the study and it seemed to the solicitor that a more than subtle change had come over the young man he had known as the bastard.

'I would have ye know, Bullstrode,' said Lockhart when they had exchanged preliminaries, 'that I have no intention of paying Death Duties on the estate.'

Mr Bullstrode cleared his throat.

'I think we can find a way to avoid any large assessment,' he said. 'The estate has always been run at a loss. Your grandfather tended to deal only in cash without receipt and besides I have a certain influence with Wyman as his solicitor.'

'Why, man?' said Lockhart brusquely.

'Well, to be frank because I handled his divorce for him and I doubt he would want some of the details of, shall we say, his sexual propensities whispered abroad,' Mr Bullstrode explained misinterpreting the question.

'I dinna care a fig what the bloodsucker does abed,' said Lockhart, 'his name is Wyman?'

'As a matter of fact you've more or less put your finger on what he does abed. Substitute for blood a certain appendage and ...'

'The name Wyman, Bullstrode, not the proclivity attendant on the appendage.'

'Oh, the name,' said Mr Bullstrode, brought back from those fantasies Mr Wyman so frequently fostered in his imagination. 'The name is Mr William Wyman. He is Her Majesty's Collector of Taxes for the Middle Marches. You need have no fear he'll trouble you overmuch.'

'He'll not trouble me at all. 'Twill be t'other way round if he so much as sets foot on Flawse Fell. Ye'll tell him that.'

Mr Bullstrode said he would but he said it uncertainly. The change in Lockhart had extended to his language which before had been that educated accent acquired from old Mr Flawse but had now broadened into something more akin to Mr Dodd's way of speech. Lockhart's next statement was stranger still. He stood up and glared at the solicitor. There was a wild look about his face and his voice had a dreadful lilt.

'So gan ye back to Hexham and tell the taxmen there that should they want to die abed and not the open air, they'd best steer clear of old Flawse Hall and gan anither route or else they'll not a-hunting go but be themselves the shoot. I will not have an ane of them come peering through my door or speiring after money that I had made afore. I'll pay my way and gie my due to them as has the need but let a taxman show his face I'll show it how to bleed. Aye, they can sweat and they can stew and they can gan to court but I'll hie here and I'll lie there and niver I'll be caught. So warn them, Bullstrode, heed my words. I dinna wish to kill but if they come a searching me so help me God I will.'

Mr Bullstrode had every reason to believe it. Whatever – and there was now no doubt in his mind that Lockhart was no contemporary but some congenital disaster – whatever stood before him and threatened so much in rhyme meant every syllable he uttered. And a man who could have his own grandfather stu... Mr Bullstrode sought a diversionary word and found it in preserved, was made of sterner stuff than the society in which he was living.

Further proof of this supposition came later when, having been prevailed upon to follow his former custom and stay for dinner and the night, he lay in bed. From the kitchen there came the sound of Mr Dodd's Northumbrian pipes and with it a singing voice. Mr Bullstrode got out of bed and tiptoed to the head of the stairs and listened. It was Lockhart singing, but although Mr Bullstrode prided himself on his knowledge of Border Ballads, the one he heard that night was none he knew.

'A dead man sits in old Flawse Hall
   Though buried he should be,
And there he'll sit within the wall
   Till blossoms the great oak tree.

Aye, blossoms and blooms the oak with bluid
   And the moss is gay with red,
And so he'll sit and so he'll brood
   Till all the warld be dead.

So saddle my horse and summon the pack
   And we'll answer the call of the wild
For I'll break the bounds that held me back
   Since I was a dyke-born child.

The old Flawse clan and the old Faas' gang
   And the troopers are back on the moss
And the warning bells will again be rang
   Till they hang me from Elsdon Cross.'

As the song died away and the thin call of the pipes was lost in the silence of the house. Mr Bullstrode, shivering more from future fears than present cold, crept quietly back to bed. What he had just heard confirmed his premonition. Lockhart Flawse was out of the dim and dangerous past when the moss troopers roamed Tyndale and Redesdale and raided cattle from the low country on the east coast. And having raided they had hidden in their strongholds in the high hills. With that wild lawlessness there had come too poetry as harsh and unflinchingly tragic in its view of life as it was gay in the face of death. Mr Bullstrode, crouching beneath the blankets, foresaw dire days ahead. Finally, with a silent prayer that Mr Wyman would listen to reason and not invite disaster, Mr Bullstrode managed to snatch some sleep.

Chapter twenty

But there were forces already at work to nullify the hope expressed in Mr Bullstrode's prayer. Mr Wyman was quite prepared to listen to reason next morning when the solicitor returned to Hexham with his warning but Her Majesty's Collector of Taxes for the Middle Marches was no longer in control of the situation. In London a far more formidable figure in the person of Mr Mirkin, Senior Collector Supertax Division (sub-department, Evasion of) at the Inland Revenue offices had been alerted to the possibility that Mr and Mrs Flawse, previously of Number 12 Sandicott Crescent and now of no known address, had withdrawn £659,000 in used one-pound notes with the intention of not paying Capital Gains Tax. This had been brought to his notice by the bank manager of the East Pursley branch of Jessica's bank who happened to be a close friend of Mr Mirkin and who had been piqued by her refusal to accept his advice. He had been more than piqued by Lockhart's attitude. In his opinion something very fishy was going on. In the opinion of Mr Mirkin it was more than fishy; it stank.

'Tax evasion,' he said, 'is a crime against society of the very gravest sort. The man who fails to contribute to the economic good deserves the most severe punishment.' Which, since Mr Mirkin's income derived entirely from the contributions of socially productive persons, was an opinion both understandable and self-serving. The very magnitude of the sum involved merely increased his sense of outrage. 'I shall pursue this matter to the ends of the earth if need be.'

But such lengths were not needed. The late Mrs Flawse had written to the bank manager informing him of her change of address. That she had changed it yet again made no difference to Mr Mirkin. He consulted the tax register for Northumberland and confirmed that a Mr Flawse, who had in fact paid no tax for fifty years, nevertheless lived at Flawse Hall on Flawse Fell and where the mother was, her daughter was likely to be. Leaving all other duties aside Mr Mirkin travelled first class at the country's expense to Newcastle and then, to emphasize his status in the hierarchy of Tax Collectors, by hired car to Hexham. Within two days of Mr Bullstrode's visit and warning, Mr Wyman found himself trying to explain to a very superior superior how it was that a Mr Flawse who owned an estate of five thousand acres and seven tenant farms had failed to make his contribution to the national Exchequer by paying any income tax for fifty years.

'Well, the estate had always run at a loss,' he said.

Mr Mirkin's scepticism was positively surgical. 'You seriously expect me to believe that?' he asked. Mr Wyman answered that there was no proof to the contrary.

'We shall see about that,' said Mr Mirkin. 'I intend to make the most thorough investigation of the Flawse accounts. Personally.'

Mr Wyman hesitated. He was caught between the devil of his past and the deep blue sea of the Senior Collector Supertax Division (sub-department, Evasion of). On the whole he decided that it might be as well for his future if Mr Mirkin learnt from personal experience how difficult it was to extract taxes from the Flawse family. He therefore said nothing and Mr Mirkin drove off unwarned.

He arrived at Wark and was directed via Black Pockrington to Flawse Hall. There he met his first obstacle in the shape of the locked gate on the bridge over The Cut. Using the intercom which Lockhart had installed he spoke to Mr Dodd. Mr Dodd was polite and said he would see if his master was at home.

'There's a man from the Inland Revenue down at the bridge,' he told Lockhart who was sitting in the study. 'He says he is the Senior Collector of Taxes. You'll not be wanting to speak to him.'

But Lockhart did speak. He went to the intercom and asked Mr Mirkin by what right he was trespassing on private property.

'By my right as Senior Collector of Taxes,' said Mr Mirkin, 'and the question of private property does not arise. I am entitled to visit you to inquire into your financial affairs and . . .'

As he spoke Mr Dodd left the house by way of the kitchen garden and crossed the fell to the dam. Mr Mirkin, by this time too irate to observe the landscape, continued his argument with Lockhart.

'Will you or will you not come down and unlock this gate?' he demanded. 'If you don't I shall apply for a warrant. What is your answer?'

'I shall be down in just a moment,' said Lockhart, 'I have an idea it's going to rain and I'll need an umbrella.'

Mr Mirkin looked up into a cloudless sky.

'What the hell do you mean you'll need an umbrella?' he shouted into the intercom. 'There's not a sign of rain.'

'Oh, I don't know,' said Lockhart, 'we get very sudden changes of weather in these parts. I have known it to pour down without warning.'

At that moment Mr Dodd undid the main sluice gates at the base of the dam and a white wall of water issued from the great pipes. Ten feet high it hurtled down The Cut just as Mr Mirkin was about to protest that he had never heard such nonsense in his life.

'Downpour indeed. . .' he began and stopped. A horrid surging noise sounded round the corner of the hillside. It was part hiss and part thunder. Mr Mirkin stood and looked aghast. The next moment he was running hell for leather past his car and up the metalled track towards Black Pockrington. He was too late. The wall of water was less than ten feet deep now but of sufficient depth to sweep the car and the Senior Collector of Taxes (Supertax Division, etc.) off their tyres and feet and carry them a quarter of a mile down the valley and into the tunnel. To be precise, the water carried Mr Mirkin into the tunnel while the car lodged itself across the entrance. Only then did Mr Dodd close the sluice gates and, taking the precaution of adding three inches to the rainwater gauge on the wall beside the dam, he made his way back to the Hall.

'I doubt he'll be coming back the same way,' he told Lockhart who had observed the Collector's submergence with relish.

'I wouldn't be too sure,' said Lockhart while Jessica, out of the kindness of her heart, hoped the poor man could swim.

There was no kindness in Mr Mirkin's heart by the time he had issued from the tunnel a mile farther on and having been bounced, bashed, trundled and sucked through several large pipes and two deep tanks, finally came to rest in the comparative calm of the subsidiary reservoir beyond Tombstone Law. Half drowned and badly grazed and with murder in his heart, not to mention water everywhere, he clambered up the granite bank and staggered towards a farmhouse. The rest of the way to Hexham he travelled by ambulance and was lodged in the hospital there suffering from shock, multiple abrasions and *dementia taxitis*. When he could speak again, he sent for Mr Wyman.

'I demand that a warrant be issued,' he told him.

'But we can't apply for a warrant unless we've sufficient evidence of tax evasion to convince a magistrate,' said Mr Wyman, 'and quite frankly. . .'

'Who's talking about tax evasion, you fool?' squawked Mr Mirkin. 'I'm talking about assault with intent to kill, attempted murder. . .'

'Just because it rained rather hard,' said Mr Wyman, 'and you got caught. . .'

Mr Mirkin's reaction was so violent that he had to be sedated and Mr Wyman had to lie on a couch in Accident Emergencies holding his nose tightly above the bridge to stop it bleeding.

But Mr Mirkin was not the only person to suffer a sense of loss. The discovery of the late Mrs Flawse in a shell crater surrounded by gold sovereigns came as a shock to Jessica.

'Poor mummy,' she said when an officer from the Royal Artillery brought her the sad news, 'she never had much bump of direction and it's nice to know she didn't suffer. You did say death was instantaneous?'

'Absolutely,' said the officer, 'we bracketed her first and then all six guns fired a salvo and we were bang on target.'

'And you say she was surrounded by Sovereigns?' asked Jessica. 'That would have made her very proud. She always was a great admirer of the Royal Family and to know that they were with her in her hour of need is a wonderful comfort.'

She left the officer in a state of some perplexity and went about the more urgent business of nest-making. She was two weeks' pregnant. It was left to Lockhart to offer his apologies to the Major for the inconvenience caused by Mrs Flawse's failure to look where she was going.

'I feel very strongly about trespass myself,' he said as he saw the officer to the door, 'disturbs the game no end to have people hiking all over the countryside and with absolutely no right. If you ask me, and out of the hearing of my wife of course, the woman got what was coming to her. Damned fine shooting, what!' The Major handed over the jam jar containing Mrs Flawse and left hurriedly.

'Talk about sang-bloody-froid,' he muttered as he drove down the hill.

Behind him Mr Dodd was about to empty the jam jar into the cucumber frame when Lockhart stopped him.

'Grandfather loathed her,' he said, 'and besides, there'll have to be an official funeral.'

Mr Dodd said it seemed a waste of a good coffin but Mrs Flawse was laid to rest beside Mr Taglioni two days later. This time Lockhart's inscription on the headstone was only slightly equivocal and read:

'Beneath this stone lies Mrs Flawse
Who foolishly went out of doors.
She met her end by dint of shell,
Let those that missed her wish her well.'

Jessica was particularly touched by the last line.

'Mummy was such a wonderful woman,' she told Mr Bullstrode and Dr Magrew who put in a somewhat unwilling appearance at the funeral, 'she would love to know she had been immortalized in poetry.'

Dr Magrew and Mr Bullstrode didn't share her certainty.

'I'd have preferred the relative pronoun to be a bit more personal than that,' said the doctor, looking at the wreaths and the jam jar contributed by Mr Dodd. It contained a vixen's brush. Mr Bullstrode was rather more concerned with the Army's role in the affair.

'"From the officers and mess..."' he read underneath a

large wreath, 'from what I have heard they should have left the mess out. It would have been more tactful all things considered.' As they left the churchyard they noticed Lockhart deep in conversation with the Major.

'It does not augur well,' said the solicitor. 'You heard what happened to the Tax Collector?'

Dr Magrew had in fact treated the man. 'I doubt it will be a few days before he's up and about,' he said. 'I put both his legs in plaster.'

'I had no idea he had broken them,' said Mr Bullstrode. Dr Magrew smiled.

'He hadn't,' he said, 'but I thought it best to be on the safe side.'

'My feelings exactly,' said Mr Bullstrode, 'I wouldn't want to pit myself against the bastard with him in so close communion with the Army.'

But Lockhart's interest in military matters was by and large pacific and concerned with preventing any further accident of the sort that had happened to Mrs Flawse.

'I'd be happy to have you put your notices up a bit closer to the house and on my ground,' he told the Major. 'It would keep people from interfering with my game.'

What his game was he kept to himself but the Major was touched by his generosity.

'I'll have to get permission from the Ministry,' he said, 'but isn't there anything else we can do to help?'

'Well, as a matter of fact there is,' said Lockhart.

Next day he drove to Newcastle with a trailer behind the car and when he returned both car and trailer were loaded to the brim with fresh electronic equipment. He made two subsequent trips and each time came back with more bits and pieces.

'Oh, Lockhart,' said Jessica, 'it's so nice to know you've got a hobby. There you are in your workshop and here am I making everything ready for baby. What was that huge machine that came up yesterday?'

'An electric generator,' said Lockhart, 'I've decided to electrify the house.'

But to watch him and Mr Dodd at work on Flawse Fell suggested that it was less the house than the surrounding countryside that Lockhart had decided to electrify. As each day passed they dug fresh holes and deposited loudspeakers in them and wired them together.

'It will be a minefield of the things,' said Mr Dodd as they ran a large cable back to the house.

'And that's another thing we'll need,' said Lockhart, 'dynamite.'

Two days later Mr Dodd paid a visit to the quarry at Tombstone Law while Lockhart, finally accepting the Major's offer of help, spent several hours on the artillery range with a tape recorder listening to the guns being fired.

'There's just one thing more I'd like,' he said when he had got what he wanted, 'some tapes of authentic rifle and machine-gun fire.'

Once again the Major was obliging and detailed off some men to fire rifles and machine-guns across the fell.

'I must say I think it's an ingenious idea,' said the Major as Lockhart packed his equipment into the car and prepared to leave. 'Sort of bird scarer, what?'

'You could put it like that,' said Lockhart and thanking him once again drove away. He returned to the Hall to find Mr Dodd waiting for him with the news that he had what was needed to make the scene realistic.

'We'll just have to be sure the sheep don't tread on them,' he said but Lockhart was of a different opinion.

'A dead sheep or two won't come amiss. They'll add a touch of death to the scene. A few bullocks would, too.'

All the while Mr Mirkin hobbled about Hexham on crutches and spent hours poring over the tax returns of old Mr Flawse in the determination to find proof of tax evasion and something that would justify the issue of a warrant. But it was a hopeless task. Old Mr Flawse had made a loss. On the other hand, one of his tax-loss enterprises had been a woollen mill and tweed-making factory and tweed-making was subject to Value Added Tax. Mr Mirkin's thoughts turned to VAT. It wasn't within his jurisdiction but came under that of Customs and Excise. VAT evasion and Customs and Excise? Mr Mirkin had found what he wanted. The Excise men needed no warrant to enter and search an Englishman's house, be it castle or cot, at any time of the day or night and their powers, unlike his own, were not subject to the limitations of magistrates, courts of law or any of the legal institutions which preserved an Englishman's supposed liberties. The Excise men were a law unto themselves and as such entirely to Mr Mirkin's envy and purpose. He went to the offices of the head VAT man for the Middle Marches and enlisted his curiosity and help.

'The best time would be to go at night,' he said, 'and take them by surprise.'

The head VAT man had raised objections. 'The Excise are not too well liked in these parts,' he said. 'I would prefer to proceed in a more open and orthodox way.'

Mr Mirkin indicated his plastered legs.

'That's what happened to me when I acted in an orthodox and open manner,' he said. 'If you take my advice you'll act swiftly at night. There's no one out there to contradict your statement that you went by day.'

'Only Mr Flawse and his wife and everyone else in the neighbourhood,' said the VAT man obstinately. Mr Mirkin sniggered.

'You didn't hear what I said,' he told the VAT man. 'The house stands six miles from the nearest neighbour and there's only Mr and Mrs Flawse there. Now if you take six men. . .'

The VAT man succumbed to his persuasion and was impressed by Mr Mirkin's willingness to join the expedition in a wheelchair. His advice about avoiding the valley and approaching by way of the dam seemed sound too.

'I shall first notify them of the need to inspect their books,' he said, 'and only if they refuse will I act according to the authority invested in me by the Government.'

And so several weeks passed and as many letters from Customs and Excise were sent and received no reply. Faced with this flagrant contempt for his office and the VAT regulations, the head VAT man decided to act. And during those weeks Lockhart and Mr Dodd continued with their preparations. They moved more equipment into the valley and on to the fells surrounding the Hall. They installed numbers of tape recorders and enormously powerful amplifiers in the whisky wall and waited for the next move.

It came with the arrival of Mr Bullstrode and Dr Magrew, the solicitor to inform Lockhart that he had learnt through Mr Wyman that the Excise men intended to raid the house that night, and Dr Magrew to confirm that Jessica was expecting a baby. Neither of them expected what happened that night, when after an excellent dinner they went to bed in their old rooms. Outside a full moon shone down on to the Hall, the fell, the Rigg, several hundred sheep, one hundred bullocks, the reservoir, the dam and Cut and half a dozen Excise men together with Mr Mirkin on crutches and Mr Wyman to help him.

Chapter twenty-one

It would also be true to say that the Excise men had no idea what to expect. They had been warned by Mr Mirkin's experience but as they stole across the dam all seemed quiet and peaceful under the brilliant moon. Having crossed the dam they took the path towards the back entrance of the Hall. Around them sheep and bullocks grazed and all was silence and shadow. The only light visible came from Perkin's Lookout where Mr Dodd sat watching their approach but, refracted through the stained glass of the little folly, it had an attractive and rather charming quality about it.

What happened next hadn't. They were still a hundred yards from the Hall when the barrage broke around them, and barrage it was. And bombardment. A thousand loudspeakers bombarded them acoustically with the roar of shells, rapid machine-gun fire, screams of agony, bombs, fresh screams, larger shells, and a high-pitched whistle of such appalling frequency that several sheep went immediately insane. Like eight men suddenly awoken Rip Van Winkle-like in the middle of the Somme bombardment or at Alamein, the Excise men tried desperately to take cover only to find that lying down was even more awful than standing up from the sound point of view. Worse still, it prevented them from getting out of the way of maddened sheep and demented bullocks startled out of their senses into panic by the terrible din.

Even in the house where Dr Magrew and Mr Bullstrode had been warned that it might be more advisable to sleep with their heads under pillows rather than on top, the sounds of battle were devastating. Dr Magrew who had been on the Somme woke with the conviction that he was back there while Mr Bullstrode, convinced that he was in dire peril from Excise men gone berserk and who being determined not to suffer Mr Mirkin's fate had taken it into their heads to bombard the Hall before entering its remains without a warrant, hurled himself under his bed and smashed the chamber pot. Gashed and bleeding he lay there with his fingers in his ears to try and keep the fearful crash of guns out. Only Lockhart and Jessica and Mr Dodd enjoyed what was happening. Provided with earplugs, specially designed ear mufflers and sound-deadening helmets they were in a privileged position.

The Excise men, lacking any such aids, weren't. Nor were the Flawse hounds. Like the sheep they went crazy. It was the high-frequency whistle that got them and in the yard they slobbered and foamed and fought to get out of the gate. Mr Dodd let them. It had been in his mind that they might prove useful yet and he had tied a length of string to the bolt. Now he pulled it and the raving pack swarmed out to join the stampede of demented bullocks, insane sheep and frantic Excise men who cascaded in a horrid panic-stricken rout back towards the dam. Only Mr Mirkin stood his ground and this involuntarily. Mr Wyman, to fend off a berserk sheep, had taken his crutches. They had done him little good. The sheep had broken the crutches and quite uncharacteristically for a normally docile and ruminant creature had bitten them in half and charged on chewing the bits. Mr Wyman charged with it only to be bitten by a Flawse hound. Several Excise men suffered similar fates and all the time the artillery bombardment continued, the rifle fire increased, the high-frequency whistle blew fit to bust and Mr Mirkin clutching his head in agony took an unwise step forward, fell and lay on an extremely large loudspeaker which was resonating at an extremely low frequency. Before he knew what was happening Mr Mirkin was transformed from Senior Collector of Taxes (Supertax Division; sub-department, Evasion of) of the Inland Revenue into a sort of semi-human tuning fork, one end of which felt as if it had been sucked into a jet engine at full power while the middle lying on top of the low-frequency loudspeaker began to rumble, stir, reverberate and bounce quite horribly. Mr Mirkin's plastered legs simply vibrated involuntarily and at a frequency that was not at all to the advantage of what lay between their upper ends. Around him the fell was clear. Sheep, bullocks, hounds and Excise men, all deaf to everything but the pain in their ears, had fled the field and had scampered back across the dam or in the case of two Excise men actually dived into the reservoir where they tried to keep their noses above the water while keeping their ears under.

As they finally disappeared from view Lockhart turned the amplifiers off and the bombardment ceased as suddenly as it had begun. Not that Mr Mirkin or the fleeing Excise men either knew or cared. They were in a soundless world in any case and by the time they reached their cars on the road and were able to voice their shattered feelings they were unable to get them heard. Only sight, smell, touch and fright remained and they stared back in wonderment at Flawse Hall. It was still incredibly standing and apparently unscathed by the bombardment. Nor were there any craters to be seen and the smoke that should have obscured their view was quite extraordinarily absent. But at least the pain had gone too and the Excise men were about to climb back into their cars and leave the scene of this frightful experience when a figure appeared climbing the road from the bottom of the valley. It was Lockhart; across his shoulder like a sack with wooden legs hung Mr Mirkin.

'You've left this thing behind,' he said, and dumped the ex-Senior Collector of Taxes across the bonnet of the leading car. The Excise men saw his lips move but heard nothing. Had they heard they would have agreed that Mr Mirkin was a thing. He was certainly not a human being. Gibbering soundlessly and foaming at various orifices he had passed beyond the bounds of sanity and would clearly never be the same again. They managed to get him into the boot of one of the cars (his vibrating legs prevented his occupying a seat in the car itself) and drove off into the silent night.

Behind them Lockhart walked happily back to the Hall. His

213

experiment in surrogate and purely sonic warfare had worked splendidly, so splendidly in fact that as he approached the house he saw that most of the windows were broken. He would have them repaired next day and in the meantime there was something to celebrate. He went into the peel tower and lit the fire in the great hearth. As it blazed up he told Mr Dodd to fetch the whisky and went himself into the house to invite Mr Bullstrode and Dr Magrew to join him and Jessica in drinking a toast. He had some difficulty making his invitation plain to them but their sleep had been so completely interrupted that they dressed and followed him to the banqueting hall. Mr Dodd was already there with the whisky and his pipes and standing in a little group beneath the battle-flags and the swords they raised their glasses.

'What are we going to drink to this time?' asked Jessica and it was Mr Dodd who supplied the answer.

'To the Devil himself,' he said.

'The Devil?' said Jessica. 'Why the Devil?'

'Why aye, hinnie,' said Mr Dodd, ' 'tis clear you dinna ken your Robbie Burns. Do ye not ken his poem "The De'il's Awa Wi' The Excise Man"?'

'In that case, to the De'il,' said Lockhart and they drank.

And they danced by the light of the fire while Mr Dodd played on his pipes and sang

'There's threesome reels, and foursome reels,
    There's hornpipes and strathspeys, man;
But the one best dance e'er cam to our lan',
    Was – the De'il's awa wi' the Excise Man.'

They danced and drank and drank and danced and then, exhausted, sat round the long table while Jessica made them ham and eggs. When they had finished Lockhart stood up and told Mr Dodd to fetch the man.

'It wouldna be kind to let him miss this great occasion,' he said. Mr Bullstrode and Dr Magrew, too drunk to disagree, nodded. 'He would have appreciated seeing those scoundrels run,' said Lockhart, 'it would have appealed to his sense of humour.' As dawn broke over Flawse Fell Mr Dodd flung open the gates of the peel tower and old Mr Flawse, seated in a wheelchair and manifestly self-propelled, rolled into the room and took his accustomed place at the end of the table. Mr Dodd shut the doors and handed Lockhart the remote control. He twiddled with the switches and once again the room rang with the voice of old Mr Flawse. Lockhart had been editing the tapes and compiling fresh speeches and it was these that the old man now uttered.

'Let us dispute, my friends, as once we did before the man with the sickle got the better of me. I take it you've both brought your reasons with you just as I've brought mine.'

Dr Magrew and Mr Bullstrode found the question difficult to answer. They were both very drunk and in any case recent events had moved so fast that they had tended to forget that old Mr Flawse, if stuffed, still seemed to have a mind of his own. They sat and stared speechlessly at this animated *memento mori*. Lockhart assuming that they were still partially deaf turned the volume up and Mr Flawse's voice filled the room.

'I care not what argument you use, Magrew,' he yelled, 'I'll not have it that ye can change a nation's or a man's character by meddling with his environment and social circumstance. We are what we are by virtue of the precedence of birth and long-established custom, that great conglomerate of our ancestral heritage congenital and practical. The two are intertwined. What judges once pronounced we now apply; 'tis common law; and what by chemistry committed shapes our cells becomes the common man. An Englishman is yet an Englishman though centuries apart. Do you not agree, Mr Bullstrode, sir?'

Mr Bullstrode nodded. He was powerless to speak.

'And yet,' continued Mr Flawse at ten watts per channel, 'and yet we have the paradox that what's called English differs century by century as well. A strange yet constant inconsistency this is that leaves the men the same and yet divides their conduct and opinions from themselves. In Cromwell's day it was religious controversy led in the field; a century and Chatham's day the conquest of an Empire and the loss of America but faith had fled the field before a clockwork model of the universe and Frenchmen dideroting on encyclopediae. Ye ken what Sully said? That Englishmen take their pleasures sadly after the fashion of their country. A century later Voltaire, that idol *persifleur* of France, would have it that we by and large have a most serious and gloomy temperament. So where's the influence of all ideas between the sixteenth and the eighteenth century on

Englishmen? Not that I mind what Frenchmen say of us; their observations have ill-accorded with mine own; or of my reading come to that. 'Tis Merrie England all the time to me and what have the French to equal Sterne or Smollett or yet a Surtees? I've still to see a Frenchman Jorrocks ride to hounds. With them it's wit and badinage that's aye the joke. With us 'tis ever action and that war between our words and what we be which they across the Channel have named hypocrisy. And what we be is all mixed up with alien blood and refugees from tyranny like a bag pudding boiled within this pot we call the British Isles. 'Twas ever thus; 'twill ever be; a ragamuffin race of scoundrels born of pirates on the run. What say you to that, Magrew, you who have some acquaintanceship with Hume?'

But Dr Magrew, like Mr Bullstrode, had nothing to say. He was silent before this effigy of the past which uttered words in parody of its own complex self. He gaped and as he gaped the old man's voice rose louder still. It was filled with fury now and Lockhart, wrestling with the remote control, found nothing would abate his voice.

'It was some damned scoundrel versifying American,' bawled Mr Flawse, 'would have it that he'd go with a whimper not a bang. 'Twere better for the creature had he been with Whymper on the Matterhorn and learnt the meaning of a fall. Well, I'll not do the same. Damn whimpering, sir, and being the world's whining beggar, cap in hand. I've not a forelock left to touch and wouldna raise a finger to it had I one, to wheedle pennies from a foreign swine be he an Arab Sheik or the Emperor of Japan. I'm true-born English to the core and so I will remain. So keep your whimpering for womenfolk and let me have my bang.'

And as if in answer to this request there was a dull explosion in his innards and smoke poured out of his ears. Mr Bullstrode and Dr Magrew looked on appalled while Lockhart, trying the switches, shouted to Mr Dodd.

'The fire extinguisher,' he yelled, 'for God's sake get the fire extinguisher!'

But it was no good. Mr Flawse was living up to his promise not to whimper. Flailing round him with his arms and shouting incomprehensible imprecations from his clapper mouth he streaked in his wheelchair across the banqueting hall, gathered a rug over his feet on the way, bounced off an armoured figure and finally, with that practicality he had always admired in his ancestors, shot into the open hearth and burst into flames. By the time Mr Dodd arrived with fire extinguisher he was beyond extinction and had flared up the chimney in a shower of sparks and flames.

'The man was born unto trouble as the sparks fly upward. Amen,' said Mr Dodd.

And so in the great hearth old Mr Flawse, the last of his line, finally fizzled out before the eyes of his two closest friends, Jessica, Mr Dodd, and the man he had always called the bastard.

'Almost a Viking's funeral,' said Dr Magrew as the charred remains flaked to ashes and the last transistor melted. It had been made in Japan, he noted, which tended to contradict the old man's final boast that he was English to the core. He was about to point this interesting anatomical and philosophical observation out to Mr Bullstrode when he was interrupted by a cry from behind him. Lockhart was standing on the oak table among the guttering candles and tears were running down his cheeks. 'The De'il has pity in him yet,' thought the doctor but Mr Dodd, recognizing the symptoms, picked up his pipes and squeezed the bag under his arm as Lockhart began his dirge.

'The last of them all is gan fra' the Hall
    And the Flawse is fled fra' the fell
But those that are left can aye recall
    The tales he used to tell.

Twa deaths he died, twa lives he led,
    Twa men he might have been;
The ane spake words he had but read
    The ither he didna mean.

And so he struggled his whole life through
    And niver in strife he ceased.
And he allus sought what was good and true
    Though hissel' to be half a beast.

'Twas all the truth he iver knew
    Since Science and God had fled,
And you couldna shake his firm held view
    That the best of men are dead.

217

But their words remain to ease our pain
  And he'd have us now rejoice
That though he's gan we can hear again
  The sound of his living voice.'

While Mr Dodd squeezed on with his tune, Lockhart jumped down from the table and left the peel tower. Behind him Mr Bullstrode and Dr Magrew looked at one another in wonderment and for once even Jessica, startled into womanly concern by Lockhart's tears, lost her sentimental streak and stood dry-eyed. She was about to follow Lockhart out when Mr Dodd stopped her.

'Let him be by hissel', hinnie,' he said. 'He gan to dree his weird awhile.'

Mr Dodd was only partly right. Lockhart was not dreeing but what came next was certainly weird. As the sun rose over Tombstone Law a thousand loudspeakers planted across the fell boomed forth again. This time the sound was not that of shell and shot but the gigantic voice of Edwin Tyndale Flawse. He was singing 'The Ballad of Prick 'Em Dry'.

Chapter twenty-two

As the final echoes of that enormous voice died away and the deafened birds in the pinewoods round the reservoir fluttered back to their perches and tried to resume their morning chorus, Lockhart and Jessica stood on the roof of the peel tower and looked over the battlements at the land that was truly theirs. Lockhart's tears were gone. They had never been entirely for the conflagration of his grandfather but more for the loss of that terrible innocence which had been the old man's intellectual legacy to him. And, like some incubus, that innocence had lain heavily upon him denying him the right to guilt and the true humanity which comes from guilt and innocence. Lockhart had stated it all unconsciously in his lament but now he felt free to be his divided self, a man of lusts as well as loves, of ingenuity mingled with compassion, of fear as well as mindless bravery, in short a man like other men. All this his grandfather's obsession with heroes and hero-worship had denied him but, in the flames that had consumed Mr Flawse, Lockhart had been born anew, his own man, never mind his ancestry or who and what his father might have been and done.

And so while Mr Bullstrode and Dr Magrew drove off down the road to Hexham and Mr Dodd with brush and dust-pan swept the ashes of his late master from the grate and, separating those foreign parts which had been the components of old Mr Flawse's posthumous animation, deposited the rest in the cucumber frame, Lockhart and Jessica stood together and were content to be themselves.

The same could hardly be said for Mr Mirkin or the Excise men now back in Hexham. Mr Mirkin in particular was not himself and no longer beside himself. He had no self to be beside. The Senior Collector of Taxes (Supertax Division; sub-department, Evasion of) was back in hospital outwardly unscathed but suffering internally the simultaneous after-effects of extremely low-frequency waves. His condition baffled the doctors who could make neither head nor tail of his symptoms. At one end he fluttered; at the other end he wowed. The combination was one they had never previously encountered and it was only with the arrival of Dr Magrew, who suggested plastering his plastered legs together to stop them oscillating, that Mr Mirkin could be kept in bed. Even so he wowed, his most insistent wow being to have his Schedule D, a demand that led to some confusion with the Vitamin. In the end he was gagged and his head encased in lead-filled icebags to stop it vibrating.

'He's clean off his rocker,' said Dr Magrew gratuitously as the Senior Collector bounced on the bed. 'The best and safest place for him would be a padded cell. Besides, it would keep the rumble down.'

'His stomach doesn't seem to be capable of keeping anything down,' said a consultant, 'and its rumble is quite revolting.'

To make the diagnosis even more difficult Mr Mirkin, unable to hear, refused to answer questions, even those concerned with his name and address, and when the gag was removed he simply wowed the louder. In the maternity ward nearby his wowing led to complaints and the demand that he be transferred out of earshot. Dr Magrew agreed at once and signed a committal order to the local mental hospital on the perfectly sensible grounds that a man whose extremities were so clearly at odds with one another, and who seemed to have lost his memory, was suffering from incurably split personality. And so with that anonymity that was entirely in keeping with his profession as a Tax Collector, Mr Mirkin, now a mere digit himself, was taken at public expense and registered under Schedule D in the most padded and soundless of cells.

Meanwhile the Excise men and the head VAT man were too taken up with their own loss of hearing to consider with any enthusiasm a return visit to Flawse Hall. They spent their time writing notes to one another and to their solicitors concerning the actions for damages which they were bringing against the Ministry of Defence for failing to draw their attention to the fact that they were, on the night of the raid, entering an artillery range. The case was a prolonged one made longer still by the Army's adamant denial that they fired at night and by the need for all cross-examination of the Excise men to be done in longhand.

Meanwhile life at Flawse Hall resumed its quiet routine. There too things had changed. The cucumbers in the frames grew larger than Mr Dodd had ever known them to and Jessica expanded likewise. And all summer long the bees in the straw hives buzzed over the heather and young rabbits gambolled outside warrens. Even the foxes, sensing the changed atmosphere, returned and for the first time in many a year curlews called over Flawse Fell. Life was returning and Lockhart had given up his previous desire to shoot things. This was partly thanks to Jessica but much more to Miss Deyntry who had taken Jessica under her wing and while instilling a dislike of bloodsports had also knocked the sentimentality out of her. Morning sickness had helped and all talk of storks had ended. Jessica had broadened out into a homely woman with a sharp tongue in her head and the Sandicott strain had reasserted itself. It was a practical strain that placed some value on comfort and the Hall had been transformed. The windows had been replaced and central heating installed to cut out the damp and the draughts but Jessica still stuck to open fires in the main rooms. And Mr Dodd still mined coal from the drift mine, though rather more easily than before. As a result of Lockhart's sonic warfare strange things had happened in the mine.

'The roof has fallen in some places,' Mr Dodd reported, 'but it's the seam itself that puzzles me. The coal has crumbled and there's an afful amount of dust down there.'

Lockhart went to inspect and spent several hours examining this strange occurrence. The coal had certainly crumbled and coal dust was thick everywhere. He emerged blackened but elated.

'It could be we've hit upon a new method of mining,' he said. 'If sonic waves can break windows and shatter glass, I can see no reason why they shouldn't be used underground to more purpose.'

'You'll not expect me to be down there with some infernal whistle, I trust,' said Mr Dodd. 'I dinna want to go out of my mind in the interest of science and there's a number of sheep and bullocks that canna rightly be called undemented yet.'

But Lockhart reassured him. 'If I'm right there will be no need for any man to risk his life and health down a coal mine ever again. One would simply install a self-propelling machine that emitted the right frequency and it would be followed by a sort of enormous vacuum cleaner to suck the dust out afterwards.'

'Aye, well I dare say there's something to be said for the idea,' said Mr Dodd. 'It's all there in the Bible had we but known it. I've always wondered how Joshua could bring down the walls of Jericho with a wee bit of a horn.'

Lockhart went back to his laboratory and began work on his sonic coal extractor.

And so the summer passed peacefully and the Hall once again became the centre of social life in the Middle Marches. Mr Bullstrode and Dr Magrew still came to dinner but so did Miss Deyntry and there were other neighbours whom Jessica invited. But it was late November when the snow lay in thick drifts against the dry-stone walls that she gave birth to a son. Outside the wind whistled and the sheep huddled in their stone shelters; inside all was warmth and comfort.

'We'll name him after his grandfather,' said Lockhart as Jessica nursed the baby.

'But we don't know who he is, darling,' said Jessica. Lockhart said nothing. It was true that they still had no idea who his father was and he had been thinking of his own grandfather when he spoke. 'We'll leave the christening until the spring when the roads are clear and we can have everyone over for the ceremony.' So for the time being the new-born Flawse remained almost anonymous and as bureaucratically non-existent as his father while Lockhart spent much of his time in Perkin's Lookout. The little folly perched on the corner of the high wall served as his study where he could sit and look through its stained-glass window at the miniature garden created by Capability Flawse. There at his desk he wrote his verse. Like his life it had changed and was more mellow and there one spring morning when the sun shone down out of a cloudless sky and the cool wind blew round the outside wall and not into the garden, he set to work on a song to his son.

'Gan, hinny, play the livelong day
And let your ways be bonnie.
I wouldna have the warld to say
I left ye only money.

For I was left no father's name
And canna now renew it,
But face and name are aye the same
And by his ways I knew it.

Some legions came, they say, fra' Spain
While ithers marched from Rome
But like the Wall their ways remain
And make in us a home.

So dinna fash yoursel', sweet son,
The name ye bear be Flawse.
'Tis so the same with everyone
And no man has nie flaws.

We're Flawse or Faas but niver fause
I pledge my word by God.
For so the ballad is my source
And my true name is Dodd.'

Down below in a warm sunlit corner of the miniature garden Mr Dodd, as happy as a skylark, sat by the pram of Edwin Tyndale Flawse and played his pipes or sang his songs while his grandson lay and chuckled with sheer delight.

About the Author

Tom Sharpe was born in 1928 and educated at Lancing College and at Pembroke College, Cambridge. He did his National Service in the Marines before going to South Africa in 1951, where he did social work for the Non-European Affairs Department and taught. He had a photographic studio in Pietermaritzburg from 1957 until 1961, when he was deported. From 1963 to 1972, he was a lecturer in History at the Cambridge College of Arts and Technology. He is married and lives in Dorset. Tom Sharpe's other books include *Riotous Assembly, Indecent Exposure, Porterhouse Blue, Blott on the Landscape, Wilt, The Great Pursuit, The Wilt Alternative, Ancestral Vices* and *Vintage Stuff.*